THINGS THAT HAPPEN in THE WOODS

NYT & USA TODAY BESTSELLING AUTHOR

JESSICA SORENSEN

THINGS THAT HAPPEN IN THE WOODS

WOODS

(STAR MEADOWS DUET, BOOK 1)

JESSICA SORENSEN

 Created with Vellum

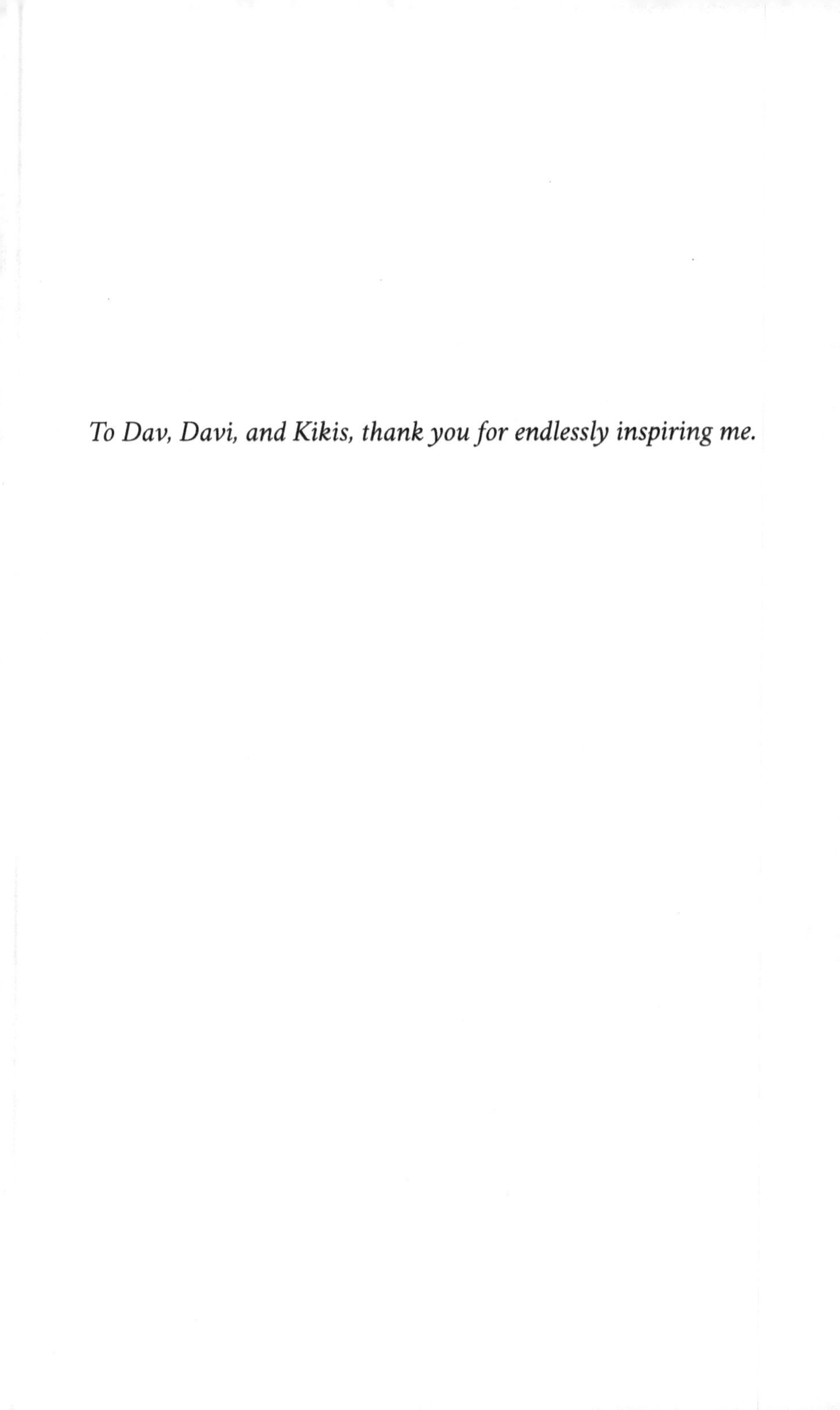

To Dav, Davi, and Kikis, thank you for endlessly inspiring me.

CHAPTER 1

My parents are yelling again. I used to get scared when they did, but now it's part of life. It's the quiet that makes me anxious, the stillness and the lack of knowing.

Not that it doesn't get annoying.

The television is on, and I raise the volume as their voices grow louder. The sofa I'm sitting on smells like flowers because my mother sprays everything with this flowery perfume. I'm not sure why she does it. If she opened the window, the scent of the roses would drift inside, at least in the springtime. It's winter now, and if we opened the window, it'd be cold and smell like snowflakes. But she likes to keep the windows and curtains closed.

"We want our privacy, Ava," she told me when I asked why she let the fresh air in. "We don't want people seeing in our house, right?"

I don't get what the big deal is. Who cares if they see? Our life is normal, isn't it?

Or maybe it isn't. I'm not sure since one of my friends refuses to play with me anymore after I told her my dad sometimes locks me in my room.

I sigh at the reminder that I'm friendless again.

Then I continue channel surfing for a show to watch. My dad is now yelling about not wanting to babysit me while my mom goes to the store. I don't understand why he doesn't. Babysitters get paid. I know this since I saw my mom give Stacy, the girl who lives next door and sometimes watches me, some money to keep an eye on me. And Stacy always seems happy to do it, so why doesn't my father want to? He rarely does, though, and it's usually for different reasons.

Today, he's saying, "I'm tired. I don't want to babysit. Plus, it's your job. Don't you forget that!" He shouts so loudly it hurts my ears.

"I know that," my mom tells him. She doesn't yell, her voice much quieter. "But I need to run some errands and taking her to stores with me is so stressful. Please can you watch her? It'll only be for like an hour."

"I have stuff to do." He's not shouting anymore, but his voice is firm.

"What?" my mom asks. "I know you have plans with your brother, but that's supposed to be later today."

"I have to go to the field and practice shooting. I only have three more weeks before hunting season starts," he snaps. "Not that it's any of your business. Stop trying to keep tabs on me."

"I'm ... Look, I'm sorry," she whispers. "I just ... I need help with things sometimes."

They keep talking, and my mom complains about how annoying I am at stores, how I wander off, how I don't listen to her.

I crank up the volume of the television.

I feel like crying whenever they talk about me like this, but I usually don't. When I do, my mom makes fun of me and tells me I'm being ridiculous. She even took photos of me a few times because she said I was acting like a baby, and she wanted me to see that.

My embarrassment and pain equals humor, I guess.

It's all really confusing—this life that moves so quickly and shows me things I don't quite understand. Maybe when I get older, I will, though.

What will it be like when I grow up and have all of this knowledge? Will life be easier and less scary? I sure hope so.

I keep trying to find something to watch as the arguing continues. It's later in the day, and not many cartoons are on. But there is a movie about a dog that I might go back to.

I click on the next channel.

And the next.

My eyes start to hurt, and then they spot over with red. I blink and click the remote button again.

On the screen is a woman with long, brown hair. She's running through the trees. She looks like she's crying, and blood is running down her arms. Someone laughs from the shadows, but I don't understand why they think this is funny. She's hurt and scared—

"What the fuck are you doing?" my dad screams. "How did you even find this?"

I jolt, almost peeing in my pants, and my head snaps toward the hallway. He's standing there, staring at me like I'm the most disgusting thing in the world.

"I-It was j-just on the T-T.V," I manage to sputter.

"What's going on?" My mom exits the hallway. Her eyes are

bloodshot, and she has a welt on her cheek. She looks like the woman who was just on the television.

"Look at what she's watching," my dad growls as he jabs a finger at the television. "How did this even happen? How did she find this?"

My mom glances at the television, and her eyes widen. "What in the hell, Ava? How did you turn this on?" She crosses her arms, waiting for an explanation.

I should say something, but I'm worried I've done something wrong. That I'll say something wrong. That they'll yell at me more.

So, I sit there, staring at them, with my tongue feeling like glue.

"She's so messed up!" my dad shouts. "Look at this! Look! She had to be looking for it!"

"I'm sure it was an accident," my mom replies. Her voice trembles a bit. "I'm sure she didn't mean to watch it."

"Bullshit," my dad seethes, his face bright red as he inches closer to my mom. "This shouldn't have happened." He points at the television again. "This is all your fault."

I feel bad I've caused another fight, and I reach for the remote to turn off the show, hoping they'll stop.

"She needs to be punished." My dad rushes over to me, crossing the room in just a few steps. "I don't need her doing this kind of shit again." He snatches the remote from me and chucks it against the wall.

It shatters, the batteries scattering. But the movie still plays.

My dad grabs my arm then and roughly yanks me off the sofa.

"Steve," my mom says, but he shoves her out of the way as he drags me down the hallway toward my bedroom.

"Make sure that gets put up someplace other than where you had it!" he shouts at my mother.

The shaggy brown carpet burns my knees as I struggle to get my feet underneath me. "Dad, please stop," I beg as I try to pull away. But he only tightens his grip on my arm. "You're hurting me."

"Good. Maybe next time you'll think before watching things you're not supposed to." He shoves me into the room, and I stumble into a small shelf that holds my dolls.

The wood cuts my hip, and the shelf tips over, sending my porcelain dolls everywhere. I fall down beside them, tears burning in my eyes from the pain in my hip and this aching sensation inside my chest, like I can't breathe.

My dad hovers over me. "If I ever catch you watching that shit again, you'll regret it." He doesn't say what he'll do to me, but he smacks me across my face so hard my ears ring.

Tears spill from my eyes as he storms away.

I sit up, cupping my cheek and crying. The tears only worsen when I notice one of my porcelain doll's faces has cracked. I pick it up, crying harder. I keep crying and crying until my mom steps into my room.

I want her to hug me.

I want her to tell me that it's okay.

I want her to tell me she won't let my dad do that to me ever again.

But all she says is, "This is your own fault." Then she tells me to take a nap and leaves me alone with my tears and broken dolls.

Sobs wrench from my chest, and my body trembles.

Over my sobbing, I can hear my parents whispering.

"You need to get her under control," my father says.

"I know," my mother quickly says. "She'll learn to behave—I'll make sure of that."

"Yeah, right. You can't even get your own shit together, let alone hers." He pauses. "I have stuff to do. You can figure out what *to do with her. And take care of everything." A second later a door slams.*

The house falls silent for a while, and part of me wonders if my mother has left. Finally, I decide to check. I'm quiet as I open the door and peer into the hallway.

No one is around, but my mother is crying in her room. The door is open, so I tiptoe to the doorway and peek inside. She's kneeling on the floor in front of the bed, and her head is lowered. My dad's gun safe is wide open, which is strange—he almost always keeps it locked. And scattered across the carpet are pieces of paper, along with something shiny and silver.

I step forward to get a better look.

The pieces of paper are actually photos of people dancing in the trees. I don't recognize them and can't tell what the shiny, silver object is, so I inch forward to get a better look.

But my mother scoops it up before I can tell what it is. Then her head snaps in my direction.

I trip backward. "I'm sorry."

She staggers to her feet and rushes toward me, but then she abruptly freezes as someone screams. A streak of bright red ribbons floats in front of my face—

Darkness abruptly clouds my head...

I hate the dark even more than I loathe the light, where at least I can see every horrible thing happening. The darkness, though, hides all the bad things. It coils around the fear and strangles it, making breathing complicated. It lets the monsters creep out from their hiding spots, their clawed hands reaching for me ...

Something is changing ...

I'm no longer in my childhood home.

I'm near the woods ...

A red ribbon floats in front of my face ...

And someone lies in front of me.

The girl I saw dead. She's there. She's always there, consuming my mind—a ghost haunting my guilty conscience.

I let her die that night—

My eyes fly open, and I bolt upright, gasping for air. My heart slams against my chest as darkness presses down on me. I fumble to find the remote, then turn on the television. The glow of the screen allows me to breathe evenly again.

Even now, years later, the dark makes me feel claustrophobic. It makes me think of the past and dark bedrooms, shadowy forests, and haunted memories I can't quite piece together. It makes me aware of the things that slip out of the darkness when they think no one can see them.

I usually sleep with a lamp on, but the bulb burnt out before I went to bed, and I didn't have any to replace it. So, I dozed off with the television on, but sleep mode must've kicked in at some point.

I take a few measured breaths as I lie back down. The other side of my bed is empty and has been for six months, ever since my ex-husband, Jason, moved out. The strange thing is, toward the end of my marriage, I hated when it was occupied. But now, as I lie here, with the lingering fear of my nightmare pulsating through my veins, I long for someone to be beside me. Not because I miss Jason. I just miss not being alone.

I hate that about myself.

I could call Jason and tell him about the nightmarish memory, but I know what he'd say. He's predictable that way.

"Go back to sleep and try not to think about it."

He wouldn't ask me what the nightmare was about. He rarely asked me anything about myself. I didn't notice it while we were together, but now, I think about it a lot—how he didn't know the real me.

I'm not even sure I know myself.

I knew a lot about Jason, though. Too much—things I wish I didn't.

But when we first got together, I never analyzed the things. In the end, though, all those things consumed my mind every single damn day.

As familiar sensations of panic come rushing back to me, I try to recall what my therapist said to do in these kind of situations.

Take a few deep breaths.

Air in.

Air out.

In.

Out—

Ring…

I blink, confused. Who the hell is calling? It's in the middle of the night.

I pick my phone up from off the nightstand. When my mom's name flashes across the glowing screen, my worry morphs into nausea. I shouldn't answer. I don't have to. I'm a grown woman and can do what I want. Maybe I wouldn't have if it wasn't the middle of the night.

Something terrible has happened—I can feel it. And while I don't want to care, I do. I wish I could cut that part of myself out—this need to worry and care. I want to snap it off of me like a decaying limb and toss it away so I won't have to decay with it.

"Hello?" I answer right before the call goes to voicemail.

"Why did it take you so long to answer?" my mother asks.

"Hello to you, too," I mumble, then sigh. "It's after midnight. You woke me up." A lie. But I learned a long time ago that when it comes to my mother, lying is the best option.

"You go to sleep too early," she criticizes. "You're young enough that you should be staying up later."

My lip twitches. "I have to work tomorrow."

"I thought you didn't work on Saturdays?"

Round and round we go. There were times when I was younger and swore I had to be living on a merry-go-round that never stopped spinning.

I yank my fingers through my hair. "Did you call for a reason? Or just to lecture me on my work and sleeping schedule?"

"Of course I called you for a reason." She gives a short pause. "It's your father. He's dead."

For a moment, I think I'm hallucinating, that I'm still stuck in that nightmare I just had.

But would this even be a nightmare?

"What?" I ask.

"Your dad, he died." She says it so matter-of-factly.

Suddenly, the world feels endlessly still. Like that fucking merry-go-round I've been trapped on has finally broke.

My father is dead.

He's gone.

I'll never see him again.

I should be crying.

It feels like there should be tears.

But nothing.

That's all I feel.

This uneven stillness.

No spinning.

Just … emptiness.

My father was right when he used to say that I was defective. Because I should be crying. At least, that's what most people would be doing. But my eyes are dry. Empty. Void. Just like my heart.

"How did he die?" I finally manage to ask.

"He fell."

That gets me to sit up. "He what? Like he fell down the stairs?"

"No, off the cliff that's on that trail you used to go to all the time. He was up there and fell and …" She pauses. "Just come home, okay? I need you here, Ava. I need you."

"I need you, Mommy. I need you," I cry as I hide under the kitchen table.

But she never comes.

Part of me wants to do the same thing to her.

But that's the thing I've learned over the years. As heartless as I wish I could be, I always seem to be the one crying and pointlessly begging for help. I've been there before with my mother, many, many times. But one of these moments stands out to me the most—just a few hours after I came running out of the woods all those years ago.

Even now, the emotions are so prominent that if I close my eyes and concentrate, I can still feel them. I can also see some of the images connected to them. But everything in them—all the faces and trees around me—are cracked and distorted, so figuring out what's a lie and what's the truth is almost impossible. But perhaps my mind splintered the truth because what happened was so horrifying that even my brain doesn't want me to see it again.

CHAPTER 2

SOMETIMES, I DON'T SEE MYSELF WHEN I STARE IN THE MIRROR. I see *her*. It's not like I resemble *her*. I'm worn, exhausted, with shadows on my cheekbones and under my green eyes. But if I stare long enough, without blinking—without reacting or acknowledging the basic need of my eyes—the images begin to alter, and *she* appears.

Even though my chest throbs, at times I find myself standing in front of the mirror, refusing to blink until my eyes sting and tears drip down my cheeks. And even then, I push harder, refusing to look away until it becomes unbearable because it's what I deserve. It's a twisted thing, this desire to see her again when it's so polluted with guilt.

My feelings about returning home are similar to this. Part of me doesn't want to return to the memories of everything that occurred while *she* was my friend. Another part of me doesn't want to go back because of *everything* else. And yet, despite all of this—despite *all* the reasons why I shouldn't—I tell my mom I will. It makes my stomach ache the moment I do as the memories buried beneath the dirt—the haunting ones, the painful ones, and the ones painted in blood—threaten to claw to the surface.

But everything was terrible. A few memories carry a lightness that shines briefly through the darkness; ones where I'm laughing while dancing by a fire, and my hand is warm from another, our fingers are laced together, and there's a greeting of a flirty smile …

Ones where I'm with *him*.

I slam the thought out of my mind.

While remembering the haunting memories can be painful, the beautiful ones are also excruciatingly unbearable because they're all interwoven.

Before I end the phone call with my mother, I attempt to get more details about my father's death, but she's evasive. But she did like keeping little half-truths from me just to drive me to the brink of insanity. Or sometimes she'd be nice for a second only to snatch it away. Comfort and security were unsteady throughout my childhood, and this inconsistency continued even after I got married. Now that I'm on the brink of a divorce, I've found a bit of steadiness, but it's so foreign and unfamiliar that I often become anxious over the quietness. I feel I'm about to lose that drop of security, though. That should be reason enough for me not to go, and yet, here I am, packing my bags.

"You know, I've heard of people not going to their parent's funeral," my friend, Clara, says as I stuff the last of my clothes into my suitcase. She's sitting on the edge of my bed, watching me with worry. "If they have issues with their parents."

It's been a day since my mom woke me up and broke the news about my father's death. Although *broke* seems like such a strange word to use. Like it was supposed to break me, and yet numbness has taken residency inside me instead.

I haven't told Clara that I feel nothing about my father's death, but she knows enough about me that she's aware of my fucked-up relationship with my family. She knows I've barely seen them since I was seventeen, but she doesn't know the whole story. I'm not sure if I'll ever tell her. Even my therapist doesn't know *everything* that happened to me.

I have a lot of secrets. But almost every one I have, someone else also owns a piece of it too. It's a frightening thing—that there are people that know about the dark things I've done. My only reassurance is that most of them will never tell, either because they have to remain quiet or because I carry some of their dark secrets as well.

"I know I don't have to go." I sit on my suitcase to zip it up, then peer around my bedroom, wondering if I've forgotten anything. "But I think I need to do this … Thanks for coming with me, by the way."

"Of course. I want to be there for you. Plus, it's not like I have anything better to do. Well, besides going to work. But, at this point, a funeral sounds way more enticing than going to that shithole for another day," Clara says as she stands up.

She's probably the most honest person I've ever met and the exact opposite of me in every way, including physical looks. Where she has shoulder-length blonde hair, blue eyes, and is curvy, my hair is long, wavy, and dark, my eyes are green, and I'm tall and lean. But we do share similarities, like we both like to wear a lot of dark colors, are obsessed with 90's music and old-school horror movies, and we like to go running. It's how we met—during a run.

I'd never gone for a run before until Jason left me. The first time I did it I was having a panic attack over the emptiness of the house and the stillness and quietness that left me too much time to think. I was so used to chaos and loudness that I felt out of place, and it left too much of an opportunity for my mind to scream at me. I called my therapist, who suggested I leave the house and go for a walk. So, I did. But the more I walked, the quicker my heart beat. So I walked faster. Eventually, I ran. I did that until I was so exhausted I couldn't think of anything, and then I went home and got a whole night's rest for the first time in months. I've been running ever since, and I met Clara during one of these runs.

While we're not very alike, it works for us. She's social, more lighthearted, and has never been married. But we're only twenty-three. It's more out of the ordinary that I've been married for six years and am getting a divorce. She also had to try really hard to become my friend. I'm not even sure why she did, and while I like that she's in my life, a piece of me wishes I'd never met her because I'm toxic. I ruin things—I ruin people.

"Is your boss still being an asshole?" I check the time on my watch.

"Yeah, he's such a pervert. He's always looking down my shirt and doesn't even try to hide it." She examines her reflection in a mirror, then traces her finger along the edge of her lips.

"You should report him."

"Ha, wouldn't it be such a lovely world if I could just go and report sexual harassment and everything would favor on my side?" She sighs, facing me with her hands on her hips. "Besides, he's the owner's son."

My lips dip downward. "I didn't know that … Maybe it's time for a new job."

"Maybe." Wistfulness flitters into her voice, a longing to make my words come true, but thinking she can't, at least until she finds another job. Even then, there's a chance another pervert will be waiting there, wearing their mask made of narcissist superiority.

"How far is the drive to this place, anyway?" She changes the subject as she sends a text.

"Like, eight hours." I lug my bag off the bed, and it hits the floor with a thud.

Her brows rise. One of them is pierced, and she fiddles with the metal stud. "Eight hours? Damn, I can't remember the last time I went on an eight-hour drive. Maybe never."

"Welcome to the land of rural towns in the middle of fucking nowhere," I say as I head out of the room, wheeling the bag behind me.

She trails behind me, continuing to text someone. "I need to look this place up and see how bad it is."

"Oh, it's bad." I head into the kitchen of my apartment that I've lived in for a handful of months.

Jason is getting the home in the divorce, along with many of our belongings. That's the downfall of being the one who stayed home and took care of everything, even though there wasn't much to take care of since we didn't have any kids. We were trying to. Or, well, that's what Jason and everyone else believed. I was secretly taking birth control because the idea of becoming a mother terrified me.

So, instead of having kids, I ended up spending the last six years cleaning, cooking, and taking care of the bills. I never really wanted to get into that position. I had dreams of doing something else with my life. Not that anything was ever a set thing. I just wondered what it'd be like to be something, like maybe a lawyer, a detective, or a writer. But I'm not very talented at anything, and when I met Jason, he suggested it might be good if I stayed home and took care of the household.

I was so young and in such a bad place that I absorbed his words like I was a dying plant and he was the sun. Only he wasn't the sun. He was a dark, polluted sky, sucking out all my oxygen. But the process was so gradual that it took me forever to realize it was happening.

And now, here I am, working at a coffee shop and I can barely afford my bills. But I feel better than I have in a long time.

Or, at least a bit freer … sometimes.

Plus, I got our dog.

I had to offer up most of the furniture in exchange for him, but the dog, Bailey, has been there for me more than anyone. In fact, he's the most important thing in my life, besides maybe Clara.

"Where's Bailey?" I ask as I peer around the small kitchen area. "I need to get him loaded in the car." I check the living room and then behind the recliner.

Usually, Bailey is waiting for me behind it, but he isn't.

"The last time I saw him, he was hiding under the table," Clara tells me as she types something into her phone. She pulls a face, and I'm guessing she's figured out Star Meadows doesn't have a coffee shop. Unless it's changed since I left. But I doubt it.

It's not a changing sort of place, which is the appeal of it to some people. It stands still, never in motion, simply existing, like I have for the last several years.

I'm afraid of these things that have stood still, that my old life will be waiting for me, perfectly preserved for my return. And so will the memories, both the good and the bad ones. All of the good ones are connected to two people. One of them gave me my first kiss, and the other gave me my first taste of safety in the form of a friendship, even if we were living in the middle of a fucking hailstorm—

"Oh my hell, there's not even a coffee place there!" Clara exclaims, yanking me from my thoughts.

"Yeah, sorry." I shove all thoughts of my past aside and return to looking for Bailey.

As I walk over to the kitchen table, my legs feel shaky. I take a deep breath, then another, hoping Clara doesn't notice that I'm unraveling. Then I look under the table and find Bailey cowering. He's a lab mix, and he's the biggest sweetheart.

"You can always bail out if you want to," I tell Clara as I stare at Bailey. *It's like he knows.* "I can handle going by myself."

Can't I? I mean, I handled living there for five years by myself. Sure, I had parents, but I was mostly by myself. And I survived because I'm here, and that means survival.

"No, I'll go," Clara assures me. "I'm just going to have to figure out this coffee situation.' She wavers then perks up. "Hey, maybe this could be my chance to learn how to make my coffee."

"That sounds like a good idea."

"Yeah, we'll just have to stop and buy some stuff on our way out. You cool with that?"

"Of course."

"Sweet. I'll do a curbside order." She falls silent as she starts ordering stuff online.

I focus on Bailey. "Come on, boy," I try to coax him out from underneath the table. "We need to get going."

He doesn't budge, and his tail is tucked between his legs. He looks so sad and frightened, so I scratch his ear. He stares at me with his big eyes.

"I know how you feel," I whisper. "I feel that way right now." I've felt that way frequently throughout my life.

Six months ago, when I moved out of the house I shared with Jason and started taking care of myself, I was scared shitless. Five years ago, I felt the same way when I left Star Meadows to create a life with him. And it was the same when I was younger, and my dad would yell at me.

But those weren't the worst times. No, there are two moments in my life where I've been the most terrified, where I found myself longing to curl up and hide.

The first was when I was fifteen years old. The day started like any other, with me bored and looking for something to do. A lot about that day is covered with canopies of shadowy branches that conceal many of the details. But a few things creep through the crevasses and into the light.

The snow falling from the gray sky.

The piercing scream.

And the blood that painted the snow.

The second time I felt that sort of fear was eerily similar, only no blood existed, only the soundlessness that death can cause.

CHAPTER 3

It takes us an hour to load everything into my car. After we do, we make a quick stop at the store to pick up Clara's order. Then she begs me to take her to the nearest coffee shop so she can get the largest cold brew they have, like if she drinks enough now, she won't need any for a week.

I order one, too, but not a large, figuring my nerves are too jittery already, and I don't need to be adding fuel to this.

Before we pull out onto the freeway, I open my GPS. It's been a while since I've been home, and I have a terrible sense of direction, so I want to be positive I don't miss one of the turn-offs. I close up my other apps, but what's open on the internet browser makes me pause.

The day before I learned about the news of my father, I craved a change in my life, and that desire led me to look into community colleges that offered GED testing.

This isn't the first time I've looked up how to get a GED. I did it a few years ago because I wanted to do something with my life other than exist. And I thought that maybe I'd even get the courage to go to community college after I did. That was the plan that was brewing in me. But when Jason discovered I was researching all of this, he planted a seed in my head, a toxic one that slowly started to kill my soul day by day.

"Why waste your time and money on something like that?" he said, slipping his arms around my waist.

I had mentioned what I wanted to do while cooking dinner. We had been married about a year or so at that point, and it was early enough that he hadn't shown all of his true colors, just sparks of orange and yellow flames when things became too dark.

"And besides, I'm going to be taking care of you for the rest of your life," he added.

Maybe he was right, I thought, but it made me feel sick.

Still, I smiled and agreed, being my typical agreeable self. But the smile felt odd, like my lips were numb.

As the days and years started to blur into nothingness mixed with raging fights, I found myself looking up GED information again. I'd read about it but never commit to taking it, too scared of another failure. It was what I was known for—that and not doing well at school. I was pretty, though. At least that's what people told me, so I guess I had that.

But I craved more, and I longed for the courage to just take the damn test. I was constantly staring at that website, trying to convince myself to do it, and Jason had caught me doing it again and became annoyed.

"I thought we talked about this, Ava," he said, reaching to shut down the computer. "You don't need to further your education when I'm taking care of you. And eventually, you'll be taking care of our children, so it'll just be a waste of money and time." He leaned down and kissed my cheek, whispering, "Besides, I don't want you to be upset when you fail. You know how you get when you mess things up." He slanted back and smiled. "So, what's for dinner?"

So, once again, I didn't take the test. Then, eventually, Jason announced he was leaving me for someone else, and I was completely panicking because I literally had nothing.

But after the panic subsided, the trauma that I'd suppressed for years seeped to the surface, and I had an emotional breakdown and had to go to the emergency room. After that came therapy. That's when things started to become a bit better.

I still have no clue where I am mentally, but the idea of taking the GED test doesn't sound as terrifying as it once did. But that doesn't mean I've gotten past the screen-staring.

"What's that?" Clara asks, startling me.

My attention darts to her. She's staring at my phone. The screen is still on the GED website, on the enrollment page.

"Are you thinking about taking it?" Her gaze shifts to me, her brows are elevated, and excitement is in her eyes.

I shrug and then shake my head. "Probably not. I was just thinking about it while I was bored the other day."

She eyes me over dubiously, then grins. "Well, I think you should."

I arch a brow. "Seriously?"

She nods. "Absolutely. It could be good for you, Aves."

Could it? Or will I fail, and it'll be the final crack that shatters me?

"Maybe," is all I say since it makes me anxious even talking about it.

I close the browser and leave the map on, then pull out of the parking lot and onto the road.

Ten minutes later, music is playing from the stereo, and the sunlight is shining through the window. Clara and I have our sunglasses on and, since it's summer, the windows are rolled down. It's hot, but the fresh air feels nice against my skin.

When I was younger, I used to lay in the backyard for hours, underneath the sun with my arms stretched out, my eyes closed, and the grass pressed against my skin. I'd get a rash from it afterward, but I never cared. Outside is where I felt calmer. Even when it snowed, I'd lie in the cold, all bundled up, letting the snowflakes kiss my skin.

Fresh air is usually good for me, so I need the windows down right now. Clara isn't complaining, so I figure we'll sweat it out for a while until it becomes unbearable.

We stay on the freeway for a few hours before taking an offramp leading to a highway. No freeways lead to Star Meadows, so the rest of the drive is on a two-lane road that weaves around the mountains.

"This road is sketchy," Clara mutters as I wind around sharp corners bordered with flourishing trees and mountains.

"I know, but I'm driving safely." I grip the steering wheel with both hands. "I've been on this road a ton of times. It looks worse than it is." That's a lie. It's as bad as it looks. But I don't want to scare her more.

She's holding onto the handle above the door with her eyes glued to the road. "Okay ..." She takes a breath. "You really had to learn how to drive on these kinds of roads?" She flicks a glance toward me.

My mind wanders back to the past, of me driving on the road with the windows down, snowflakes spilling into the interior of the car …

Music is playing from the stereo, and the singer is screaming lyrics of anger and rage, about the cruelty of the word. I can feel what they're deep inside my bones. I can also feel the smoke telling me it will be okay.

Whispering me little lies …

Promises that everything being okay.

Numb. I feel so numb. And numb is better than everything else.

She laughs. "Isn't this so much fun?"

I smile. It's real. I think, anyway. "Yeah—"

"Ava!" Clara cries as I start to swerve off the road.

I jolt and swerve back onto the road, not too fast, or I'll risk overcorrecting the car.

Clara breathes profusely as she gapes at me. "What the hell just happened?"

"Sorry," I tell her as calmly as I can.

The truth is I scared myself, too.

"Do you want me to drive?" she offers. "Maybe you need a break."

"I'm fine." My hands are sweaty, but I don't want to remove them from the steering wheel to wipe them off. "I promise it won't happen again."

She tosses me a wary look but settles back in the seat.

I continue to drive, keeping my head in the present.

I love to drive places. Some people might think flying is much better. But being on planes gives me anxiety. I like rolling down the windows, letting in the fresh air, cranking up the music, flipping through songs, and belting out lyrics. I like stopping at fast food places and grabbing snacks from the gas station. I like being able to stop and look at the scenery. I love being able to breathe.

What I like is having control. There's no other way to put it. It's plain and simple. Only, it's not that simple at all.

Understanding the complexities behind my desire to control everything took me a while. And when I started to grasp it, the knowledge began to unravel something in me, like the windy road I'm driving on. I know where it's going—the route we're on. It's the entire point of this road trip. And yet, even though the final destination is on the GPS, I feel anxious, out of control, and lost.

Because while I'm aware of the physical location of our destination, I'm not quite sure where I'll end up mentally.

And I hate it.

That not knowing.

That hits me about three-quarters of the way there. My stomach clenches at the reality. I try to blame it on all the Cheetos I ate. It's a lie. But the lie is easier to accept. Isn't that usually the story?

I attempt to lie to myself for another few miles, telling myself that stomach-wrenching nausea will pass. But eventually, vomit burns in my throat.

I spot a pullover area. It's near an overlook with a view of cliffs bordering a river gliding over rocks. It's beautiful, but I can also see the horrifying idea of falling off the cliffs.

My phobia of heights developed when I was younger, and my family would go into the mountains. I would cry hysterically whenever we drove on the mountainside or hiked. My parents never cared and would either ignore me, tell me to shut up or make me get closer to the ledge to scare the phobia out of me.

"What's going on?" Clara straightens in her seat as I pull over into the turn-out spot.

"My stomach's being weird." I shove the car into park.

Bailey perks up in the back seat, wagging his tail and peering around.

"I'm just going to get out for a second in case I throw up."

She reaches for her seat belt. "Do you want me to get out with you?"

I shake my head and hold up my hand. "Nah. I don't want to make you watch me puke my guts out on the side of the road."

Despite my fear, I still get out of the car and walk to the other side. I don't look directly at the cliffs. Instead, I stare at the gravel, focusing on breathing and not emptying the contents of my stomach.

Air in, air out, Ava. Take deep breaths. Don't let the pain get to you.

But ultimately, the pain wins. I brace my hands on my knees and vomit. When I'm finished, I feel better but a little weak and lightheaded.

I slump against the side of my car and take a few measured breaths, trying to let fresh air return to my lungs and clear out the dizziness while I look out at the cliffs. The sight makes breathing more complicated, but I do it anyway.

My therapist says facing my fears in baby steps is good for me. It's not like I have to walk to the ledge and peer down. I just need to stare at the jagged rocks and the water dancing across them. I need to focus on the beauty of it.

Can you see it, Ava? Can you see past the fear and see the beauty in it?

For a brief second, I can, like my brain has snapped a photo of the shadows and the light mixing, of the water and of the rocks uniting, of the cliffs, of the vast space between them, and of the ground contrasting with each other.

But then my phone rings, and the photo fades, like a damaged set of Polaroids I had when I was younger.

I took a bunch of pictures with my camera, and for some reason, the images only stayed on the film for a moment before fading. I could never get them back, those snapshots of memories I was trying to keep.

Ironically, later in life, I'd find myself wishing I could forget every single one of my memories. And some of them did fade, like old photos left out in the sunlight, all damaged and blurred. But others stayed. Every line, shape, and shade are all there, never to be forgotten, no matter how much I want to leave them in the sun to wither and die.

Since my head is hurting, I ignore the call.

About thirty seconds later, a voicemail arrives. I almost don't check it, but then decide I probably should.

Pushing away from the car, I head toward the driver's side while dialing my voicemail. It clicks on, and a recording plays of someone breathing heavily into the line.

And just like that, I'm forced back to a time when I was hounded relentlessly by calls like this. And while that doesn't seem alarming, the first time it happened was also around the same time teenage girls began disappearing from Star Meadows.

Three girls, to be exact.

Their bodies were never discovered and in the end, the police declared them runaways. Their evidence? They were drug addicts and dropouts, so there was no way their disappearances were anyone's fault but their own. The entire town believed that without too much of a fuss. Well, except for the girls' parents.

Me? I couldn't stop thinking about what happened in those woods only months before they started vanishing. Even now, I question if the incidents are somehow connected. But I never had any proof. Just like I never figured out who was calling me back then.

Maybe those calls never meant anything, though, and it was only an odd coincidence that I was receiving them at the same time girls began disappearing. Perhaps this call doesn't mean anything. Still, it makes me uneasy that I received one on the day I decide to return to my hometown.

I move to put the phone back into my pocket when it rings again. This time, the call is from my mother. I could answer it. I'm holding the phone. Instead, I silence the call and climb back into the car, pretending nothing happened.

Something I've always been good at.

CHAPTER 4

THE PAST...

I'M STARING AT THE FOUR WALLS OF MY BEDROOM THAT ARE covered in photos of celebrity guys I have crushes on. I sometimes like looking at them and dreaming of what it'd be like to date them or to date in general. I've never dated anyone, but I want to. But no one ever seems to pay attention to me.

Loneliness. I can feel it in my bones, like they're hollowing out from the lack of substance filling my life. I want to change this. I want to feel something other than the vast space of this room and empty this house.

It's too quiet here, mostly because my parents are hardly ever home. I'm not even sure where they go. Sometimes they tell me. Sometimes, they don't. Even at seven years old, I can remember being in my house alone, playing with my toys and trying to convince myself ghosts weren't real. I was afraid of the quiet, of the vacancy, of the what-ifs that could exist in the stillness. It was a weird thing to think about, and I longed for it to stop, for my mind to just be silent.

And yet here I am again, lying in my bed, with silence wrapping around me like flesh over muscle and bone. And familiar trepidation is congesting my chest.

This time, it's not ghosts I'm afraid of. No, I'm worried this will always be it for me. That I'll forever be alone. That this mundane ordinariness is all there is. It's depressing. There is no poetic way to put it.

Endless boredom. It's terrifying. Maybe even more so than ghosts.

I decide to turn on some music to distract my mind. I put on a sullen song and focus on dissecting the lyrics. For a while, it's enough. But even that becomes boring.

I do have a few friends. I wish I had more, but talking to people makes me feel like I'm being choked. How ironic is that? The girl who hates boredom and loneliness also has a phobia of talking to people. I am a basket case, just like the song is saying.

After listening to a few songs, I finally work up the courage to drag my ass off my bed and call Livia, who I consider my best friend. I don't know if she considers me as hers. At times, I get this feeling she doesn't even like me, yet she hangs out with me at school and sometimes after. And sometimes she wants to go to the movies, she'll invite me, but not always. That'd be okay, except she often rubs the lack of an invite in my face. But she's easy to talk to and doesn't mind the quiet like I do. Plus, we both like the same music and movies, and we have similar clothing styles.

I walk out of my room and into the family room to call her. The area and my bedroom are in the basement, and it's dark down here. My parents sleep upstairs where large picture windows allow sunlight to shine in, even in the winter. Another room is upstairs, too, but when we moved to the snowy town of Star Meadows a few years ago, I thought having my own space sounded like a good idea. That having an entire basement to myself would be fun. I was in a weird mood when I made the decision, angry with my parents for making us move in the first place. I had friends. I had a life, and I worked hard to get it since I had to overcome this fear of talking to people. It had taken me forever to achieve this, and once I felt like I was almost getting this sense of security in my life, my parents announced we were moving hours away. And any security I felt was gone. So were my friends.

I often worry this funk I've been existing in will be my life forever.

But I try not to think about that as I grab my phone and sit on the sofa. I don't text Livia because, more than likely, she won't respond. Instead, I dial her number and cross my fingers she'll want to do something.

She just got her driver's license, and it's late May, so the snow has almost melted. Usually, it wouldn't have, but it was a mild winter since the winters here are usually intense.

I chew on my fingernail as I listen to the phone ring. I'm fidgety and nervous. It's the dumbest thing. I've known Livia for three years. We're not strangers, and yet I go over what I'm going to say to her in my head.

Her mom answers after three rings. "Hello?"

It's odd that her mom answers her phone, but Livia told me her mom has boundary issues and likes to pry into her life.

"Um … Hey … Is Livia there?" As I drag out my words, it

makes me pull a face at myself.

I am such a loser.

"Yeah, hold on," she tells me.

I hear some rustling around—I think she might be taking the phone to Livia.

"Someone called you," Livia's mom says. "I answered it because you carelessly left your phone on the counter."

"Sorry," Livia replies. "Who is it?"

"I think it's Ava."

"Great," Livia murmurs with annoyance.

I summon a deep breath, preparing for potential rejection.

"Hello?" Livia says into the phone.

"Hey, it's Ava." I cringe at how uneven my voice sounds. "Do you want to do something? My parents are gone, and I'm bored."

"I can't," she replies. "I'm going to the movies with Zoe."

I smash my lips together, hoping she'll add a: *you should come with us.*

Instead, she says, "So, yeah, I can't do anything with you today."

"Oh. Okay." My disappointment is evident. I open my mouth to ask if she can do something tomorrow.

But she mutters a quick, "Bye," and then hangs up.

I force out an exhale, as if my lungs can push out the entire weight of her rejection, but that doesn't work. My lungs must be weak or something.

I release another breath before I return to my room, but I stop in the middle of it, not wanting to climb into bed again.

Restlessness stirs inside me, along with envy that my friends are hanging out without me. They're both my friends, too. I'm just closer with Livia. Although Zoe can be nicer. I could call her and see if she'll invite me, but that seems pathetic. And Livia would be irritated. But maybe I shouldn't care. I *shouldn't* care. I shouldn't. So, why the hell do I?

Because I'm pathetic.

Because I'm stupid.

Because I'm tired of being alone.

Alone. Alone. Alone. The girl no one wants to be around. That has to mean something, right? Because there can't be something wrong with everyone else, so it has to be me.

"*Gah*," I let out my frustration as my thoughts move too fast.

Then I sink down to the floor that's covered with dirty clothes, CD cases, shoes, and half-burned candles. The brown carpet is barely visible underneath the mess, my bed is unmade, and food wrappers are piled on my dresser. My mom told me to clean my room a few weeks ago. She thinks I did, but only because she hasn't been down here since then.

I could clean it. It's not like I have anything better to do. But the idea seems like it'll feed the boredom.

My mind starts racing again with reasons as to why I'm so bored. It's too much at this point.

I need to get the hell out of this room. I'll go for a walk. We live near the foothills of the mountains that enclose the town. The town's population is spread around several miles of acres, so the probability of running into someone is low. That's the one thing I love but also hate about this town. It makes no sense. How can I want to be around people—dream about it—and at the same time fear it? Can you fear the desire of something?

I get up and put on a pair of old jeans, sneakers, a long-sleeve shirt, and a coat because, even though the snow has melted, it's likely around forty degrees outside. I'm not sure if it's sunny or cloudy, but I guess I'll find out.

I zip up my coat and start to head out of my room when an idea occurs to me, one that might make this walk more adventurous.

I backtrack to my room, open the cupboard that holds some of my CD cases, and reach behind the top row to retrieve a pack of cigarettes that I found at the fairgrounds the other day when I went walking around town with Livia. The pack looked like it had gotten wet. At least, that's what Livia said.

"They're probably ruined," she told me, bunching up her nose at the pack.

I opened it and peered inside. Some were falling apart, but not all of them. "They might not all be."

"So?" She crossed her arms and gave me this disapproving look. "Why would you want them, anyway? Smoking is so bad for you."

I could tell if I kept the pack, she would judge me. I didn't want that, but I wanted the cigarettes. I'm not even sure why.

Ultimately, I had set them back down where I had found them. Then we walked away, but Livia needed to stop and use the bathroom on our way out. While she went, I had gone back, picked up the cigarettes, and stuffed them into my pocket.

And for a brief moment, I had felt … well, something other than emptiness inside me. I just didn't know what it was.

But now I wonder if I smoke one if maybe I'll feel something again.

So, I grab the pack, stuff it in my pocket, along with a lighter, and head out of the house.

The sky is cloudy and gloomy with the taunt that it might curse the land with snow again. I try to ignore it, zip up my coat, and hike across the front yard and start down the road that leads away from my yard.

Boot tracks are imprinting the dirt, and they look fresh, which means someone has been walking around out here. That's a little weird since we live out in the middle of nowhere, but our neighbors sometimes do come out for walks here.

Dismissing the boot prints, I keep hiking up the road. Ten minutes later, I arrive at the mouth of a canyon. A trail is at the entrance of it that weaves through the towering hills that are blooming with trees. For about three miles, the path is relatively flat, and then it starts to ascend upward around the hills. That's where I always stop. I hate that I have to, but I can't seem to get over my crippling fear of heights.

Maybe today, though, I'll be able to overcome it.

That's what I attempt to convince myself as I start up the muddy path that's dotted with various footprints. I hike for a while, taking my time while fiddling with the pack of cigarettes inside my pocket. I'm not sure how far I should walk before I try to light one. I don't want to get caught, and yet the idea that I could makes my heart sputter excitedly. It's like I'm excited and scared at the same time. The feeling kind of makes me dizzy, but I'll take that over the steady decline I've been feeling lately.

Finally, the excitement becomes too overwhelming, and I

duck off the path and into the trees. I take out the pack of cigarettes, my fingers trembling as I open it—I'm not sure if it's from the cold or adrenaline rushing through my body. Whatever the reason, it takes a lot to get one of the cigarettes out. Then I put it between my lips, dig out my lighter, and attempt to light one. It takes several flicks before the flame ignites. Then I put the flame to the end of the cigarette and light it like I've seen people do in movies—

The paper crinkles. Livia was wrong. They're not ruined. They're just fine—

I hack out a cough as smoke puffs into my mouth. I cough so hard I see stars. No snowflakes. Wait … those are real.

Shit, it's snowing. And hard. And I'm at least a few miles away from home. I should take off, and run home before it turns into a full-on blizzard. I've heard of people getting stuck in these types of situations, where they're in the mountains when a storm rolls in and they can't find their way out. When they get found, they've gotten frostbite and lose toes and fingers. Or on occasion, a storm takes a life. It's rare, but it happens; And what if it happens to me?

Panicking, I hurry out of the trees. I still have the cigarette in my hand and smoke is lacing the air, along with my breath. The air is quiet like it always is with a storm.

But then it suddenly isn't.

Suddenly, the air, it's not as still.

In fact, it's shaky, like an earthquake, a slow build-up that threatens destruction. And eventually, it does, as a piercing scream cuts through the stillness.

I swear a red ribbon floats by me. Then everything goes dark.

CHAPTER 5

A lot of tourists drive through Star Meadows in the summer since the highway leads to one of the entrances to Yellowstone. They usually stop in town to shop in the quaint stores that sell knickknacks of outdoorsy things that most people will rarely use. Then, after spending a few days roaming around, they realize they like the noisy side of life. That being in the quiet is more complicated than being surrounded by noise because it lets you dissect your own thoughts way too much until they're all hacked into pieces. And, for some people, that's difficult because it means seeing things about yourself that perhaps you don't want to acknowledge exists. I know this because I've lived in the quiet for too long.

It was something I also heard when I was younger, and I had a brief job at a gas station. Some customers would come in and talk about how pretty the town is. Some would ask for directions. Some would ask me how it felt living in a place so pretty. A few, though, asked me how I didn't go crazy living somewhere that didn't even have a coffee shop.

I wanted to reply with, "How did you not know I'm not crazy?" I mean, I could've been. I thought I was.

Honestly, maybe I am.

But, out of politeness, I would lie and merely say, "For some people, the lack of things is what's appealing."

Usually, people accepted that answer.

One man in particular didn't.

He looked at me with an amused sort of smile and asked, "What about you? Do you find it appealing?"

He was in his twenties, and I got the impression he was flirting with me. I'm not even sure why I thought that. I could have been totally wrong. If he was, though, I should've been revolted. He was old—too old for me at sixteen.

And yet, deep down inside, I felt flattered at the possibility that someone was paying attention to me. No one ever did. And, back then, I was naïve about the dangers of older men who paid too much attention to young girls.

All I knew was that I wanted to reply in a clever way that would make me feel cool because I wanted to feel cool for once. I wanted to be noticed. To not just be this thing that existed. But my anxiety got the best of me, and instead, I let out a flustered, "It's okay, I guess." The words came out rushed. I'm sure I sounded like an idiot.

But he gave me this smile, one that let me believe he didn't think I was an idiot.

"Hmm … I guess I'll have to take your word for it," he said as he paid for his soda and chips. "I'll see you around, Ava." He winked at me before walking away from the counter.

At first, I was confused how he knew my name, but then I remembered I was wearing a nametag. I also didn't get why he acted like he would see me again if he was just passing through.

He was right, though.

I would see him again. At a party a few months later.

And I would regret being polite to him because he hit on me all night then tried to kiss me, leaving a horrible taste in my mouth and a faint scar on my mind.

And still, I was too polite about it.

I've always hated being polite. I don't understand why I can't just tell the truth. It'd make things easier. At least, it feels that way. Then I wouldn't have to spend so much time trying to decipher what people actually mean. I also wouldn't spend so much time lying.

But I was taught to be polite. I mean, it's not like my mom and dad sat me down one day and gave me a lesson on politeness. It was through little things, like when I told my grandma the truth when she asked if I liked her casserole and I said it was kind of dry.

My grandma got so upset that she didn't speak for the rest of dinner. Afterward, my mom took me to the guest bedroom and spanked me, per my dad's request. Before she did though, she told me she was going to and asked me if I knew why. I honestly didn't, and when I told her that, she replied, "Because you hurt Grandma's feelings."

And then she spanked me.

And it fucking hurt.

But pain for pain, I guess. At least, that's what I was taught.

I was four years old when that happened, and even though

I was confused at the time, looking back, I think that's when I started fearing telling the truth and started to ponder the idea of lying to protect myself.

"My ass is starting to hurt," Clara declares as we near the outskirts of the town where the land is dotted with the occasional log cabin or old brick home.

"Yeah, mine, too," I tell her. "But we're getting close."

She eyes the mountains, and then the line of cars in front of us. "Why is there so much traffic?" she wonders as she puts her hair up into a high ponytail.

I crank up the air conditioning. "It's tourist season."

It's mid-summer, so the highway is extremely busy. Passing cars isn't an option due to the long line of vehicles going both ways. But briefly, I contemplate punching the gas and seeing if I can make it. I don't, though, mostly because I don't want to be responsible for hurting anyone else that I care about.

A few minutes later, we're passing the welcome sign to Star Meadows. My chest constricts at the sight, and this deep desire to turn around tugs at me. Honestly, I don't even know where home is. The walls I spent years living in? The bedroom where my bed is? The garage where I park my car?

It sounds so simple—these things that make up my life. But every home has its secrets, and trust me, mine is no exception. My house is so crammed with secrets that I'm surprised it hasn't crumbled from the rot and decay of them yet—

I jolt as my phone rings and, for a nearly blinding moment of panic, I dread that *unknown* will flash across the screen. But it's my mother again.

I haven't answered any of her calls. I need to, though, to give her a heads-up that I'm almost to the house.

Letting out a breath, I press *talk* on the phone and put it on speaker.

"Hello." My voice sounds flat, devoid of emotion. Controlled.

It's the only way I can be, because if one single sliver of emotion slips through, the whole entire dam I built will break.

"How close are you?" my mom asks. She sounds upbeat yet drained. She gets that way when she's highly stressed. Her moods push and pull from each other, and chaos sometimes follows.

"About ten miles away." I slow down with the line of cars in front of me.

Some cows are standing in the acres of land that line the road, and someone has stopped in the middle of the road to look.

"Give me an exact location," my mom replies. "I need to know what time you'll get here so I can have your room ready."

"It's fine if it's not," I tell her. "I can get the bed ready myself."

"No, I don't want you to do that." She's all sugary sweetness now, and it's making me uncomfortable. "I can take care of the room. I'm sure you and Jason are exhausted from the drive."

Clara's attention snaps to me, her brow arching. *"You haven't told her yet?"* she mouths.

I shake my head and bite my lip.

I bite it so hard I taste blood.

I haven't told my mother yet.

Told her the truth about me and Jason.

About what's happening.

And I know when I do ... when I tell her the truth that lies in the walls of my house ... the politeness she's using will evaporate like the sunlight during a storm, and nothing will be left but darkness. Cruel and empty darkness.

"Look, Mom, I have to go. Traffic is bad." I hang up on her.

"What the hell, Aves?" Clara lowers her sunglasses and gapes at me. "Why haven't you told her you're getting a divorce?"

I shrug as I adjust my sunglasses. "It's complicated." While Clara knows a bit about me, she doesn't know everything.

She knows I don't get along with my parents, but she doesn't know all of the gory details. And I don't want to tell her, partly out of worry she'll freak out about being here *with* me and partly because she might freak out about being *near* me. Because, as terrible as my parents are, I'm equally as awful. At least, I was in the past. And now, here I am, entering the place that carries memories of every horrible thing I ever did.

My secrets are hidden everywhere—in the half-abandoned town, in every curve of the streets, in the crevasses of the buildings.

But the thing that holds my darkest secret of all is the woods.

CHAPTER 6

THE PAST...

It's the start of my junior year. I used to hate the beginning of the school year and the panic of going into the unknown. It's a contradiction—starting school every year. I've done it before—It always goes the same—yet I still don't know what will happen.

That panic isn't present today, though. Perhaps because I grew up over the summer, got my driver's license, and bought my first car with the money I saved up from working two jobs. Or maybe it's because I'm doped up on so many prescriptions that numbness has become my best friend.

That's okay. Feeling nothing at this point is better than feeling the fear I've grown so accustomed to. It's a little weird not being able to feel it, like I lost a finger or something, and yet it feels like I still have a finger, like I have a phantom limb. This didn't happen right away. It took several prescriptions to get me to this state of numbness. A lot of work was put in by my doctor and parents, and they succeeded. Everyone seems happy about it. Well, happier than they were when I was having my meltdowns.

I wasn't a huge fan of the pills at first, because they made me feel all fuzzy. The fuzziness does have its perks, though. Like, for instance, I'm about to walk into school and don't feel as if my heart is about to self-destruct.

Feeling *nothing* is better than feeling *everything*. At least, that's what everyone keeps telling me. But sometimes the numbness scares the hell out of me.

I park my car in a vacant spot near the exit, so leaving for lunch will be easy. I'm supposed to be meeting Livia at the front of the school so we can walk in together. I haven't seen her in a few weeks because she's been busy. I have been, too, with my job at the gas station.

I sling my backpack over my shoulder and climb out of the car. People are standing around, hanging out and talking. I wish I was doing the same thing, but I remind myself that I'll have someone to talk to when I head inside. So, I focus on that as I start across the parking lot and toward the school.

I remain invisible until I pass by Hunter Frankton. He's one of the most popular guys in school. Gorgeous, with blond hair and blue eyes; he is even on the football team. He's also the walking cliché of those popular guys that are in movies. He's an asshole too, and him looking at me can't mean anything good. Maybe he's looking at someone behind me.

I nonchalantly glance over my shoulder. The only person in the vicinity is Ms. Collington, an English teacher. She's around fifty, with short gray hair, and she's sporting a red pantsuit. So, unless Hunter has a fetish for older women, he's unquestionably looking at me. He could have a thing for older women, though. Who the hell knows?

If I've learned anything over the last few years, it is that people have a shit ton of secrets. Ones they don't want anyone else finding out about, and they'll do anything to keep them a secret.

As my thoughts turn down that dangerous road, I brace myself for the panic that usually crashes over me. Yet, all I feel is disconnected.

Guess the drugs are doing their job.

My parents will be thrilled to discover this.

I should be thrilled, too, but again, the disconnect.

I rotate back around with a dull sensation nibbling at my chest. I frown when I note Hunter is still staring at me. Then, to make matters worse, his lips cock into a grin.

It's never good when guys like Hunter smile at you, unless you're a girl like Raya Stepforton. Then it more than likely means he's smiling because he likes what he sees. But when you're a girl like me, a smile from a guy like Hunter usually means he's going to mock my pants, or shoes, or my lipstick that matches my top. So, instead of waiting around to find out, I fix my attention straight ahead and hurry off, pretending he doesn't exist.

A few seconds later, I arrive at the entrance to the brick building Livia is there, tapping her foot while glancing around, as if searching for someone. When she spots me, she hurries over.

"Oh my god, you're so late," she hisses at me. "What the hell, Ava? We agreed to meet at eight-fifteen."

I glance at my watch. "I'm only two minutes late."

"You're always late, though." She flips her hair off her shoulder. "And that's two minutes less that we have to walk around and find our classes."

"We already know where they are," I point out as we enter the school and step into the busy hallway. I expect my anxiety to make a grand appearance and can *almost* feel it prickling inside me. "We've gone here for two years already."

"So? That doesn't mean we've been to all the classrooms." She rolls her eyes then digs a piece of gum out of her backpack. "Hopefully, my locker won't be down the east hall where all the freshmen are. I've heard it happens sometimes. Freshmen are so annoying."

She keeps prattling on and on about the hallway and lockers and freshmen, but I zone out, my thoughts centering on one thing.

Or, well, one person.

I knew I was going to have to see him. I spent hours worrying about it at night and trying to come up with a plan to avoid him. It was stupid. I was stupid. Because, in the end, no one can stop me from having to cross paths with him.

No one can stop me from having to feel the fear I am right now.

Even the drugs can't stop it.

Trystan Evenford, one of the most popular guys in school. He's even more popular than Hunter. Star quarterback, straight-A student. All the girls are in love with him. All the teachers think he's the politest guy in school. He's also my cousin. Our fathers are brothers, and while I've spent many summers at barbeques with Trystan and his family, I've never felt comfortable around him. For a long time, I wasn't sure why. While we weren't friends, he'd wave to me at school. Considering how lonely I've always been, I should've been grateful for this. And yet, I never felt gratitude. In fact, I often wish he'd pretend I didn't exist like almost everyone else did. There's no real reason for me to feel this way about him, except for one moment. One single moment that made it so every time he looked at me, a chill clawed up my spine.

I was thirteen, and my family was over at Trystan's family's house for dinner. After we ate, the kids went downstairs to watch a movie. Being the only child in my family meant I had to hang out with Trystan and his brother and sister, who were younger than us. Because of this, we ended up putting on a cartoon. It was boring. I can remember thinking that. Trystan must've thought so, too, because he changed the channel and his siblings protested immediately.

"Oldest gets to choose," he told them as he flipped through the channels. "Right, Ava?" He glanced at me with this weird little smirk on his face.

I shrugged because I honestly didn't care. "Sure."

His smirk grew. Again, I didn't know why.

Then he settled on a movie. But I wasn't sure if it was even a movie. All I knew was that a man and woman were on the screen, and they were kissing and touching each other.

My attention shifted to his brother and sister on the floor. I was horrified to discover they were watching it. I knew they shouldn't be—and neither should I.

I was about to say something when Trystan told them, "Kelly and Eric, cover your eyes."

They protested at first but ultimately, they did what he said. Then he let the show play further.

I wanted to cover my own eyes.

I wanted to leave.

But Trystan kept looking at me with this smirk on his face, like he was daring me to leave. I had this icky feeling that if I did, he'd make fun of me. I don't know why it mattered, yet it did. So, I pretended I was okay when really, I was staring at the spot on the floor in front of the television. And that biting chill appeared like teeth on my flesh. I felt uneasy, but I was trying not to freak out.

Then Trystan placed a hand on my leg. I startled, and he snickered. A beat of silence ticked by where I was frozen. His hand was still on my leg. I wanted to tell him to remove it, but I couldn't find my voice.

His fingers trailed upward … I wanted to scream, but my throat felt as if it were shrinking.

I couldn't breathe.

But at the sound of the footsteps coming down the stairs, Trystan yanked his hand away and quickly changed the channel back to the cartoon. "Kelly. Eric. Uncover your eyes. The cartoon is back on."

The moment they did, Trystan's mom entered. Then she paused in the doorway.

I'm not positive what was behind the pause. If she merely stopped for a second, or if she somehow knew what had been going on. Whatever the reason, she never mentioned anything about it. She simply smiled then headed over to the laundry room that was adjacent to the room. Trystan got up then and went into the bathroom.

And me? I rushed upstairs and told my mom I had a stomachache.

She said I should go lie down in the car. I did and an hour later, we went home.

I never spoke about what happened. But at the time, I couldn't stop thinking about when I was younger, and my dad yelled at me for watching the same kind of show. I wondered if Trystan's mom was aware of what he was watching.

After that, I became even more anxious around Trystan, and it was like he knew and enjoyed it. And every so often, he would give me that little smirk.

He's doing it right now as I make my way down the hallway. Only, this time, it feels more sinister than that day in the basement. That day felt more like a teasing taunt, almost a dare for me to tell on him, but this smirk feels threatening.

I get the vibe that he knows about the woods. I've had my suspicions about this for a while, that he's hiding in the fog that's been haunting my brain every single day for the last three months.

"I have to go to the bathroom," I mutter to Livia as I slam to a halt.

Then I spin around and take off, hurrying in the opposite direction as Trystan. People are filling up the hallways as I bolt toward the restroom with vomit burning at the back of my throat. Little flashbacks flicker through my mind of me doing the same thing months ago, only now I'm running through people instead of the woods. They could easily be trees, though—their faces are just blurs—and most of them are completely oblivious to what could happen in the shadows of this world.

I envy them for that.

But the envy is fleeting as I make it into the bathroom.

Then I run into an empty stall, collapse on my knees, and puke up the toast I ate this morning. My stomach lurches even after nothing is left, as if it can somehow purge me of everything else.

Unfortunately, even when I'm finished, that gnawing ache that's been inside me for months now is still present.

I pull myself up from the tile floor and exit the bathroom stall, wiping my mouth with the sleeve of my shirt. I'm no longer alone. Clover Walshingford is standing at the sink, applying some maroon lipstick.

Clover runs with an edgy crowd. She has blonde hair, and blue eyes, and wears heavy eyeliner and lipstick. She's wearing torn black jeans and a crop top with a plaid shirt pulled over it. We've never spoken except for in middle school when we were in a group project together. Even then, we barely said anything to each other. Not because she's mean. She's just intimidating. I'm not quite sure what it is about her. That she has confidence, maybe? That's not something I am familiar with.

They say you fear the unknown, but what I'd give to know her unknown.

I remain quiet as I approach the sink, turn on the faucet, and wash my hands. She continues to put on the lipstick, but her gaze flicks to me. Then she returns her attention to her reflection as if I'm not there.

Or so I think until she says, "Rough morning?"

I glance around, wondering if someone else is in the bathroom, because no way in hell is she talking to me. But, apparently, she is since no one else is here.

"Um … yeah." My confusion is evident.

It falls quiet for a beat as I finish washing my hands and shut off the water.

"Yeah, I've been there," she says as she leans back from the mirror and caps her lipstick.

I'm not positive what she means, but I pretend to get it and nod.

She offers me a smile that makes me question if she knows I'm a liar.

I feel twitchy and struggle to stay calm as I dig out my pills from my bag.

She tosses her lipstick into her bag. "I love your boots."

"Thanks." I find my pills in my bag and without thinking, I take them out.

The moment I do, she glances at them, and I realize I shouldn't have openly taken them out. Stuff like this is what fuels rumors, and the last thing I want is for people to talk about me.

"What're you taking?" she asks. Then, before I can put the bottle away, she leans over and reads the label. "Nice. I was on those for a bit when I was a sophomore."

I want to ask her why, but that seems personal. So, instead, I twist the lid off. "I've been on them for a few months."

"Do they make your head foggy? They did for me. That's part of why I liked them so much."

"They make me feel sort of numb."

"That's cool, too. I like numb. And foggy. And crazy." She smiles at me.

I smile back.

I feel like we're trading a secret, but I'm missing part of the exchange. Still, I'll take it.

She sticks out her hand. Her fingernails are painted a dark green, like the forest. "Mind if I have a couple?"

It seems wrong to give her my prescription pills. But maybe my right and wrong meter is all messed up. Everyone else seems to think so. That the stuff I've seen that I think is wrong is just me overreacting.

"Yeah, sure." I dump two into her hand.

Smiling, she tips her head back and swallows them. Then she grabs her bag off the floor, saying nothing as she walks away. I think she used me for the pills. I'm not even sure how I feel about that; if I care or not.

But as she reaches the door, she spins around. "Your name's Ava Evenford, right?" she asks, and I nod. "If you want to hang out at lunch or something, a couple of my friends and I are leaving campus."

My heart leaps in my chest. I swear it's the first time it's done this. Truthfully, I thought it was dead in the cavity of my chest.

I aim to sound calm as I say, "Yeah, okay, sure."

"Awesome. Meet me at the front of the school after the bell rings." The corners of her lips tug upward before she exits.

I free out a tremulous breath I didn't even realize I was holding. My heart continues to beat vibrantly as I swallow down two pills. Then I collect my stuff and exit the bathroom.

The panic that appeared early has now faded. But then I enter the hallway and see Trystan walking through the crowd. It's then that I realize the panic isn't gone; it's just been lulled to sleep by a distraction.

Now it's awake again, ever-present and biting.

Sucking in an inhale, I make my way down the hallway

toward my locker. I can feel eyes on me—maybe Trystan's—but I don't look up. Eventually, the sensation fades, either from the drugs or because Trystan can no longer see me. I start to relax as I reach my locker.

But in the snap of a twig, all of the relaxation is stolen away from me. Even the drugs can't pull me back. Because written on my locker in either blood or red paint are the words:

Die slut.

CHAPTER 7

"So, this is where you grew up?" Clara asks as we sit in my car, staring at my old childhood home.

I parked out front of the house, away from the garage, so the front door is close to us. Bailey is awake in the back seat and is excitedly looking around, on high alert.

The house's layout is odd; the garage is on the side by the lower level, the porch wraps around half the house but ends halfway on the east side, and another section continues on the other side. It's an older place but has been remodeled except for the attic, which is spacious, dusty, and creepy. So, a stereotypical attic.

"Yep," I reply.

I should feel something other than nausea when I look at it, but I don't.

"It's pretty," she notes. "Older, but I like older houses."

"Don't let the prettiness fool you," I mutter as I get out of the car. "It's got ugliness hidden underneath that new paint and freshly stained deck."

"That's ... dark," she tells me as I slide the seat forward and let Bailey out of the car.

He does a circle then starts smelling the bushes and grass surrounding the place.

"It's the truth." I head for the trunk to grab my suitcase.

Clara rounds to the back of the car, too. "Are you going to be okay staying here? Because we could always stay at a hotel."

A hotel sounds nice, but completely undoable. I'm on a budget. Plus ... "You can't get a hotel room here during the summer unless you book a year in advance."

Her eyes go huge. "What? Seriously?"

I nod. "Yep. Like I said, tourist season."

Shock continues to consume her features as she processes this information.

I pop the trunk to collect our bags. By the time I'm closing the trunk, my mother has wandered out of the house. She starts to wave but freezes when she notes Clara. Her arm lowers to the side and, while I can't see her face, I'm guessing she's frowning.

Sighing, I drag the bags around to where Clara is. She has her phone out but is looking at my mom. She smiles and offers a wave, which my mother doesn't return.

"Don't take anything she says or does personally," I whisper as I wheel her bag up to her, the gravel crunching underneath the wheels.

"Oh, I won't," Clara assures me with a wicked grin. Then she looks at my mom again, smiles, and waves exaggeratedly.

With her forehead creased, my mom steps off the front porch and hurries down the dirt path toward me. She's wearing a nice pair of pants, a button-up blue silk shirt, and strappy sandals. Her hair is curled, and she looks like she recently got highlights. She has on makeup to the point where she looks ten years younger.

This isn't the mother I remember, the one who liked to look as plain as possible. What the heck is going on?

"I'm glad you made it," she says as she reaches us, her gaze flicking to Clara then me. "Where's Jason?"

And this is the point where I should tell her.

About the divorce.

About what happened.

About the abuse.

About how I caved to everything, conformed, molded into what I thought I was supposed to be—the perfect little obedient doll.

But I know what would happen if I told her.

If I told her about the torment.

About the pain.

About the suffering I've been through over the last few years.

Mentally and physically broken.

And how it took me forever to realize it was torment. That life wasn't supposed to be that way.

And I know what her reaction will be since I've heard it from her before.

This is your fault.

You made him angry.

Why can't you just behave?

It's a thought that's been in my mind for years. It's why I stayed.

My fault.

My fault.

My fault.

All of it is my fault.

Everything that occurred from the day I was born, to the day in the woods, until this instant where I'm standing here, in front of her, has mapped out my life for me. I could tell her that—tell her everything—but natural instinct is a potent little bitch, so I end up lying. I'm a coward. But I'll take that over having to deal with her disapproval.

"He had to work," I lie, gripping the handle of my suitcase.

Clara casts a glance at me, and she clearly disapproves, but I give her a pleading look, silently begging her not to say anything.

She keeps her lips zipped but doesn't appear thrilled about it as she draws her sunglasses back down over her eyes.

Like I said before, Clara is blunt. And blunt is as far away from lying as one can get.

Too truthful, some might say.

Free is how I see it.

"He couldn't come." The lie is almost robotic, like I can't even feel my lies anymore. My mouth moves on its own accord and spits them out. "He had stuff to do, so I brought a friend of mine. Clara, this is my mom. Mom, this is Clara."

"Hey, Mrs. Evenford," Clara says to my mom.

"Hello." She eyes Clara over, judging her short cut-offs, the tattoos on her arms, and the piercings in her nose and ears.

"So sorry to hear about your husband," Clara adds politely while tucking a strand of hair behind her ear.

"Yes, well, it definitely is terrible, isn't it?" my mom replies, dusting something off the front of her shirt.

It's weird hearing her speak like that. She was so emotional growing up—either angry, sad, rude or, on occasion, happy. Her happiness was almost as overwhelming as her anger. It's like she was trying to drown me in all sorts of emotions to the point where I could scarcely breathe whenever I was around her. Then, right before I was about to pass out from lack of air, she flipped and that rage would rise up, yanking me out of the water and forcing life back into me. Or she'd leave me alone for days, and I'd feel like I was floating in that water, waiting for the next storm.

"Are you okay?" I ask her as Bailey lets out a bark. She is my mom after all, the woman who brought me into this world through screams and pain. She used to tell me all the time about it, about how it was so awful she never wanted to do it again, and that's why I'm the only child.

Like a light switch, she shifts from emotionless to happy, a smile spreading across her face. "Oh, I'm fine. You guys probably should come inside and start getting unpacked." She glances at the dog. "You can put your dog in the fenced area." She points to a section of land wrapped in barbed wire and old wooden posts just to the house's side.

"Okay." I start to walk toward Bailey.

"Oh, and some of your aunts and uncles are coming over for dinner," my mother says and I freeze.

My stomach clenches as I pause and look at her. "Which ones?"

"Uncle Stephan and Aunt Marissa," she says, shielding her eyes from the sunlight. "We thought we'd have dinner and reminisce about your father."

"What about their kids? Are they coming over, too?" My tone wobbles, causing Clara to turn and look at me with concern.

"Well, they're not really kids anymore, are they?" My mom starts toward the house, calling over her shoulder, "But yes, they're coming, too."

My palms dampen with sweat. I feel like I'm fifteen years old again, standing out in those woods, terror pulsating through my veins.

"What about … Trystan?"

"Of course Trystan is coming." She pauses near the front door and looks directly at me as she grips the door knob. "He was like a son to your father, Ava. You know that."

No, I know for a fact that's total bullshit. Trystan despised my father. He even once told me that, before I refused to be around him.

"I could ask my dad for you," I told him. We were twelve, and Trystan wanted to learn how to work on cars, something my dad was good at. He did it for fun when he wasn't working, and in this small town, he didn't work too much. He made a lot of money, though. I'm not sure how much. I just knew we were never hard up for cash.

Trystan let out a dry laugh. We were sitting outside in the front yard, and the sun glared in his eyes, yet he didn't squint, like he was enjoying the sting or trying to blind himself.

"I'd rather eat dog shit than ask your dad for help," he said with hatred.

I winced from how scalding his voice was, but I didn't argue. Couldn't. My father was an asshole—

I jerk from the memory as Bailey starts barking at some horses on the property next door. He's so happy, like he's tasting freedom for the first time.

Well, at least one of us is having fun.

I look at my mom. She's about to go inside.

"No, he wasn't," I call out, surprising myself and baffling her.

She has the door open but pauses with her brows knit. "What?"

I rarely speak my mind, but for some reason, I find myself wanting to, to let her know she doesn't know everything. "Trystan didn't like Dad."

"Oh, Ava," she says in that tone that lets me know she thinks I'm clueless. "Trystan loved your father, and your father loved him."

Liar. Does she really believe it? Or is she just clueless?

Why does this even matter?

I don't know, but for some reason, it does. Or maybe it matters to me that I get to speak my truths. Because I am not a child anymore. I am not moldable like I used to be.

I'm not.

I'm not.

I. Am. Not.

Before I can comment any further, my mom calls out, "Come inside after you're done putting your dog away, and we can get you two settled. I don't have an extra bed for your friend to sleep on, so she'll either have to sleep on the sofa or the trundle in your old bedroom."

"Trundle?" Clara whispers to me. "What the hell? Are we like twelve?"

"I can sleep on it," I offer. "And you can have my bed."

"No. I can sleep on it. I think you'll need better rest than I am," she mumbles, eyeing the front door as my mother closes it. "I think she's upset that I'm here."

I shake my head as I hike down the hill that leads to the fenced-in area and call for Bailey to follow.

"No, she's just unhappy Jason isn't," I tell Clara

"You should probably tell her what's going on. Maybe she'll be understanding about it," she replies as she follows me.

"Maybe." But I know what my mother will say. She'll try to convince me to stay with him. I know this because of what happened right after Jason and I returned from our honeymoon. Jason and I had returned to Star Meadows to pack our stuff and move to Idaho, where Jason had been living on and off for a while. We had been in California for a week, enjoying the sunshine. That's what the story was, anyway. But nothing about the vacation was relaxing—I had bruises to prove that. The most prominent ones were on my throat.

I tried to cover them up, but it was in the middle of summer, and wearing a turtleneck wasn't an option, so I was left to use my hair and makeup as a shield. It was working okay until my mom came to my room to help me pack. Jason was at his parents' house, packing up his stuff.

My mom peeked into my room and frowned. "Where's Jason?"

"He went to pack up his stuff," I said as I tossed some books into a box. They landed with a heavy thud.

"You should be more careful with that stuff," my mom reprimanded.

"My arms are tired," I muttered, chucking more books into the box.

Everything about me was tired. My arms. My brain. My soul.

"Well, you still need to be more careful." She entered the room and peered around at the poster and magazine cutouts still hanging on the wall. "You should probably take these down now that you're married. I'm sure Jason doesn't like looking at them."

His name felt heavy in the air, a sound that caused the exhaustion inside me to deepen. Maybe because we were still fighting? We had fought over the honeymoon about dumb things, like where to eat and money. But one fight in particular was brutal, hence the marks on my neck.

It wasn't the first time he'd hurt me, but it was definitely the worst. And deep inside a place I didn't want to admit existed, I had been truly afraid of him when he wrapped his fingers around my neck.

"It's kind of insulting to keep them up, don't you think?" She looked like she expected me to agree with her, something I did a lot, even when I didn't want to. It was just easier to be agreeable when it came to her.

"Not really," I found myself saying, and she blinked in shock. So, I tried to explain it to her, hoping she'd understand me. "I catch Jason checking out other women sometimes. And he talks about women he thinks are hot."

She stared at me momentarily then did something oddly unexpected. She came over and took me by the hand. I jolted.

My mother rarely touched me, and the connection was a mixture of ice and warmth.

"Come sit down with me for a second," she said, steering me over to the bed.

We sat down, and she continued to hold my hand while looking me in the eye. "Men are different from women. You need to understand that as a wife. While Jason may look at other women and talk about them, it doesn't mean you should. Your father always does this with me, but it's all just an act. And if I ever did the same, it'd hurt him." She smiled like she was sharing a valuable secret with me. "Men's egos are fragile, and it's up to us to protect them—it's part of being a good wife." She brushed her fingers across the bruises on my neck, and I realized she knew they were there. "Give him what he wants, and he'll take good care of you. That's an important lesson to learn." She lowered her hand. "If you don't, he'll continue to get angry, and might eventually leave you. And you don't want to end up alone, do you?" When I didn't answer right away, she frowned. "A high school dropout isn't going to be able to take care of herself, you know that, right? These are the consequences of you making all those stupid choices. And I'm not taking care of you anymore."

I was seventeen years old when she told me this.

I was seventeen years old and so damn confused about what she was saying and how I got to that point. It's not like I couldn't remember, but I felt like I was a puzzle with a bunch of pieces shoved in the wrong place.

My throat felt thick as I nodded.

She smiled. "Good." Then she stood up. "Do you want me to help you rip down the posters, or can you do it yourself?"

"I can do it by myself."

"Okay." Still smiling, she walked out of the room.

I sat there, perplexed and not even sure why. Why had I expected more from her? Considering her history and how easily she dismissed the dark things I told her, I should've been completely unshaken.

But I wasn't.

I was crammed with confusion that felt like it was cracking me apart. I had bruises on my neck, and she didn't even ask me where they had come from. Because she already knew—she had to.

She just didn't care.

Why would she? She knew my dad used to beat me and never gave a shit. Maybe I was the messed-up one. Maybe I cared too much about all these dark things that seemed to be a constant in my life. Perhaps something was wrong with me. Maybe what I thought was wrong was more normal.

I swallowed hard. My neck muscles hurt as I did, but I ignored the pain. Then I got up and tore the posters down, one by one, until all of it was erased. Until nothing was left but blank walls and a torn mess of paper on the floor.

***

I LOCK UP BAILEY IN THE FENCED-IN AREA BEFORE HEADING inside. The property that encompasses the house is a massive piece of land, so I don't feel too bad about locking him up.

Clara goes with me, in awe of the mountains and space.

"You can literally smell the trees," she remarks as she breathes in the air.

I press my lips together. I remember thinking the same thing when my family first moved here. Now the scent makes me feel sick.

Swallowing the sensation down, I move to lock the gate. And that's when I spot them—daisies growing in the field. Suddenly, that clenching feeling in my stomach shifts to my chest. It happens every time I see one because it reminds me of *her*.

"What're you looking at?" Clara tracks my gaze to the white flowers sprouting in the grass. "Daises?"

"Yeah … They don't usually grow on our land, so it's weird seeing them," I say, tearing my gaze away. I suck in an inhale, then say to Clara, "Come on; let's go inside and get this over with."

We exit the field, and I lock the gate behind us. Then we make our way to the house..

Inside, it smells the same and looks so similar that I almost feel like I've stepped back in time.

"You okay?" Clara asks when she notices me suck in a slow breath.

I nod, scratching my wrist as my gaze sweeps across the spacious living room. The walls are as bare as I remember. My mom rarely put up any photos. I'm uncertain if it's because that wasn't her thing or if she was gone too much to care.

"The place looks the same," I say as I wander farther into the room.

"My childhood home looks the same, too," she tells me like

it should reassure me that this is normal. "It's like my parents are too afraid to change anything."

Maybe that's how my mom is, too. But I hate the reminders of the past everywhere. Those lack of photos reminds me of all the family vacations we didn't go on, my zero hobbies, and the lack of family togetherness. The lack of everything. Just vast bareness filling each room. And yet, there were so many times that I felt as if this place was so small, as if the walls, floor, and roof would crush me.

But right now, it's lonely to look at, and that loneliness weeps all the way to my bones.

"Are your parents not huge fans of taking photos?" Clara asks as she observes the room.

I shrug, not divulging the truth, mainly because my mom is standing only a handful of feet away from us, trying to eavesdrop.

"I don't know." I'm annoyed I'm already reverting to my old patterns.

Little lying Ava. She's back.

My mother plasters on her fake smile as she leads us down the stairs, like a hotel manager taking guests to their rooms. Of course, the basement is a far cry from anything resembling a hotel. It's dark and dusty, and its few windows are covered by plastic to protect the cold winter air from getting inside.

"Here you go." My mom halts in the doorway of what used to be my bedroom.

I don't step in right away. I linger outside the doorway that leads to a room that used to feel like a tomb.

"Thanks, Mom," I mutter after an uncomfortable amount of silence stretches by. I'm unsure what she's waiting for, but she wants something. "We're good if you need to go do anything else."

"I do," she tells me. "I need to go get ready for dinner. I haven't even started cooking yet. And then, after dinner, we're supposed to spend some time with everyone, telling stories about your father."

I straighten, as if someone has snuck up behind me and stabbed me in the neck.

"Do we have to?" I sputter.

"Of course," my mother snaps, her fake politeness briefly slipping away, but she hastily collects herself. "Dinner is at six. Don't be late."

With that, she walks up the stairway, closing the door behind her.

Clara arches a brow at me. "She didn't lock us down here, did she?"

"There's another exit." I avoid answering her question.

While I don't want to believe my mother would lock me in the basement, it wouldn't be the first time.

CHAPTER 8

THE PAST...ONE MINUTE AFTER LEAVING THE WOODS

My legs feel like they're going to break, but I keep running. My feet crash against the frozen dirt. I can smell the trees. They're so close. Too close.

Screaming.

I trip.

Stumble.

Dirt scatters in the air along with the snow.

"Ava!" someone shouts.

More screaming …

Screams.

Dirt.

Snow.

Trees.

Dirt.

Snow.

Footsteps.

Footsteps.

Footsteps.

Screams.

My mind slams back to moments ago as I run through the woods, but everything is so hazy.

How did I get here?

Why am I running?

A red ribbon floats in front of me, then darkness.

Eventually, it starts to fade.

Blood is trickling against the dirt.

Drip. Drip. Drip.

"Help me," a voice whispers.

Tree branches canopy above, and snow is everywhere. I swear I can see faces through the branches of the nearby trees, but their skin has cracks in it. That doesn't make sense, so maybe they aren't faces.

Or perhaps I can't see right.

"Help me," someone begs as quietly as the melting snowflakes hitting the ground.

"Shh ..." someone else whispers. It's a deep voice, low and eerily calm. "No one's going to help you. No one ever does."

I should run. Whatever is out here can't be good.

I still have the cigarette in my hand. It's burned out, but the smell of smoke is burning my nose. How can this thing between my fingers smell so bad?

"Please," the voice pleads through a choking sob.

I step toward the voice. I am a dumb, dumb girl, just like my father always said too much in everyone's business. That's what women are, according to him.

And yet, it doesn't stop me.

I continue walking further. The snow is starting to create a light layer of snow on the ground. It crunches under my boots.

A branch snaps.

"What was that?" someone says just from my other side.

A scream pierces the air, but it's cut off mid-sound.

That's when I see the fire on the other side of the trees—

"Ava!" the voice echoes across the vastness of the mountains and yanks me from what I think I saw moments ago.

I can't recall much of anything.

Why can't I remember?

"Come back!" they yell.

I only run faster, my breath fogging in front of my face.

I run. And run. And run—

Everything goes black. I can't hear. I can't think.

Then all I can see are red fragments of what is happening around me. They pierce my brain like shards of glass, slowly digging through the crevasses of my mind and filling my head with blood.

I need to get up.

I need to run.

My legs wobble as I stand.

I hear my name shouted, but I start running again. I run so fast that I'm unsure how far I've gone or how much time has passed. My feet thud against the snowy ground for what feels like forever until I finally arrive at the main road that leads out of the woods. No cars are driving down it, so I continue running toward my house, my feet dragging against the asphalt as I do. The air has stilled, but I'm not convinced they're gone. No, I'm pretty sure their owners are still out there, watching me through the shield of the trees. I can practically feel them.

Eventually, exhaustion overtakes me and I slow to a jog.

But I refuse to stop moving because if I do, I know I'll be dragged back into those trees.

Finally, my red brick home comes into view, and my parents' truck is parked out front. My parents are home, and while I'm relieved to see this, I wonder how long I've been out in the trees.

Minutes, hours, a day? Time is beginning to blur. Everything is distorted. I think something might be wrong with my brain.

I quicken my pace and reach my house, barreling inside and slamming the door behind me. The lock clicks as I slide it over. It's the loveliest sound I've ever heard.

I press my back against the door while struggling to catch my breath. *Air in. Air out.*

"Ava?" My mom appears. Just past her, my father sits at the kitchen table with a glass of juice in front of him, and he has his phone out. He's not looking at me; he's staring out the large window to his right where the snow is falling so thickly now that not even the mountains are visible. He has a coat on and thick boots, like he was just about to go outside. To look for me, maybe?

"M-mom," I sputter breathlessly. "Mommy …"

I can't get anything else out. It's like my brain is trying to reassure me that she's really here and not a figment of my imagination.

She notes my clothes, and then at my hands. She doesn't utter a word. When I detect a slight gulp from her, I notice the mud on my clothes, and the soaked fabric of my pants and jacket. And dried blood and dirt cover my palms.

"M-mom." I chatter. "S-something h-happened. There's … there's someone else out there."

She doesn't ask questions. She merely puts her hand on my shoulder.

"Let's get you cleaned up." She steers me toward the stairway.

It's the first time she's made me feel safe. And while her hand on my shoulder is foreign to me, it's comforting. I feel calmer as she guides me down the stairs instead of having me go there alone.

I'm not alone.

She gets me clothes and a towel. Then we head toward the bathroom. There, she sets the clothes and towel down on the counter and turns on the water before facing me. "Take a shower and get washed up. I'll be right back."

I've started to shiver. And chatter. I think I might be in shock.

"I need to tell you something first," I say as she walks toward the doorway. "I need to tell you what happened. And we need to help her."

"Shh …" She smooths her hand over my hair. "Take a shower first so you can calm down. Then we'll talk, and we can help her."

"S-send help now," I chatter. "Please … to the woods."

She nods, and relief attempts to shove through the fear consuming every inch of my body.

I'm so frozen. And aching. And I feel icky and gross, dirty inside and out. So, I nod back, my body trembling as I enter the bathroom. She shuts the door, leaving me alone.

I feel trapped. I tell myself to breathe while slipping off my boots, wet socks, and jacket. Each movement aches, pain searing through my limbs. I wince, my eyes closing …

"No—" The scream is knocked out as I fall to the ground, my shoulder blade hitting a rock.

I yank away from the memory and reach around, lightly touching the spot. Then I wince.

Sucking in another breath, I carefully strip off my shirt and turn around so my back is facing the mirror. A bruise, almost as dark as the ash at the bottom of a fire, is splattered across my flesh. I reach back and touch it, and wince again.

It fucking hurts, but the pain is real. Weirdly, I find a sense of comfort in that.

I touch it again.

And again.

And again.

Until it's so sore that it's all I can focus on. Then I lower my hand, take off my pants and underwear, and climb underneath the water. It's scorching. Too hot against my chilled bones. So I adjust it, turning the knob until basically no warmth is left. Then I start to scrub the dirt off my skin. The water below me turns brown and eventually bleeds to red.

I scrub. And scrub. And scrub.

Screams.

Blood.

Screams.

Blood.

Pain.

Help me—

My shoulder pulsates as I yank myself from the images searing through my mind.

The water is ice-cold now, and my hands look like prunes.

How long have I been in here?

I shut off the water, climb out, and wrap the towel around me. The air is quiet as I dry off. So still. Like right before it started snowing in the woods.

I'll be okay.

I begin to get dressed, shivering as I put on the clothes my mom gave me—a T-shirt and a pair of pajama bottoms. I leave my hair wet and walk out of the bathroom. I expect my mother to be waiting for me on the other side of the door, but all that welcomes me is the basement's darkness.

I cross the room and start up the stairs. The door at the top is shut, and when I turn the door knob, it won't budge.

Did my mother accidentally lock it?

"Mom," I call out, knocking on the door.

Silence is my only response.

I knock again. "I think you locked the door on accident."

Nothing. The house is so quiet.

Did they leave for some reason?

I knock again, this time raising my voice. "Mom!"

Nothing.

I tell myself to calm down, that I'm safe in my own house.

I. Am. Safe.

"Mommy," I call out again, tears spilling down my eyes. "We have to help her!"

Silence.

In the woods, my mind and body begged for everything to be quiet, but right now, I want to hear anything but it. A whisper. A breath. Any sign that I'm not locked down here alone.

I hurry back down the stairs and head for the other door

that'll take me outside. But that one is locked, too. I rewind over what my mom said to me before she left me to take a shower. She said we could talk and that she'd send help for the girl still stuck in the cage of the trees. But she never did ask where the girl was, so how can she send help?

"Mom!" I bang on the door and scream so hard my chest feels like it's about to burst.

Nothing follows my pitiful cries but a grave of silence.

I collapse to the floor and curl up in a ball. The tears spill out, like a wave crashing over me. And I let it take me away, carrying me into the darkness of my own nightmares.

I am alone.

CHAPTER 9

Being in my old room is a weird experience. Maybe because it's not my room anymore. Or perhaps it never truly was. Maybe I never had a home until the apartment I live in now.

"Your walls are so bare," Clara says as she rotates in a circle, taking in everything.

"It didn't use to be like this," I tell her as I shove my suitcase into a corner. "I used to have posters of guys and stuff hanging up, but my mom had me take them down before I moved out."

She fiddles with one of her bracelets. "You had posters of guys on the wall? That's so weird to picture you being like that. I mean, you barely talk to guys now."

I stare at a calendar on the wall, one of the few things left up. "I don't want to date or anything—ever. Not after everything that's happened."

"Everyone going through a divorce says that, but it rarely

happens." She smiles as she sits down onto the edge of my bed with a bounce. "I bet, in a year, you'll be ready to get back out there."

Doubtful, I think but don't say aloud.

We descend into silence as she checks her messages on her phone. I check mine, too, but I don't have any.

"Are you freaked out about having to talk about your father tonight at this dinner thing?" she suddenly asks as she stuffs her phone into her pocket. "Because I got this vibe you weren't thrilled about it. Plus, I know you and your dad didn't get along very well."

"Very well," I find myself mumbling, which causes her brows to furrow.

I can see questions appearing in her eyes. Before she can ask them, I sink onto the edge of the bed beside her and admit, "I'm not thrilled about the entire night, mostly because I don't like my extended family."

"Yeah, I picked up on that, too." She wavers, crossing her legs. "What's the deal with them? Are they like assholes? I have this uncle that says the most sexist shit, and I can't stand him. What makes it worse is that during family get-togethers, almost everyone gets uncomfortable with the shit he says, but no one will tell him to shut up. I lost my shit once and told him off, but my mom stopped me in the middle of it."

"How old were you?"

"Like sixteen. My mom's kind of a bitch."

"My mom is, too."

"Yeah, she seems kind of bitchy." She briefly pauses. "She seems a little off. Is it because … because your dad just died?"

I shake my head and then shrug. "Maybe."

"Is she normally like this?"

"Sometimes."

She searches my eyes then sighs. "Look, I don't want to pressure you to talk or anything, but you're giving off some bizarre vibes, Aves. Like you're restless and angry, and I'm not sure what to do. But it feels like I should do something."

She can sense anger flowing off me? Weird since I'm not feeling much of anything at this moment.

"I just hate it here; that's all." I shift on the bed, pulling my knees to my chest. "I hated it as a teenager, and I never wanted to come back. Yet, here I am."

"Well, you kind of had to come," she extends me an excuse.

"No, I didn't. Just because he died doesn't mean I'm obligated to attend his funeral. You said it yourself." And I'm questioning if I should've taken her advice.

She chews on her lip. "Does your town have a bar?"

I snort a laugh. "This is Wyoming. This town has a lot of bars, and not much of anything else."

"You want to go get trashed? I know you're not a huge drinker, but maybe it'll help."

I shouldn't.

I definitely shouldn't.

Because drinking is bad.

Drinking is for sinners.

Drinking makes you do bad, bad things.

But drinking also makes you forget.

The latter caused me a lot of trouble in my life.

That's what Clara doesn't know about me—that I used to drink all the time. It took a lot to stop because it was so easy to forget about everything when I was wasted. And high. And everything else in-between.

Because of this, I should say no. I worked hard not to drown my pain and sorrow in alcohol. But I also worked hard to stay away from this place because it breaks something inside me that's not ever really fully fixed.

I stand up. "Sure. Let's go get wasted."

She grins. "Really?"

"Yep, really." I grab her hand and yank her to her feet. Then we embark up the stairs.

For a brief moment, I expect the door at the top of the stairway to be locked, but it opens up. Relief washes over me as I turn for the front door.

Clara stops me right before I open it up. "Wait—aren't you going to tell your mom we're leaving?"

I should. That's what normal people do. But it's something I've rarely done in my life. Still, I turn back around to tell her. Not that I'm going to a bar, but that I'm leaving the house. I pause before I even make it into the kitchen, though.

My mom is whispering from somewhere close by. "No, I don't think she does … I really don't … I know, but … Okay, okay, I'll try to find out if she does … But I don't even know how she could … Fine … I'll be careful … Yeah, I get how important this is … I know she's fragile right now, but I promise she won't talk."

She falls quiet. Then I hear her walking toward me. I barrel for the front door, but she reaches me before I can escape.

She slams to a stop, clutching her phone to her chest. "What're you doing?"

She's worried. But why? Because I overheard what she said? That was nothing, yet it seemed to mean something to her.

Who was she talking to?

Her lips part and then shut. Part then shut. She glances at Clara then at me. She says absolutely nothing. It's the first time I've seen her speechless, at least toward me. Even when I came home so drunk I could barely stand, she had all sorts of foul words for me.

"Is there something you want to ask me?" I question suspiciously.

She blinks then smooths her hand across the front of her silk shirt. "No." Just one word, but I've seen my mother lie many times to the outside world, about the bruises on my arms, about why we were late to things, about how good of a man my father is.

Then she notes my wallet in my hand and frowns. "Are you going somewhere?

I offer her what she's offered me—a lie. "To the store to buy some deodorant. I forgot mine."

"Oh, okay." She stares at me longer, and I can't tell if she wants to tell me the truth about what she just lied about or if she's trying to figure out if I'm lying. Or maybe it's neither. "Be back by six."

I resist a shake of my head. It's insane she still thinks she can tell me what to do. But I nod, anyway. Another lie. I won't be back by six. I won't be back until the sun has fully set, the moon is consuming the sky, and the shadows have taken over to the point where nothing else can be seen.

I used to be afraid of the night when it was too dark to see anything. I worried that monsters would come out and snatch me away. But as I got older, I realized that monsters walk around in the softness of the daylight just as much as they do in the suffocating darkness of night.

It was a brutal, terrifying day when I learned this. That not even the sunlight can keep the monsters away. And as I endeavor out into the outside world of a town I know is full of monsters, I can't help but fear that some of them might be out and about tonight.

"OH MY GOD." CLARA SPUTTERS A LAUGH. "THIS IS THE BEST bar in town?" She looks utterly dumbfounded. "Seriously?"

"Yep." I unfasten my seat belt. "Well, at least it was when I was a teenager."

I'm parked in the back parking lot of the bar that is smack-dab in the middle of the stores that line the main street of Star Meadows. It's getting late, and the sun is starting to cast a pinkish-orange glow across the sky as it descends behind the mountains, but it's still bright enough that the town is fully visible.

So is the horror in Clara's eyes as she warily eyes the two-story wooden structure that looks like it belongs in some sort of 1980s horror movie.

"How did you even get in if you were that young? I mean, I get the fake ID thing, but I know you moved away when you were only seventeen. And I've seen photos of you when you were that old, and you looked younger than seventeen."

I slip the keys out of the ignition. "No one gives a shit here about that kind of stuff—at the bar or in this town."

"Your mom seems like she would give a shit."

"For appearance, yeah." I attempt to grapple with the emotions stirring inside me. "There are two kinds of people in this town—the ones who party, who get high and drunk all the time, and they don't give a shit who parties with them, and then there's the certain type of people who care too much about everything. But the main focus is appearances. They just care if their friends and family believe they care. It's all about the illusion of your life. I know for a fact that some of the most religious people have way worse vices than some of the people who hang out on weekends getting high and wasted. Because those people, they don't give a shit what other people think, so they usually don't have a lot of secrets …" I trail off, realizing I went off on a rant.

When I direct my focus to her again, her jaw is practically hanging to her knees.

"Wow, that's the most I've ever heard you rant." She points at me. "I kind of get what you're saying, though. This family lived next to me when I was a kid. They were supposedly this picture-perfect family that went to church, did charity work, and was part of the neighborhood watch. Almost everyone thought they were perfect, nice, and sweet." She pauses, this strange look crossing her face. The kind of look someone only gets when they know about the underlying darkness that can be hidden by sunlight. "I never thought they were, though."

I want to ask, but I'm unsure if I should since I hate discussing certain subjects.

"Because I knew it was all bullshit," she continues. "I knew that the mother was a total robot, that the kids were, too. And the father … he was the worst." Her gaze lowers to her wrist. "But yeah, anyway, I get what you're saying." She clears her throat then looks up at me, forcing a smile. "So, are we ready to go get drunk off our asses?"

No.

Not at all.

Why am I here?

Why did I come?

Who am I anymore?

Who was I ever?

My previous desire fades now that I'm here as thoughts of one of the worst times of my life prickle at the desolate space of my memory. After that day in the woods, drinking became a prison for me, my own poisonous cage of torment.

At first, drinking and partying felt like my sanctuary, my protection against all the chaos and badness that consumed almost every inch of my mind. What I didn't realize was, it wasn't keeping things away from me but locking me away from everything else. It made it easy for people like Jason to find me and slip into my self-created cage of hell.

And it almost killed me.

A part of me wanted it to.

Because all I could think about at the time was her.

My best friend.

The only person who ever cared about me.

And how did I repay her?

I fucking let her die.

CHAPTER 10

THE PAST... THREE MONTHS AFTER THE INCIDENT IN THE WOODS...

Die slut.

Die.

Slut.

Slut.

Slut.

I don't know which word is worse, but both are branded in my mind like they're still branded on my locker. I haven't used my locker since I found the words painted on the metal, like scarlet letters for everyone to see. I've been carrying around my books all day to the point where my arms are exhausted. But out of sight, out of mind, right? No one really knows the locker was mine, anyway. Well, except for whoever painted *"die slut"* on it.

But maybe they didn't know it was my locker. Perhaps it was meant for someone else.

My thoughts laugh at me.

Die slut.

Slut.

Slut—

Ding. The bell rings.

I gather my belongings and head for lunch. Normally, Livia and I meet at one of our lockers for lunch, but Clover invited me to lunch, and I want to go with her, even though I'm a little anxious about it.

I make my way toward the school's entrance, pushing through the crowd with my arms tucked in. My earlier sedation has worn off due to the locker incident, and self-consciousness has crept back into me. When Clover invited me to go with her, I felt more confident then and that's why I said yes. Now that nagging uncertainty is gnawing inside me, whispering all sorts of shit from how ugly I look to how much of a freak I am.

"Ava!" I swear I hear someone shout my name. But that doesn't seem right.

I continue walking through the main quad.

"Yo, Ava!"

For an instant, I don't want to look to see who's yelling my name because I'm worried that Trystan will be there.

Although it's definitely a girl's voice…

I turn around and scan the people around me. When my gaze lands on the front door area, Clover is there, smiling at me.

"Hey!" She waves.

I wave back, lost, and probably looking like a freak.

She laughs then motions me over.

I pause briefly before making my way to her. She has no books or a backpack, but she is holding a small case that looks like a wallet. It's red and has a plastic daisy on it. Daisy isn't too common around here, but they grow in some fields farther back in the woods.

"Okay, so the ride is going to be a little crowded because we had to take Jane's car, which is literally the size of a box," she tells me as we start for the door. "You know Jane, right?"

I nod. Everyone knows Jane. Just like everyone knows Clover. "Yeah, I think she's in my math class."

"Awesome." She pushes open the door, digs a pair of sunglasses out of her jacket pocket, and slips them on. "A few other people are going with us, so we'll have to lap it up," she continues as we head down the sidewalk toward the parking lot. "A little advice: if Greg is with us, don't sit on his lap, no matter how polite he is about it." She glances at me, and through her voice, I hear her eye roll. "He always has a hard-on. So, unless you're into getting your ass used as a rubbing post, I'd recommend trying to get a seat or sitting on someone else's lap."

Everything she's saying is overwhelming. Plus, she's talking so fast. It's like she's so confident in every word that leaves her lips that she doesn't have to pause and think about what she'll say.

Uncensored. What must it be like?

She keeps talking as we walk past people and cars backing out of parking spaces. I attempt to stay present in the conversation as much as possible, but I'm pretty sure I might be coming off as some kind of weirdo, and it's almost all I can think about. And it's something she confirms when we stop beside a small, red car.

"You don't talk a lot, do you?" she asks with her head angled to the side.

I want to lie. Say *no, I do*. Be cool. But this walk toward the car has proven her words to be true. Plus, like I said, she seems like the sort of person who is confident in every word she says.

"I do sometimes, but not a lot," I reply with a shrug.

Her lips curve into a grin. "I'm going to make it my mission to break that out of you." She reaches for the handle of the passenger side door. "Trust me; by the end of the month, you're going to be so confident that you're not even going to recognize yourself anymore."

That doesn't seem like a possibility, but I desperately crave what she's offering.

She opens the door. Music is blasting from the stereo, and at least a few people are talking at once.

"Fuck, I hate this song," someone groans.

"Dude, I'm not sitting on your lap," someone else says.

"Shut up, Jenna," a guy snaps.

"All of you shut up!" Clover hollers as she lowers her head into the car. Then she turns the music down. "I brought someone with me, and you guys better be nice to her or else."

"Or else what?" I hear someone say with amusement in their tone.

And then, suddenly, everyone's' gaze shifts to me. Greg, Jenna, and a guy named Ellis are squished in the back seat of the car, Jane is in the driver's seat, and the passenger seat is the only one available.

I grow self-conscious at their stares. Jenna's face is obscured from my vision since she's sitting in the middle, and the same goes for Ellis. Greg's, though, is pressed up against the window, and he has a smirk.

For a horrifying instant, I worry he's aware of my secret. But he doesn't associate with Trystan or any of his friends. Maybe he heard about it some other way, though.

"She can sit on my lap," Greg says, winking at me.

"Um …" I'm not sure how to react.

Clover smacks him on the side of the head. "Don't be a fucking pervert, or you'll scare her off."

"He scares everyone off." Jenna flicks a lighter and lights up a cigarette. Right there, in the school parking lot. It's a gutsy move, and I discreetly glimpse around to see if anyone is watching us.

"Fuck off, Jenna," Greg whines while rubbing the spot on his head where Clover slapped him. "You're being such a bitch to me today."

"Oh honey, I'm a bitch to you every day," Jenna clarifies, smoke puffing from her lips. "You're just too self-centered to notice."

"Shut up," Greg snaps then noticeably composes himself. "Can I please just sit in front?"

"Nah," Clover tells him. "The back seat's a good look for you."

"I don't even know what that means," Greg mutters, glaring at her.

That would make two of us, Greg.

But then I rewind and realize Clover said she's sitting in the passenger seat, which leaves me sitting in the back seat, probably on someone's lap.

Clover eyes me over, and then a smile plays at her lips as she looks back in the car.

"Hey Ellis, you don't mind if Ava sits on your lap, do you?" she asks, still smiling.

That's about when my heart stops.

Ellis Averyton is one of those guys who's not necessarily popular but noticeable. He's mysterious, quiet and, according to rumors, likes to get high and party a lot. I used to have a crush on him in middle school. Not that the crush faded. I just got a lot more crushes in high school.

A smile touches his lips. "Yeah, that's fine with me."

Nerves weave through my gut, partly out of excitement and partly out of anxiety. I used to dream about a guy noticing me. In fact, I dreamed about it a lot. But now conflict is rising inside me.

"Are you getting in?" Clover asks.

I realize I've zoned off. Luckily, Clover appears to find this amusing.

"Um … yeah." I sound like a moron who's never had friends, which is untrue. But it does remind me that I left my friend without telling her where I was going.

I should go back in, find her, and let her know, but we technically didn't make plans. And I don't want to make these guys sit around and wait for me. Besides, I can always text her and let her know.

Sucking in a breath, I climb inside, apologizing when I bump into everyone. Then I squeeze my way over and sit down on Ellis's lap.

My bag is still on and weighs about ten pounds, thanks to my refusing to go to my locker. Ellis notices this and shifts his weight, saying, "Man, what the heck do you have in this thing?"

I grimace. "All of my stuff … I didn't have time to go to my locker."

Little lying Ava, your lips are becoming so acquainted with these toxic little words.

"Here. Let's put it in the back, okay?" Ellis says to me.

I start to take off the backpack, but he slips the handles off my shoulder for me. When I look at him, slightly confused, a smile touches his lips.

My heart flutters, but my stomach twists. It's hard to know which one to trust. Touching is complicated because the deprived part of me craves it while the broken part of me despises it.

Don't touch me.

Just don't.

Run!

He's careful not to touch me too much, something I'm grateful for.

When he gets the backpack off, he tosses it into the back of the hatchback car.

"Everyone good?" Jane asks with her hand resting on the steering wheel.

The question is followed by a series of, "yep," "sure," and a, "I will be when you suck my dick" from Greg. That response earns him another smack from Clover.

"Shut the hell up or your ass can get out and walk." She rotates back around in the seat, shaking her head. "Why the hell do we bring him with us?"

"We don't. He just shoves his way into the car," Jane

replies, cracking the window as she steers toward the parking lot exit. "Like a dog."

I look at Greg, shocked they're talking rudely about him right in front of him.

"You know what, Jane?" he snaps, shoving up the sleeves of his shirt. "You can let me out."

"Sounds good to me," Jane quips, slamming on the brakes in the middle of the entrance.

Someone honks a horn, but Jane remains unfazed as she shoves the shifter into park, looks over her shoulder at Greg, and arches her brow. "Go ahead. Get out."

"Seriously?" he huffs, flabbergasted.

"What? I'm just doing what you asked," she retorts, annoyance ringing in her tone.

"Yeah, but …" Greg rakes his fingers through his hair as he looks around at everyone, like he expects someone to jump in and help him out.

No one does.

Clover shoves the door open, climbs out of the car, moves her seat forward, and then she gestures for Greg to get out. Greg gapes at everyone, dumbfounded. Then his eyes eventually narrow on Jane.

"Why do you always have to be such a bitch?" he snaps as he slides forward to get out.

"You know why I'm doing this," Jane replies, flicking her cigarette out the window. "I mean, I wasn't going to make a scene about it when you got in the car, but since you clearly want a scene, here you go." She glares at him. "Stay the fuck away from Jamie, you date-raping motherfucker."

Holy shit, did she seriously say that?

No one seems to react, and Greg zips his lips shut as he hops out of the car.

The moment he does, Clover slides back in and shuts the door. "I'm glad you kicked him out. I know he's your cousin, but I'm tired of pretending that's enough of a reason for us to always forgive him for stupid shit."

"Agreed," Jane says as she drives forward. "My mom will probably freak out when she hears about this, but I'm getting tired of it, too. It's like she just wants us to dust everything underneath the rug—our entire family is that way."

"Not mine," Clover replies while staring out the window. "We love airing out our dirty laundry."

I feel way out of my element with how openly they're talking to each other. Not that I can't relate to Jane. I can way more than I can ever admit because, unlike her, I'm terrified to speak about my family aloud. How is she not afraid she'll get punished? Do her parents not punish her?

Everyone grows quiet momentarily, and Jane flicks her cigarette out the window. Tension is drenching in the air and seeping into my pores.

Finally, Clover breaks the silence. "Well, Ava, welcome to our fucked-up family." She tosses me a smirk from over her shoulder.

Jane blows out a weighted sigh. "Yeah, sorry, Ava," she tells me as she steers down the road, thrumming her fingers on the steering wheel. "I didn't mean to freak you out." Her gaze finds me in the rearview mirror, and she offers me an apologetic look.

I wonder about Greg, what lies beneath his flesh and blood, what hides in the center of his chest behind the prisoning bones. A beating heart? Darkness? Or something rotting and ugly, like a heart starved of oxygen and screaming to be fed.

I don't know what to say—I never do.

"It's fine," I tell her. "I'm not freaked out or anything." How much truth those words carry, I'm unsure since my emotions are just whispers of a breeze quiet these days.

Jane returns her attention to the road as she picks up a pack of cigarettes. With a flick of the lighter, she lights up again. The end of the cigarette crinkles and then smoke laces the air, the scent nearly smothering as a memory tugs at me, one of me in those trees, standing in the muddy dirt as snow tumbled around me. Everything felt as if it were moving in slow motion, trickling, trickling, trickling, until that scream shattered it. After, everything moved so rapidly that my brain couldn't even remember all the details. Just fragments, pieces—

"You want a cigarette?" Clover asks, looking at me.

I blink, my brain stuck between the present and the past, and words become lodged in my throat.

The smell of the smoke is nauseating, yet I still take a cigarette from the pack. I'm not sure why. Because I don't want to look like a loser? Or am I curious if it tastes as bad as it did the last time I tried one? Or maybe I just don't know what else to do.

My mom once told me I have no direction in my life, that I'm going nowhere and will continue to do so if I do stuff like upset people by talking about things I'm told not to speak of, if I keep making bad choices like that day in the woods.

"You're never going to amount to anything if you keep

going down this path, Ava," she said as we sat in the living room.

I was staring out the window, hugging my knees to my chest. I felt wrong inside. Just wrong. Nothing else. And my mom was telling me the things I felt and thought were wrong, that everything was wrong.

She was right, in a way.

She took a sip of her hot chocolate while mine remained untouched, the steam rising from the mug and lacing through the air like fog on the surface of a lake. "If you don't learn how to stop worrying about everything, your life will get stuck in this place where you are now. Some things you just have to learn how to move past." She paused then stressed, "Silently." She took another sip of her hot chocolate and some dribbled onto her white blouse.

She didn't seem to notice, but I couldn't stop staring at the way the ugly brown tainted the white, like blood against the snow. My head hurt to know the truth yet begged never to see it again.

"Not everything has to be talked about," she continued. "Sometimes, letting stuff go is the best way to handle things."

I kept staring at the stain on her shirt. I wasn't blinking. My eyes started to burn, and yet I kept staring at it.

Blood trickles in the snow ...

Blood drips from my hands ...

Blood seeps from her nose ...

We lock eyes.

She looks dead.

I feel dead, but my heart is beating, so that has to mean I'm still alive, right?

"Ava," my mom snapped so loudly I jolted.

"What?"

She shook her head. "You are the most difficult girl. You need to pay attention. This is important." She stared at me, her voice firm as she spoke. "You will not speak about what happened in those woods. You can't. Too much is on the line, Ava. And you're going to move past this."

I wasn't even entirely sure what she meant by *too much was on the line*. What was she hiding? She never did quite fully explain.

My dad entered the room then, looking from me to my mother.

He was wearing a coat and put on gloves as he asked my mother, "Did you talk to her?"

"I'm still talking to her," she replied, setting her mug of hot chocolate onto the coffee table. "But, as usual, she's being difficult."

He glanced at me again, not saying anything. He rarely spoke to me. I wasn't sure why. He always talked to other people, like his father, the leader of our church, and some of the husbands who live in the area. He had hunting buddies and guys he played sports with. He was always chatting with them. I wanted him to speak to me and tell me everything would be okay. That was all I wanted. Just those words. Nothing less. Nothing more.

But he didn't say anything, and the saddest part was that I wasn't surprised.

He fixed his attention on my mother as he zipped up his coat. "Make sure she understands the importance of this, no matter how many times you have to drill it into that thick head of hers." He walked away then, without so much as a glance back at me. But I did hear him mutter, "Fucking cursed with a daughter. I wish I had a son. Things would be so much easier then. Less dramatic. Women are always about the goddamn drama."

I tear myself from the memory as I pop the cigarette between my lips and wait for Clover to hand me a lighter. She extends her hand toward me with one in her palm, and I reach for it, but Ellis beats me to it. He also steals a cigarette from the pack.

I think he's going to light up, but he flicks the lighter and moves it toward the end of my cigarette. As I realize he's lighting it for me, I lean in. I also mentally prepare myself for when that smoke goes down my throat. I've done this before. Once. And it was awful. But I can't hack my lungs out in front of these people or they might not want to hang out with me anymore. They'll stamp me with a loser sign and kick me out of the car—I just know it.

So, when the end of that cigarette starts burning, I do everything I can to keep it together. My lungs feel like they'll explode as I hold in the cough trying to claw its way out of my throat. It's like that scream I bottled in while I was in those woods. It burned the same way.

"You good?" Ellis asks me. The corners of his lips are twitching, and I suspect he's trying not to laugh at me.

Loser, loser Ava. I've been stamped with this label before, starting back all the way to kindergarten when I once peed my pants because I was so afraid to ask the teacher to use the bathroom. Adults were so scary, and they yelled so much. And Mrs. Kay, my teacher, was no exception to this. She talked loudly, was short with the kids, and had strict rules. I worried she'd get mad for interrupting the lesson if I asked her. I tried to hold it, but eventually, I couldn't.

I started to cry when I became aware of what happened, and everyone laughed at me. And Mrs. Kay scolded me, called my mom, and told her that maybe I wasn't ready to be at school, that I was too immature.

My mom disagreed and made me continue to go. So, I spent the rest of the year getting teased. Fortunately, by first grade, everyone had forgotten about it. That didn't mean that I wouldn't be called a loser again.

I exhale the smoke as smoothly as I can. "I'm good," I tell Ellis. Then I smile. It feels weird and stiff. It's been so long since I've done it, and I'm unsure if any emotion is behind the movement. It might solely be a movement, just muscle memory.

He lights up then and hands the lighter to Clover. He looks at me, but I don't look at him. I only glance out of the corner of my eye at him every once in a while. His attention is making me feel self-conscious.

Why is he looking at me?

Do I look weird?

Does he know I have a secret gnawing at my insides?

Those thoughts continue spinning through my mind like a stuck record. But the noise stops when I spot someone walking down the sidewalk.

Her name is Camilla Anmerline, and I haven't seen her since the woods. I thought I'd run into her at school today, but with where she is right now and the direction she's heading in,

I doubt she was even at school. Her head is tucked down, and her blond hair is blowing in the wind. I can't see her face, but she seems to have a heaviness she's carrying around with her.

"Is that Camilla?" Ellis asks.

I think he's talking to me, but his eyes are on Clover. I'm relieved because I don't think I can speak about Camilla.

Clover nods as she takes another drag of her cigarette. Her eyes are locked on Camilla as we passed by her. "Yeah, I think so."

"It's definitely her," Jane says then pauses as she ashes her cigarette out the window. "Did you guys hear that rumor about her?"

My heart thuds in my chest. Do they know what happened?

"That she was locked up in a mental institution over the summer?" Clover replies with smoke circling her face.

My heart twists. *Is that true?*

"I heard she was in the hospital." Ellis slants forward and reaches around me to ash his cigarette out the window. "Because she tried to kill herself."

Air … I can't get it into my lungs.

Jenna says, "That's what I heard, too."

"Hmm …" Clover mutters, her attention still fastened on Camilla as she ducks off the sidewalk and crosses a patch of grass, heading for a set of older apartments near the town park. "Well, either way, something must have happened to her this summer because she dropped out of school."

A scream sears inside my throat, but I swallow the fucker down.

I know what happened to Camilla, I want to yell. *I know. I know. I know.*

The truth.

It's at the tip of my tongue. *Just say the words. Say what you know. Speak.*

It should be so easy.

Like breathing.

Only, sometimes breathing is complex—choosing to put life into your lungs.

"You can't ever talk about this, Ava." My mom gripped my shoulders. She'd been shaking me hard as she ignored the tears spilling down my face. "And even if you did—if you ever tell anyone—no one will ever believe you. That's just the way things work. So it's better to keep it to yourself and let it go. Just forget it ever happened. Just forget."

Forget, Ava. Forget.

I move the cigarette toward my lips and take another inhale. This time, it's not as hard to breathe in the smoke. In fact, it burns away the scream inside my throat. And for a moment, all those memories smother away. But then everything inside my body starts screaming again as my phone lets out sharp, loud beeps. And it's not just mine that goes off. All of our phones do simultaneously.

Ellis is the first to grab his, since it's sitting on the seat beside his hip.

"It's a missing person's alert," he mutters with his phone in front of him.

I can see his screen. He has the notification open. It has a photo of a girl on it, and I recognize her face. Her name is Lucy, and she's a year younger than me. She used to be in the same church classes as me, but she stopped attending a few months ago. Rumors began spreading that she got into drugs. And that was just the start of it. I heard things like she robbed a bunch of houses, was dating this man in his thirties, and was selling herself for drug money. Everyone was talking about it, including my parents. I felt terrible for whatever was happening to her, whatever it was.

Things only worsened when Lucy's family stopped attending church, probably because of the rumors. I even heard my mother talking to my aunt about how she bet they felt too ashamed to go anymore because their daughter was an embarrassment.

"Does anyone know her?" Clover asks as she stares at the missing person's info for Lucy on her phone.

"I do," I say. "She's in the grade below us and used to go to my church."

Clover arches a brow at me. "Used to?"

I shrug. "She hasn't been for a while. I've heard people say it's because she got into drugs, but I don't know if that's the truth."

"Everyone always says they got into drugs when they don't want to know the truth." She puts her phone away then, and so does everyone else.

Everything seems to go back to normal, but Clover remains quiet. She trades a glance with Ellis, who also sinks into silence.

Clover's words echo in my head. What did she mean by it? What truth?

Maybe I'm reading her wrong right now, but for some reason, she almost looks as if she's afraid of something.

CHAPTER 11

I've always found bars obnoxiously loud, even small town ones. In fact, those might be louder and rowdier than city bars. The entire room is made of wood from ceiling to floor; even the bar is made of wood paneling. The tables and barstools match the décor and the lights are woven with artificial antlers. It's outdated yet strangely works for the place.

Clara's demeanor reveals how she feels about being here; tension is humming off her as her gaze travels across the packed space in front of us. "Wow," she mutters as she clutches onto her wallet and phone. "I mean, I've been to a few smaller town bars, but this is a whole new level of … I'm not even sure what word to put in there."

"Run down?" I offer as I step up beside her, equally as tense as I try to see if anyone I used to know is here.

About half the people at the bar are double my age, though a few look younger. I can't spot any familiar faces, but a lot of the last years I spent in this town are blurry, just a stream of dazed, dull drunkenness and foggy gray highs. It's difficult to recall things when no brightness or colors exist within the memories.

"Well, I guess we'll have to make this work," Clara declares as she shucks off her jacket. She hands it to me, and I elevate my brow.

"Do I look like a coat hanger?" I ask with a smile so she knows I'm kidding.

She eyes me over. "Kind of."

I shove her, and she laughs as she stumbles.

"I don't even know why you wore a jacket," I tell her as I drape it over a chair at an empty table. "It's in the middle of the summer."

"It goes with my outfit," she explains, combing her fingers through her hair. "And it's not even that hot here."

"True," I agree as she walks backward toward the bar.

"What do you want to drink?" she asks.

I notice a few guys eyeballing us, and it makes me uneasy.

"Water's fine," I reply, trying not to twitch.

Trying not to expose myself.

To overact, as I've been so often told.

Just relax.

Take it easy.

Stop being so uptight.

"Pretty girls like you should be smiling," Jason said to me during the first days we spent together. So, I did. I smiled through the pain and discomfort of what was going on in my life and told myself that I shouldn't even feel the way that I did, that I should feel better and even flattered that he called me pretty.

Clara rolls her eyes. "I'm not getting you water." She spins on her heel and saunters over to the bar.

I pull out a chair to sit down. Then I glance around again, unsure what the hell I'm even doing here.

When I left Star Meadows, I practically ran away and didn't look back. And I didn't want to come back. The problem is where I ran to wasn't any better. This town had always felt like a prison, and my home felt crushingly small, the air constantly scalding, like it was about to burst into flames. I spent years in that smoldering that threatened to burn me alive until one day it did. But I didn't just burn. I *ignited*. Part of me wanted to stand still amid those flames until nothing was left but embers.

But, for some reason, I fought against it. Sort of. Although the flames still taunted me for years afterward.

I'm still trying to decide if I made the right decision to escape them, if the reason I did was purely survival instinct. In fact, I question this every day. Right now, I may question it more than ever since one of my darkest secrets walked into the bar.

Back in high school, before the day in the woods, Camilla was considered one of the most gorgeous girls in school. She was sweet, and kind, and made talking look so breathlessly easy. *The perfect girl*, people said. Sometimes, I wished I was like her. It would've made life so much easier. That's what I believed at the time, back when I was young and naïve. Back when I didn't understand the darkness that lay inside people, back when it was difficult to tell what was real because of the disguises people around me wore. The smiles they painted upon their lips. The twinkle in their eyes. The way they talked, like honey and sugar and all sorts of other sweet things. These people were far worse than those who walked around wearing shadows on their faces, who whispered the truths of their dark minds aloud. I learned that it's the people who hide their darkness that usually let it slip out when least expected.

"I'm going to watch you burn," Jason whispers. His voice sounds as cracked as his face looks. "You stupid bitch. I'm going to make you pay for that."

His hands are around my neck and I lay there, broken, defeated, and ...

Dead inside.

But then I take a deep breath.

I am not dead inside.

Or maybe I am, and my lungs just refuse to quit fighting.

Can someone still breathe and be dead?

I wonder this about Camilla as she enters the bar. She kind of looks dead. It's horrible to think, but she does look awful, like life has not been kind to her.

She doesn't notice me as she moves deeper into the bar, her gaze zeroing in on the bartender. She stumbles over to him, scratching her arm. She's thin, but I wouldn't say frail. She looks like a lot of energy is building up inside her, a ball of need rolling around, driving her forward. She has sores on her arms, which leads me to wonder if the drink she's seeking will barely feed the monster screaming inside her.

"You okay? "Clara appears by my side, startling me so severely I jolt.

"Um ... yeah." I glance at Camilla again and note the bloom of a purple and blue bruise on her cheek.

I wonder how she got that.

Did she "fall" like I used to "fall" all the time when I was married to Jason? Same goes for when I lived with my parents. Anyone who really paid attention would've probably started to become suspicious. Unfortunately, at these times, I didn't really have someone in my life who looked at me long enough to see past the seemingly put-together family.

It's incredible how easily people will see the fakeness if it matches their perception of what they want life to look like.

"Do you know her?" Clara asks as she hands me a glass filled with clear liquid.

"Who?" I play dumb as I tear my eyes off Camilla.

The scent of vodka is whispering silent promises to me of a night, telling me it can make this pulsating agony inside my chest disappear.

"Okay, I can tell you're lying to me right now. And now I'm even more curious." Her gaze bounces from Camilla then back to me. "Who is she?"

Sometimes, in moments like these, I wish for the days when I was friendless and alone, that posters on my walls, reading articles about how to get the guy I've been crushing on, and reality television were my only friends. When I didn't have to answer questions, tell the truth, to pluck at the little slivers of my messed-up past that have been lodged inside my veins for years. It's fucked up. I know. But I can't stop the thoughts from biting at my mind.

"I used to go to school with her." Not a complete lie.

"Really?" She stares at Camilla again, and I can almost see her mind spinning all sorts of ideas.

It's apparent Camilla is suffering from a drug addiction.

And now Clara is wondering who I was in high school. She's aware that I used to drink a lot and sometimes did drugs, but I never got into the extent of how bad I was drowning in it. Now she's probably wondering if I was a drug addict. Did I use to look as bad as Camilla? Did my addiction become so powerful that it ate away everything else about me until I was nothing but a skeleton of what I used to be?

The answer is yes to all these questions, but it's not how I defined myself back then. I knew who I was and still sometimes am.

A liar.

The edges of Clara's lips tug downward. "Was she like this back then?"

I could say yes. But my addiction is connected to something I don't want to discuss. The thing I'll never tell—can't tell.

I let her die.

"No," I lie.

I don't take a drink. I want to *desperately*. And maybe I would have, but then I see another familiar face, and I get uncomfortably distracted.

Oh my hell …

Ellis.

Fuck. Apparently, this damn bar is memory lane tonight.

He looks a bit older, his brown hair is shorter, and he's less thin and leaner than when I knew him in high school. And yet, he still looks the same. Just healthier. And instead of being dressed head to toe in black like he used to, he's sporting a gray button-down shirt with the sleeves rolled up and dress pants. But underneath it, he still resembles the guy I used to know, the one I partied with my junior year, the guy who gave me my first real kiss, the guy who was with me the first time I drank tequila, the guy who I got high with many times—the guy who was beside me in my darkest of moments.

With how healthy he looks, I doubt he's taken the same road as Camilla. He looks good, but that doesn't mean I want to see him.

Panicking, I hand Clara my drink.

She nearly spills it as she takes it from me. "What the hell, Aves? You spilled it all over me."

"Sorry … I have to pee." I take off before she can ask more questions.

I keep my head low as I bolt across the bar, weaving through people until I reach the bathroom. One other woman is by the sink, drunk off her ass, stumbling around in front of the dingy mirror as she tries to touch up her makeup. I want to splash some cold water on my face, but I don't want to go near her, so I lock myself in the bathroom.

I stay in the stall for a few minutes, breathing in and out while I sit on the toilet. It smells in here, and a wet substance pools around the toilet. It's disgusting, but I've done worse than sit by piss.

I mentally curse myself for coming here. What was I thinking? I should've suspected I'd end up crossing paths with people I used to know—

My phone rings, and I latch on to the distraction as I dig it out of my pocket, assuming it's my mother wondering where the hell I am. But it's from an unknown caller again. That same anxiety I felt earlier today on the side of the road rises inside me.

I start to put the phone into my pocket, but then the caller leaves a voicemail. I try to tell myself that it doesn't mean anything, that getting calls from unknown numbers is common and is probably just a spam call. But my fingers tremble as I press the button to listen to the recording.

At first, it's quiet, but then a soft noise of shifting rises in the background, and it goes on for about thirty seconds. I'm about to hang up when I hear something that makes me instantly tense.

And for a second, I'm not sitting in the stall. I'm lying back in those trees enclosed by branches and snow.

"Help me." The sound of Camilla sobbing drifts through my phone. *"Please ... someone help me."*

CHAPTER 12

THE PAST...

I WENT TO LUNCH WITH CLOVER AND HER FRIENDS EVERY DAY this week. They have a system where they smoke and drive for a while before getting some food and heading back to school. It's nice to have something to do and be around people who don't constantly make me feel like our friendship is an obligation, like with Livia. But I'm not even sure if Clover is my friend. Sure, we eat lunch together, but we haven't hung out after school or anything. With everything going on in my life, though, I appreciate her being nice to me, especially since being at school feels like I'm continuously tracing my finger along the edge of a razor.

I never reported the locker incident, and I avoided going to it for the entire day. But the next day, someone—I'm guessing the janitor—had cleaned it off by the time I arrived at school. I worried I'd be called into the office about it, but the school seems content on pretending it never occurred, which is fine, I guess. I honestly don't want to discuss it with anyone, like the counselor or the principal. I can only imagine how that'd go. They'd ask me who did it, and if I was being bullied. If I decided to be truthful, I'd tell them I'm pretty confident I know the culprit, which would lead to *why would I think that?* And that is a question I can't answer, not because the idea of speaking the words scares the hell out of me.

You can never tell anyone, Ava. No one will believe you.

"Hey, slut." Clover strolls up beside me as I'm collecting my books to take home with me for the weekend.

I stiffen at her choice of words. *Has she heard a rumor about me?*

So far, no one has mentioned the slut incident, but I overheard people whispering about a locker being painted with the word. But the gossip about that rapidly faded as news about Lucy quickly spread.

Some are saying she overdosed, and that her body is in the mountains somewhere. Others speculate she ran away. But the darkest rumor is that someone in our town killed her.

A murderer in Star Meadows? It's odd to think that a place so small could have one. Most of the people who hear this rumor don't believe it. Me? I know monsters reside here.

When I look at Clover, she's smiling, and her blue eyes glitter with amusement.

I relax a smidgeon. "Hey," I reply as coolly, trying not to let on that my heart is sputtering inside my chest.

Slut. Slut. Slut.

"So, I heard a rumor about you." She crosses her arms and leans against the locker beside mine.

"What rumor?" I play dumb, but deep down, I'm terrified she knows the terrible truth about me.

"The one where you've never been drunk before." Her grin broadens as she fiddles with the diamond stud in her nose. "Dude, is it true?"

I start to relax but then realize what she said. "Who told you that?" Because, so far, I've barely told anyone anything about me.

She laughs as she straightens her stance. "No one. I was just messing with you. Although, I think I might be right about this." She assesses me. "Am I?"

I squirm as I stuff a book into my bag. "No."

Her brow arches. "Really?"

"Yeah." I'm such a liar. But I don't want to look like a loser, either.

"Oh, my bad," she says, and I can tell she knows I'm full of shit. But for some reason, she lets it slide. "Okay, drinking slut, you want to go to a party with us tonight?"

Clover is probably the bluntest person I've ever met, but she has this way about her that even when she calls people things like *drinking slut*, it somehow sounds like a good thing.

"Yeah, sure." I bump my locker shut. "Where's it at?"

"It's at this party spot we go to a lot," she replies as we start toward the exit doors.

The final bell rang a few minutes ago, so the hallway isn't too crowded.

"What's the address? And what time should I be there?" I ask, weaving around a group of guys in basketball uniforms.

I swear they glance at me as I pass, and then one of them smirks.

Slut. Slut. Slut.

Die.

But I can't tell if I'm being paranoid or not.

Truthfully, I think I might be losing my mind.

"Don't worry about that—we'll pick you up," Clover tells me as she combs her fingers through her hair. "And you can spend the night at my house if you want to. That way, we can stay out later since I don't have a curfew." She glances at me. "Because I'm guessing you do."

How does she know that? I don't even know that since I've never gone out before. Not really, anyway. I go to the movies with Livia and sometimes spend the night at her house, but my mom usually picks me up. Or, well, she used to. During the summer, when I got my driver's license, I barely went out as I drifted through the months feeling empty. I blamed it on what occurred in the woods, but now that I think about it, I may have been this way my entire life—drifting aimlessly.

Maybe things are changing, though.

As I accept Clover's offer to go out, I feel something I haven't ever felt—a spark of excitement maybe? I'm not positive what it is since it's so foreign, but it's definitely a spark of something.

That spark gradually fizzles, though, as we pass by Livia. She hasn't talked to me since I started spending time with Clover. I texted her once to tell her I couldn't meet her for lunch, and she replied with an "Okay." And that was that. She's been spending time with a group of people that are popular. She's done that occasionally, but I guess she's one hundred percent in their group now. Part of me speculates she was waiting for me to leave her alone so she could live the life she desired.

Zoe is with her, too, and she hasn't spoken to me either.

Livia is laughing about something. A group of guys go over to her and her new friends, and start discussing the game this weekend. Livia begins flirting with Greg, the guy Jane kicked out of her car earlier this week.

Part of me wants to warn her about him, but the other part is afraid to enter the territory of people I don't know. Maybe I could text her and give her a heads-up.

"Die slut," someone coughs.

My back stiffens as my gaze skims the faces around me. No one is looking in my direction, but one person is nearby who might have said it. Blond hair, tall, and he's wearing a jersey.

Trystan.

He's walking away from the group and toward a hallway on the other side of the quad. He's not looking at me, but that doesn't mean he wasn't a moment ago.

"Shut the fuck up, or I'll slit your throat."

If I focus hard enough, the faint memory sounds like it's being said in his voice.

"Hey, are you okay?" Clover asks with a crease between her brows.

"Yeah, I'm fine." *Did she hear what someone called me?*

Her frown deepens, and then she sighs. "You shouldn't let them get to you." She nods toward the people standing in the middle of the quad. "They're all sluts. They just like to pretend they're not." She loops her arm through mine. "Not that I think you're one."

So, she did hear what they said.

I wait for her to ask me questions, but she doesn't. Instead, she smiles as we reach the exit doors.

"Come on; let's get the hell out of here. It's the weekend, baby, and it's time to escape this hellhole and party."

Weirdly, I find myself smiling.

* * *

When I arrive home after school, my mom is in the living room with my aunt Marissa. They're discussing a community charity event they're attending tonight that'll go into the early morning hours. This isn't an anomaly; they go to those things a lot.

I attempt to sneak downstairs without being spotted, but either my mom saw my car pull up or she heard me come inside.

"Ava," she calls out as I'm closing the front door.

Sighing, I drop my backpack in the foyer and go to the living room. They're sitting on the sofa in front of the window, drinking lemonade and eating cookies.

Seeing my aunt Marissa—Trystan's mom—makes me think of what happened at school today. It had to be Trystan who called me a slut. I don't know how I know this. I just do. Just like I have no proof he was in the woods that day, and yet I'm almost positive he was. It's an inkling in my gut, a twinge in my bones, a clawing in my brain.

I could tell my mother what he called me in school, but the last time I tried to tell her something horrible was done to me, she locked me in the basement for days and made me question everything that happened.

The haze started on day one and swelled deeper into my brain the longer I was locked down there. Late at night, while I was asleep, she placed food and water at the top of the stairs. But I'd barely touched it.

On day two, I tried to break the door open by pounding and kicking it. That resulted in my father screaming at me through the door. On day three, I had a mental breakdown. That day, I lay in bed, staring off at nothing, feeling delirious, detached, and so damn lost. I couldn't feel anything anymore, and that made me question if anything was real.

I still feel that way sometimes.

Not right now, though. No, right now, I'm focused on the party tonight, and that makes an excited hum run through my veins. It's a bizarre sensation to feel after walking around practically comatose for so long. The emotion is so potently new that I'm bouncing with jitteriness.

"What are you doing?" my mother asks as I enter the room.

My palms are sweaty, and my heart is fucking hammering inside my chest. Does she know about the party? How would she?

"Um … I was going to my room," I say.

She sips the lemonade and then sets the glass on the table. The look she trades with my aunt next sends me into full anxiety mode.

"There's something we need to talk to you about," my mother says, returning her attention to me. "It's about a rumor your aunt and I heard."

I swallow hard. "Okay."

"Some people in our community say they've heard you're being … promiscuous." My mother crosses her arms as she reclines in the sofa.

Is she kidding me? She knows what happened to me—she saw the aftermath.

Then again, she acted like she didn't fully believe me.

"It's not true," I say quietly.

"Are you sure?" she questions with her brows lifted. "Because many people are saying this. People who we know and trust."

My fingers curl inward, and I stab my fingernails into my palms. "Well, it's not true. And whoever told you that is either lying or gossiping."

She eyes me over. "I don't know, Ava. You have been acting a bit odd the last week or so. And your aunt Marissa said she was at the school the other day, substitute teaching, and she saw you leave for lunch with some kids who looked like troublemakers. Who were they? And what happened to Livia?"

Shit. I didn't consider that my aunt sometimes substitute teaches at the high school and could've seen me leaving with Clover, who I know my mother would never approve of me spending time with, especially since her and her friends were smoking in the car.

Wait—did my aunt see me smoke?

No … My mom would've brought that up already in the form of a smack across the face. And if my dad learned about it …

I resist a shudder and attempt to play it cool.

I shrug. "Livia and I stopped talking to each other."

My mother shakes her head. "Why? You two have been friends for years."

"You should call her up and apologize for whatever you did," my aunt chimes in. "Friendships like that don't come around that often."

Dammit, she's so nosey. It drives me crazy.

I dig my fingernails deeper into my palms. "Who said *I* did anything?"

"One of you had to have done something, or your friendship wouldn't have just ended," she informs me, seeming so sure of herself.

It's an unnatural attitude for her. When my uncle is around, she's typically quiet and submissive.

"No one did anything," I mutter. "We just stopped being friends."

My aunt rolls her eyes. "Teenagers are so stubborn. I don't get it. Why does everything have to be so overdramatic?"

"I know. I sometimes wish I had a boy so I didn't have to deal with this," my mother agrees. "Boys are so much easier."

"They really are." My aunt collects the cup of lemonade and takes a sip, eyeing me over the brim of her glass.

I want to scream that her son is terrible, but I'll probably get grounded or worse if I do, so I bite down on my tongue until I taste rust.

"You need to stop hanging out with those kids." My mother reaches for her phone as it buzzes. "Or you'll end up like that Lucy girl."

My brows pull together. "The girl that went missing?" Why is she bringing this up?

"Missing?" my aunt sneers. "That girl did not go missing. She's a drug addict that ran away. Her parents are just too naïve to admit it."

"How do you know that?" I wonder, shifting my weight.

"Because the police just called off the search for her"—my mother sets her phone face down on the coffee table—"and changed her status to a runaway." She takes a bite of a cookie she considers something. "I'm only going to tell you this once, Ava. You'll clean up your act so the rumors about you will stop. I don't want anyone to have an excuse to tarnish our family's reputation. Do you understand me?"

So many words scratch at my tongue, but I swallow them down, and they land in my throat like shards of glass.

"I understand," I manage to say. Then I turn to walk out of the room.

"And Ava?" my mother calls out.

I pause, gritting my teeth. "Yes, Mother."

"These rumors better not have any truth to them," she warns. "For now, I'm giving you the benefit of the doubt, but if I keep hearing these things about you, I'll assume there's some truth to it. And if there is, you'll pay for it. I won't have a daughter who sleeps around and becomes the town slut."

Slut.

Die.

I have to mentally count to keep my composure. "Okay."

"Good," she responds.

I'm surprised she isn't punishing me over the rumors. I'm unsure why; if she doesn't believe them, or perhaps she's giving me a get-out-of-jail-free card because of what happened that day in the woods.

Or maybe she simply doesn't want to deal with me right now.

If the latter is true, this will come back to slice me open later.

* * *

Before my mom and aunt leave for the event, she comes

into my room to tell me where she's going. I'm sitting on my bed when she enters, and then she chews me out about my messy room. I promise her I'll clean it tonight, but I won't. It's not like she comes to my room often enough that I need to worry about it.

"You're father and I will be late tonight," she tells me. She's now wearing a blue, floor-length dress. "Make sure to lock up the house when it gets dark."

"Okay."

I'm not sure what to do about the party. Clover said I could spend the night at her house, but the probability of my mother letting me do that is zero.

So, how in the hell am I going to the party tonight?

Since I can't develop an idea yet, I keep my lips zipped.

She turns to leave but then pauses. "Do you …? How are you doing with your medication?"

I blink at her, confused. Why hasn't she asked me about this since she picked up the medication from the pharmacy? And about a week after I started taking them, she canceled my therapy sessions because, as she put it, "It's not a good look for our family for you to be going to a therapist. People will think you're insane."

I wanted to tell her that maybe I was, that I felt like this wasn't how things were supposed to be, but I merely nodded.

"They're fine," I tell her.

"Okay, well … That's good, I guess." She stares at me, as if she wants to say more.

And it's fucking weird.

"All right, well, I'll see you tomorrow." She leaves my room, thinking I'll obey.

And why would she think anything else? Usually, I'm a good girl and do what I'm supposed to. But in the past, I've never had another option.

Tonight, I have options.

Tonight, I'm not going to sit in my room or on the sofa in the basement, eating dinner by myself with the ghosts of the empty house haunting me, whispering secrets in my ear that nip and bite at my flesh—secrets that I've buried and want to forget. But every time I look out the window, the reminder is there, like a photo left in the sunlight to melt and warp.

I need to figure out a plan.

I rack my mind until Clover texts me to say she's headed to pick me up. It's close to seven o'clock, and the sun is setting over the sharp peak of the mountains.

Even though I'm still unsure what to do, I start getting ready. What am I supposed to wear, though? I decide on torn jeans and a T-shirt. I hope my outfit isn't too casual. I wouldn't know since I've never been to a party.

As I'm standing in my room, listening to the stillness of the empty house, it dawns on me—a plan. I could go to the party and sneak back into the house in the morning. My parents won't check on me when they get home—they never do. All I need to do is leave the window unlocked.

Do I dare risk it? I've never been a risk-taker, but I want to go out tonight. Besides, everything I've never been and always have been isn't what I want to be anymore.

Or I could take one step further and do something to help my mother get off my case about these rumors of me. I could tell her I'm spending the night at Livia's so we can work on mending our friendship.

I sit on the idea and decide to go for it. It's the first time I've done something like this, and it makes my stomach twist with nervousness. My mom doesn't reply to the message, but more than likely she's busy with the event.

I comb my hair and put on a bit of lip gloss and eyeliner. By the time I'm finished, Clover has texted me that they're at my house.

I hurry and grab my phone and ten dollars in case I need some cash. Then I rush up the stairs and throw open the front door. Clover is standing on the front porch, and the moment I see her, I realize my wardrobe choice wasn't the correct one.

She's dressed up in a pair of wide-legged jeans and a cropped halter top that has daisies on the straps. She also has daisies in her hair—real ones, I think. She looks pretty, and I'm envious of it.

"Is that what you're wearing?" she asks as she studies me. She doesn't say it like I'm some hideous beast. It's a simple and straightforward question. That's how she usually is. I like that about her—that she doesn't have this nasty side to her. Well, except when it comes to Greg. But that's justified.

I tug at my T-shirt. "I wasn't sure what to wear."

"Hmm …" She taps her finger against her lip, then casts a glance back at a small, blue truck.

Someone is sitting in that driver's seat, so I assume it's not Clover's truck.

She holds up her hand at whoever is in the truck and yells, "Give us five minutes!" Then she spins around to face me again. "Let's go raid your closet."

"Um … okay," I say.

"We don't have to," she adds. "I just thought maybe I could help you pick something more party-esque."

"No, it's fine." I step back and motion for her to come inside. "I'm just unsure if I have anything better in there."

"I'll figure something out." She winks at me and walks inside, her gaze skimming along the foyer's walls. "Which way's your room?"

"This way." As I start down the stairway, she trails behind me.

When we enter my room, her jaw drops.

"Wow, your room is hot. Seriously, I did not expect this." Her eyes are on the posters covering my walls.

"Expect what?" I wonder.

She shrugs. "For you to be so guy crazy."

"I'm not," I insist, picking at my nail polish, discomfort weaving through me.

Slut.

Slut.

Slut.

"Shut the fuck up, or I fucking slit your throat."

"That's not a bad thing, Aves." She lightly nudges her shoe against mine. "Own it, okay? You like hot guys. I like hot guys." She grins at me. "Not let's make you a hot girl, okay?"

I nod, unease still stirring inside me that she said I was guy crazy. My grandma once visited our house, and my mom let her stay in my room even though we have an extra room. But at the time, it had been full of paint supplies due to my parents remodeling the house. So, my grandma got the room, and I got the sofa, which I didn't mind. What bothered me, though, was that my grandma told my mother the following day at breakfast, "How do you let her decorate her room like that? It's disgusting. Do you know what kind of girls put up posters of guys on their walls? Ones that sleep around." She had violently stabbed her waffles with her fork. "She's going to end up pregnant."

I felt embarrassed and confused, and other things I couldn't quite sort through. I was thirteen then, so I understood what getting pregnant and sleeping around meant, but I was puzzled why she'd believe I'd do that. I mean, I couldn't even talk to guys without getting anxious.

My mom gave me the darkest glare I'd ever seen. "Go take those down now. I've already told you this, Ava."

It was a lie. She hadn't been in my room since I'd put the posters up. This is how my mom was around her mother, though—constantly trying to impress. Constantly trying to be agreeable.

Obey.

Obey.

Obey.

And I always did.

Usually.

I didn't take those posters down. I'm surprised she didn't mention it tonight, but she seemed more focused on my dirty room and my lack of compliance.

I've been doing that more and more lately.

I'm sure as hell doing it tonight.

Ten minutes later, I'm dressed in cut-offs, a gray crop top, and knee-high socks. I don't have shoes on because Clover told me she has some in the truck that will go with my outfit.

Right before we leave my room, she stops. "Hold on." She

studies me with her head angled to the side. "Something's missing."

There's a lot of things probably missing, I want to tell her.

Decidedly, she plucks one of the daisies out of her hair and tucks it into mine. "There we go. Perfect," she says with a smile. "And it's kind of fitting for you."

My brows knit. "Why?"

A smile tugs up her lips. "Because daisies mean innocence."

I frown. *Is that how she sees me?*

Because I'm not. At all.

"How do you know that?" I wonder.

She shrugs. "I like to look up the symbolism of things." She checks her makeup in the mirror. "Daisies have a few meanings—loyalty, love, positivity, new beginnings—which I totally think you're about to have." She wipes a smudge of lipstick off her lip. "I also read that they used to mean the ability to keep secrets."

My next breath gets stuck in my throat. "Really?"

"Yeah, I think it's meant between friends or something. I can't remember." She shrugs and then faces me. "And hey, I've got a secret I can tell you right now to start our Daisy friendship."

"Um … okay," I say warily because I don't want any more secrets.

She grins. "You look hot, and I know someone who will agree with me. Although, you probably could've worn your T-shirt and jeans, and he still would've thought it. But this way is *so* much more fun."

Before I can ask who she's talking about, she grabs my arm and yanks me out of my room. We leave the house, and I walk barefoot to the truck, the ground cold against my feet. When Clover opens the passenger door, I spot Ellis sitting in the driver's seat.

He's so cute. He always is and without any effort. Tonight, though, it looks as if he's tried to look even better. He's sporting a long-sleeved gray shirt and dark jeans, and he doesn't have his usual knitted cap on, so wisps of his dark hair are falling into his eyes.

When our gazes collide, his lips pull into a smile. He's done this every time I've seen him this week. This time, things go down a bit differently as his gaze drifts up and down me.

"Wow." He blinks a few times. "You look …" He wavers, as if choosing his words carefully. "Good."

"Thanks," I mumble, shifting my weight self-consciously.

Clover is leaning over the passenger seat and digging around in the back for the boots. "She doesn't look good. She looks fucking hot," she says.

Ellis drags his teeth along his lip. "I was trying to be a gentleman about it, Clove. Maybe you should try it." He smiles at me, and I return it. But inside, I feel wobbly.

I'm not used to the attention.

I like it.

I hate it.

I don't know what I feel.

It's an uncomfortable sensation, like I'm carrying a thorn around in my hand that's pressed against my skin, not breaking it, just there, reminding me of its existence.

Clover reaches over and swats Ellis playfully on the shoulder while continuing to dig around in the back seat.

Ellis laughs while gripping the wheel, his gaze flicking back to me and then to her.

"What're you even looking for?" he asks.

She sits back with a pair of clunky, worn boots in her hand. "These. My girl needs shoes. Or did you not notice she's shoeless?" She has this insinuating look on her face and a hint of amusement in her eyes.

Ellis clears his throat as he looks away from her. "We should probably get going."

A smirk curls at her lips. "Why are you suddenly in a hurry?"

I feel lost and out of my element as to what the hell is going on.

"Shut up," Ellis mutters under his breath.

Clover snickers, then hands me the shoes. "I'll let you ride in the passenger seat." She winks at me, then hops over the console and into the back seat.

Still totally perplexed, I climb in, shut the door, then start to put on the socks and boots.

Ellis offers me another small smile, and while I give him one back, that invisible thorn in my hand nicks the flesh, and a few droplets of blood trickle out. I have no clue why I feel this way. Why I'm so nervous? Ellis is nice. He smiles. He's never done anything that'd lead me to believe he's a bad guy. And yet, I can't seem to settle down as we drive away from my house with the shadows of the trees in the distance.

Will things always be this way?

Will there always be a windstorm of nervousness inside me about every little thing?

Will I always be lost?

Will I always be scared?

Will I always be that girl hiding in the shadows, waiting for the monster to come out and tear her apart?

Will I always feel like I never entirely escaped those trees, that the branches still hold me down and shred me with their wilting flesh?

The feeling keeps swelling inside my chest until I can no longer breathe. I worry I might pass out. I can feel it—the dizziness, the stars bursting across my vision—

"Let's pregame," Clover abruptly announces. She has a bottle in her hand that's filled with clear liquid.

I get a glimpse of the label. *Vodka.*

I've never drank before, but I thought about it during those times in my basement when I sat alone with nothing but the television and books to keep me company. I wondered what it would be like to be at a party, drinking and dancing, completely relaxed. That's how I pictured it from the knowledge I have. My parents don't drink, not that I'm aware of. But who knows? Early this summer, I learned people are good at hiding who they are.

I mean, look at me.

Clover twists the cap off the bottle and takes a swig. Her face contorts, but just slightly, so I figure it can't taste that bad. When she hands the bottle to me, I take it and immediately the potent scent engulfs my nostrils.

"It smells like rubbing alcohol." I don't mean to say the words aloud. They accidentally slip out.

Clover snorts a laugh. "Yeah, that's kind of the point." She gives a short, considering pause. "Have you never drank before? Or have you just not drank vodka?"

"Just vodka," I lie, not wanting to look stupid.

Amusement sparkles in her eyes. "Okay."

"It's okay if you don't want to drink it," Ellis tells me as he steers down the road. "Clover just thinks everything we do needs to involve drinking."

"Um, yeah, because it's fun," she says as she sinks back into the seat.

The sunlight has begun to descend below the mountains, painting a pinkish-orangish glow across the curves of the hills, the trees, and Ellis's eyes. If I don't think too hard about anything, I might even say everything around me looks pretty.

"It's okay. I want to try it." I raise the bottle to my lips.

It's almost unbearable. But I manage to choke a swallow down without spitting it out. The burn, though, flares through my throat, stomach, and even my eyes. For a moment, I believe I might die from being unable to breathe again.

For a moment, I don't want to.

Eventually, I manage to take an inhale through my nose. It's loud enough that Ellis and Clover notice. I exhale, then brace myself for the ridicule I know will come.

Because it always comes. *Always.*

"Dude, you should see your face right now." Clover takes the bottle from me. "I'm proud of you, girl. For a moment, I thought you were gonna spit it out." She tips her head back and takes a long gulp.

I exhale shakily, then wipe my lips with the back of my hand before twisting around in the seat.

Ellis looks at me. He's not smiling. "You really don't have

to drink if you don't want to," he tells me as he turns up the heater.

Later on, when I look back to this moment, I wish I'd taken his advice and I'd stopped right there and avoided everything that lay ahead of me.

But the truth is, whatever direction I'd gone in at the moment, I probably would've self-destructed either way. It was inevitable from the day I hiked into those woods.

Or maybe it happened before that.

Perhaps I was destined to self-destruct from the day I took my first breath.

THE PARTY IS IN THE CENTER OF A CLUSTER OF TREES IN THE middle of nowhere. I should be freaking out, but my surroundings are spinning enough that the trees look more like blobs than anything else. And that makes my memories of the last time I was in the woods more misshapen and hazy than they already were.

And in the middle of it all is a fire blazing against the darkness, and the mob of people around are drinking and chatting.

"Jesus, why are there so many people here?" Clover mumbles as Ellis parks the truck beside a row of vehicles. She has a compact mirror out and is checking her reflection, the glow of the firelight reflecting in her eyes.

"Isn't anyone worried they'll get busted?" I wonder as Clover snaps her compact mirror shut.

"Nah." She tucks the mirror into a small backpack she

brought with her. "It's far enough up in the mountains that there's a minimal chance the cops will drive up here unless someone tips them off. And even then, they likely won't do anything other than slap us on our wrists, confiscate everyone's drugs and alcohol, and send us on our way. Then they'll go off and party on their own."

"Is that true?" Because I'm learning that sometimes Clover can be a bit on the dramatic side when talking about the shittiness of this town.

It's clear she despises this place. I'm not positive why. Sure, I loathe this town, but I'm aware of my reasons. What are hers? Did something happen to her here? Or does she simply despise it because it's too small and doesn't have much in the line of things to do?

"Unfortunately, yeah." Ellis is the one to answer as he slips his keys out of the ignition.

Clover slants forward and reaches for the bottle of vodka that I'm holding. "So, E," she says to Ellis, "are you volunteering to be DD, or are we gonna sleep in your car?"

"I don't know …" His gaze strays to me for some reason. "It all depends."

Clover arches a brow. "On what?"

He shrugs while tracing his fingers along the top of the steering wheel. "On if everyone can stay the night."

"Are you sure that's what you mean?" A teasing grin plays on her lips as she unscrews the lid of the bottle, and Ellis throws her a dirty look. She downs a swallow, her face contorting as she does. Then she lowers the bottle and fixes her attention on me. "So, did you tell your mom you were staying at my house?"

I shake my head. "Her and my dad were gone to a charity thing when I got home," I lie, mostly because I don't want to explain the complication that is my mother.

"Are you going to stay the night at my place?" she asks, wiping her lips off with the back of her hand. "Or will you need a ride home?"

I hesitate. I checked my phone a few minutes ago as Ellis's truck was inching up the bumpy dirt road that led to this place, and she still hadn't responded.

"I'm good," I tell them.

"Are you sure?" Clover checks as she rummages around in the back seat until she finds the wallet she always carries, the one with daisies on it.

"Yep." I sound more confident than I feel.

I'm rewarded with a smile from Ellis. Then he gets out of the car, and I follow, flipping the seat forward so Clover can get out.

She grabs the half-drunk bottle of vodka then bumps the door shut. "All right, let's find Jane, and then we can go get wasted," she declares, then skips toward the firepit.

I inch toward the front of the car, a trace of nervousness trying to bite its way through the booze in my system.

Get wasted? I already feel wasted. Everything is wobbly and slightly blurry.

The woods.

I vowed never to go into them again, yet here I am.

Maybe it was a mistake coming out tonight? The voice in my head is faint tonight and slurred enough that it's easy to disregard.

"You good?" Ellis' boots scuff in the dirt as he steps beside me.

"Yeah, absolutely." And weirdly, it doesn't feel like as much of a lie as it should.

Smiling, he places a hand on the small of my back. "Come on. I'll introduce you to some people. Hopefully, that'll make you feel a bit more comfortable."

"Thanks," I say. Then, just because my lips feel numb, I add, "Why are you so nice to me?"

He pauses, his head cocking to the side. "You say that like no one's ever been nice to you."

I'm unsure how to respond since I'm unsure if anyone has ever been nice to me.

For a flash of an instant, I swear I detect pity in his eyes, but it fades so quickly I can't be certain.

"I'm nice to you because you're sweet and quiet and nice. And pretty, which I know will make me sound vain, but it's true." He gives a considering pause. "And I find it interesting how you always seem to be thinking deeply about something, but you never say much aloud." He reaches up with his free hand and softly brushes his fingertip along my temple. "It makes me wonder what's going on inside here."

I don't know what's stranger, that he's curious about what I'm thinking or that I don't panic over his touch. I've dreamed of being touched by a guy like this, but I've been anxious around everyone after the incident in the woods. Right now, though, I feel completely and blissfully numb.

"Maybe you'll tell me some of your secrets tonight," he says, lowering his hand to his side.

That remark chisels through the wall of numbness in me. I

think he notices, too, since his expression falters. Thankfully, a guy wearing a baseball cap approaches us and offers a distraction.

The two of them start chatting about something that happened at the last party, and my mind wanders …. to the trees … to the fire … and to …

Camilla?

Camilla is here?

I tense when I spot her on the opposite side of the fire. She isn't looking at me and has a cup in her hand. A guy with dark hair is sucking on her neck while she stares off at the trees. As his hand feels her chest, she flinches but doesn't budge. It's as if her soul has withered like the ash at the bottom of the fire.

Guilt creeps inside me, winding around my stomach, circling my chest, and slipping to my throat.

Snow drifts around me as I lie on my face, the snow damp against my cheek.

"Help me," she begs. "Please." A sob wrenches from her chest as someone approaches us, their boots crunching in the snow.

The person stands there momentarily, and then they crouch down and trace their fingers across her back. Her body jolts, and her fingernails dig into the snow.

"Shh …" they whisper.

I blink against the blurriness, trying to make out their face. Everything is distorted, but I swear they look familiar—

Camilla's eyes lock with mine. I want to look away, but I can't. I want to tell her I'm sorry for not getting help, for not telling someone who would've helped her. I want to ask her if she remembers everything because maybe these empty graves in my mind would finally be filled.

Her gaze is unwavering as she lifts the cup to her lips and takes a drink. Emotion floods her eyes. I can't tell what it is. Anger? Confusion? Understanding? She carries my gaze for a second longer before she stands up and walks away.

My heart is frantically racing, as if we just ran out of the woods again.

"Are you okay?" Ellis asks as I suck in an uneven breath.

He and the guy he was talking to are now staring at me like I've lost my damn mind.

What they don't realize is that I lost it a long time ago.

The day I ran out of the woods, I told my mother that Trystan might have been part of the group that hurt Camilla and me. She asked me if I was sure, and I wavered because I wasn't. I couldn't see the faces anymore, but it was a feeling in my stomach. When I told her this, she uttered words that made me question everything.

"Sometimes, when something bad happens to us, Ava, our mind plays tricks on us because it can't cope with reality." She draped a blanket around me. "And perhaps you just think you heard Trystan because you don't know who it was, and your mind is just trying to fill in the holes. So, unless you're certain it was him, I don't think we should accuse him of it." She gave me a pat on the shoulder. "We wouldn't want to throw accusations that could be false and ruin other people's lives, now would we?"

Before this, I had been more confident I'd heard his voice, and that he wasn't alone. But I didn't recognize any of the other voices. When my mother said those words to me, it smeared doubt all over my brain like the blood that had been on my flesh just hours before that. And so nothing ever came of it. Now I'm left questioning everything I believed I witnessed and heard that day.

"Come on; let's go get a drink," Ellis tells me, nodding toward the coolers.

I nod, and we head over to them.

I spend the next handful of hours drinking and smoking with Ellis, Clover, and some people they introduce me to. The night is fun, light even, with the starlight and moonlight trickling down on us. The more I drink, the easier it becomes to convince myself that the day in the woods was merely a nightmare. Maybe it was. Perhaps my mom was right—my mind was playing tricks on me.

"It makes it easier, right?" A voice startles me out of my daze.

I'm sitting by the fire on a log, and Ellis is beside me, talking to the guy with the baseball cap again. And Clover … well, I'm unsure where she wandered off to.

When I look to see who spoke to me, Camilla is sitting on a log beside mine. She's staring into the crackling fire.

Her gaze slides to mine. "I mean, being drunk. It makes it easier not to remember what happened."

Everything briefly stills, like someone pushed pause on my life. But then it slowly moves again.

She's right. Even the mention of it from her doesn't create a lightning storm inside me, like it usually does.

"Did you tell anyone?" she asks, surprising me.

When we spoke again, I thought she'd unleash her anger and tell me I was horrible for never sending help.

"My mother," I answer quietly.

"I'm guessing she didn't care." It's not a question—just a speculation.

I nod, clutching at the beer bottle in my hand.

"Guess I made the right choice then," she utters, her gaze skating to the fire. "Not to tell anyone."

I think about the rumors of her going around, how she was in a psychiatric hospital, and how she tried to take her own life. I've never been certain if those rumors carried any truth, but considering what I've done, I wouldn't be surprised.

"Do you …? How much do you remember?" I ask as I pick at the label on the beer bottle

"Right now, I don't remember a damn thing, and I'd like to keep it that way," she says, slanting back. She digs something out of her pocket and pops it into her mouth. Then her eyes drift shut.

I'm about to ask her what she took when the guy that was sucking on her neck earlier moves up beside us. Now that he's in the glow of the fire, I can get a better look at his face.

His name is Ben, and I've seen him hang out with Trystan.

Worry stabs inside me. What if Trystan is here? Will he tell on me for being here? What if he drags me into the woods?

Ben's attention shifts from me to Camilla. "Is she gonna come party with us?"

Something about how he says it causes a chill to slither up my spine.

"No, she's not," Ellis is the one to reply, his cold tone not matching his usual easygoing personality.

A smirk creeps up on Ben's face. "I didn't realize you two were dating. My bad."

My gaze strays to Ellis, expecting him to clarify that we're not.

But all he does is glare at the guy and say, "Get the fuck out of here, Ben."

Ben raises his hands and lets out a fake laugh. "Man, someone has anger issues."

The muscle in Ellis's jaw spasms. "Leave now before I fucking make you."

Ben mutters something about Ellis being a little bitch before he reaches down and drags Camilla to her feet. She glances at me one final time, and I want to grab her from him, but they're already walking away.

I'm on the brink of attempting to get up and chase after her, if my legs will allow me to, but Ellis draws my attention to him.

"Stay away from him, okay?" he tells me as he pokes the fire aggressively with a stick. "He's a real piece of shit. He gets girls addicted to drugs so he can string them along and use them until they die."

"*What?* Who did he do that to?" I ask, thinking of Camilla and how out of it she looked.

"My sister." He tosses the stick into the fire then slips his fingers through mine. "Just stay by me tonight, okay?"

I nod, my heart abruptly awakening. I suddenly don't feel as drunk. In fact, I feel wired, my body breathing with life.

Ellis goes back to talking to the guy with the baseball hat on. They speak to me a few times, but I can't grasp what they're talking about since half my brain is fixated on Ellis's hand in mine and how warm his skin feels. And the other half is searching for Camilla. I want to find her and warn her about Ben, but I can't spot her anywhere. I attempt to stand up a few times to search for her, but the spouts of dizziness make me sit right back down.

At some point, sleep overtakes me. One minute, I'm sitting by the fire and leaning against Ellis, and the next, I'm waking up in the passenger seat of a car, and something is beeping loudly.

"What the hell is that?" Ellis murmurs. He has the driver's seat leaned back, his eyes are shut, and his head is resting against the door.

I blink a few times, attempting to clear the fogginess from my mind. Eventually, I wake up enough to become aware that my phone is what's beeping.

Shit. Shit. Shit. I never checked my phone to see if my mother said it was okay for me to spend the night at Livia's.

I fumble to get my phone out of my pocket and exhale in relief. The call isn't from my mother, but from an unknown number.

"Hello?" I answer, my voice scratchy and my head pounding.

"Dude, Aves, please don't take this the wrong way, but please shut the hell up," Clover groans from the back seat. She's lying on her side and has a jacket over her. Only one daisy remains in her hair now.

"Sorry," I whisper to her then say quietly into the phone, "Hello?"

No one answers.

At first, it seems like they hung up, but when I check the screen, the call shows as still connected.

I put the phone back to my ear and hear heavy breathing.

"Who is this?" I whisper, rotating toward the door.

We're still parked in the woods, and a few cars are around us, but not nearly as many as last night. The firepit is a pile of ash, and dew covers the ground, the leaves on the trees, and the windows.

While I was fine last night with being in the heart of the woods, now that the alcohol has faded from my veins, I feel the simmering of anxiety scratching at me again, so I force my gaze away before I tumble into a panic attack.

More heavy breathing fills the line and then *click*, the call ends.

"Who was it?" Ellis asks as he sits up and rubs his eyes with the heels of his hands.

I shrug. "I don't know. The call was listed as unknown, and the person on the other end never said anything. They just breathed heavily."

"That's weird." He lowers his hands from his eyes. "Maybe it was a spam call. I get them a lot."

"Me, too." Still, I don't ever hear heavy breathing.

Anxiousness webs through me as I check my messages. What I find does cheer me up a bit. My mom finally replied to my text at about midnight.

Mom: Good. I'm glad you're working on your friendship with her. I like Livia. She's a good girl. But be home early, because we have a family lunch to attend.

I'm so thankful that I didn't get busted that I don't even care that I have to go to a family lunch.

"Everything okay?" Ellis asks as he adjusts his seat upright.

I nod and manage a smile. "Yeah, I think so."

He returns my halfhearted grin, and the memory of him holding my hand brushes at my brain like a soft kiss.

"What's that smile for?" Ellis questions.

I shrug, pressing back the smile. "I'm not quite sure."

It's the truth, too.

I'm not sure if I'm smiling because he held my hand last night or because I didn't get caught going to the party. Maybe it's both.

What I do know is that when all of our phones suddenly go off, any amount of happiness evaporates like the evanescence of the morning. Because it's another missing person's notification.

A second girl has gone missing from our quiet little town.

CHAPTER 13

THE VOICEMAIL ON MY PHONE IS REAL. I TRY CONVINCING myself it's not, but after checking multiple times, it remains there.

I'm clueless about what to do.

I have no idea why it's happening.

What I do know, though, is I need to get the hell out of the bathroom because I can't hide in here forever, even if I desperately want to.

"You can't hide forever, Aves," Clover used to say all the time. She typically said it to encourage me to come out of my shell and to be who I was without pretending. But I didn't know who I was back then. I still don't, but I'm trying to.

I summon a few shallow breaths before exiting the bathroom. When I enter the bar area, Clara is standing near our table, talking to Ellis.

I'm about to take off, go outside, and drive away, be the worst friend ever, which is nothing new to me—I've been far worse of a friend in my lifetime—but Clara spots me before I can. She arches her brow, and I wonder what Ellis has told her.

Then Ellis makes eye contact with me.

It's been years since we've been around each other, and yet the instant our gazes collide, I'm slammed back to that moment in my life that took the broken pieces of me and smashed them into dust. I knew from then on that I'd never be the same again. And I'm relatively sure Ellis shattered with me. Now, here we are, years later, and our connection is still prominent. That connection where, for a split-second, we exist in the exact horrifying moment, feeling the same pain and guilt, the same stillness that only comes with death. It was so brief, like a whisper of a breath, a slam of a heartbeat, a pleading last word.

I thought I could run away and forget—I desperately tried to. Part of me even stupidly believed I succeeded. But standing here and looking at him, the truth smacks me hard. I didn't escape. Not really. I was just running in circles with the truth constantly nipping at my heels.

And I have the same connection with Camilla.

Both of these connections are frayed, but they still exist. But I wish I didn't have them. I wish they dissolved so I'd never have to remember. As I make my way toward Ellis, though, memories I buried try to resurface and I have to take a desperate breath from the years of suffocation.

It's painful to the point where my chest is throbbing. Between this and the voicemail I just received, tonight is heading toward a potential disaster.

"Hey," Clara says as I reach them. She has a strange expression that I can't quite decipher. "So Ellis was just telling me that he used to know you from high school."

"Yeah …" I glance at Ellis, and that tug I used to feel toward him yanks tighter.

"I'm sorry about your father," he tells me as he picks at the label of the beer he's holding.

I don't know what to say to that. *Thanks?*

"Do you still live here?" I ask instead.

There, that's easy, right, Ava? And that's what you need. That's all you want. That's what you never seem to get, though probably because you don't deserve it.

He shakes his head while brushing strands of his hair out of his eyes. "I live in Mountain Valley now. I'm just back for a bit because of work."

He's holding my gaze, and I despise it. I used to like it when he looked at me. Now it makes me feel like I'm breathing razors.

"Really?" I look away, unable to endure the weight of his stare any longer.

Unfortunately, my gaze lands on Camilla.

She's still at the bar, talking to the bartender. I think she might be arguing with him.

"What do you do for work?" I ask Ellis as I watch Camilla throw a bowl of peanuts at the bartender and then spin around. Her face is red, her eyes are raging with hunger, and they lock right on me.

The bar fades away for a second, and we're back in those woods, snow falling around us, the air so silent it felt like time wasn't moving. And that voicemail—those sounds—they're playing in my head on repeat.

My temples pulsate.

Vomit burns my throat.

But I swallow it down.

Like I swallow down the truth.

Until I can only taste the bitter lies on my tongue.

"I'm a detective," Ellis answers then pauses. "I'm actually here working on your father's case … I'm not sure if your mother told you that. I know how she is."

Camilla stares at me for a slamming heartbeat longer. Then she glares.

It throws me off balance. She's never looked at me that way before.

Our eyes remain locked for a second longer before she breaks the stare and storms out of the bar.

That's when Ellis's words register.

My gaze snaps to him. "Wait … what? My father's case? What are you talking about? He died because he fell off a cliff."

He rubs his lips together, studying me. "There's some suspicion surrounding his death, and when the autopsy came back, it revealed he died prior to the fall."

"What?" Clara whispers as she gapes at him, then at me.

"How did he die then?" I sound weird, my voice uneven and much lower than usual.

His gaze sweeps across the bar then lands back on me. "I'd rather not talk about this here. We want to keep some details from the public for specific reasons, but I'd like to talk to you … maybe tomorrow?"

Wait … am I a suspect?

Why my mind first goes there first is beyond me.

I try to remain unruffled, but who knows if I miss the mark.

"Yeah, I can do that. Just let me know the where and when."

I wait in fear for him to answer.

What if he says the police station?

Why do I care? I didn't kill my father.

But Ellis knows I hated him.

"Do you want to meet at the Star Meadows diner tomorrow afternoon?" he asks. "Say … like at like one o'clock?"

I nod, unable to form words.

My father was murdered …

By *whom?*

"Good." He visibly relaxes, leaving me to question why he was stiff. Is he nervous for some reason? "Can I buy you a drink and maybe talk for a bit? It might be weird to sit around and talk after what I just dropped on you, but we can talk about other things." He smiles.

That smile. It's the same. He was such a nice guy. Probably one of the few nice guys I've met in my life. He was so cute, sweet, and a talented artist who liked talking about philosophy when he got stoned. The only time I ever saw him angry was when he saw Ben that night.

"Oh, wait, hold on," he says before I can respond. He retrieves his phone from his pocket and frowns at the screen. "Shit, I have to go to the station for something." He looks at me as he pockets his phone. "I'm sorry. Raincheck on the drink?"

"Sure." I don't plan on taking him up on that raincheck,

though. I don't want to be in this town long enough to be able to cash in it.

He smiles again, and I don't like how my stomach flutters. "You look good, Aves. Better than the last time I saw you."

I smile back, the movement tight and unnatural, like when I first met him. "Thanks."

Because I do look better, but only because I'm not doped up on every substance I can get my hands on.

Before he walks away, we trade numbers. Then I'm left standing in the bar, feeling like I've been punched in the throat.

You look good.

Better than the last time I saw you.

Your father is dead.

He's been murdered.

We need to talk to you.

Don't utter a word, Ava, or I will fucking kill you.

"Are you okay?" Clara asks over the chatter and rowdy music filtering through the air.

I tear my gaze off the door and look at her. "Yep," I lie.

She looks at me dubiously.

Ignoring the look, I grab the shot she's holding and down it in one long gulp.

For a moment, it makes the lie feel a bit more believable.

CHAPTER 14

Snow flutters from the smoky clouds, and red rose petals splatter across the frost-kissed ground. I'm lying on my side, and my cheek is wet from the melting snow beneath me. Laughter echoes from somewhere, along with shouting. The noise makes my eardrums burn, but it's less painful than the pain searing through my limbs.

I want to get up, but my bones feel broken, like the snapped branches around me. I need to force myself to stand because the snow is seeping through my clothes and flesh to the point where the cold is biting me.

Get up, Ava.

Get up.

I push up, and my head groans in protest. I let out a moan, reaching up and touching the side of my head. My fingers brush against a wet substance that at first I think is snow, but then I notice how sticky it is. I move my fingers away and see blood coating my hands.

My breathing increases, and fog circles my face as I frantically peer around at the rose petals that aren't rose petals at all.

Blood.

Blood is everywhere.

My eyes lock on something else. A girl around my age is lying face-down in the snow. She looks dead, her eyes nearly black.

I stare at her in shock. Is she dead?

But then she whispers, "Help me."

I want to—desperately—but I can't seem to move.

"Help me," she repeats. "Please, Ava."

I realize I know her from school.

Camilla.

I trip toward her but freeze at the sounds of crunching snow—footsteps from right behind me.

"Oh, Ava," the person whispers. "I thought I told you to lay down and stay still."

That voice ...

I know it. I start to turn around to see who it is—

Smack.

Something heavy hits me on the back of my head, and everything goes black.

A red ribbon floats in front of my face ...

The images change, fade, and morph into something else.

I'm sitting on a log in front of the fire, and Ellis is holding my hand. He's talking to a guy wearing a backward baseball cap while he skims his thumb along my knuckles. A smile tugs at my lips. I remember this quiet place where I felt content, if only for a moment.

"You and I, new bestie, are gonna be friends forever," Clover says from the other side of me. She slants back and tips her head toward the sky. "Even after we die. I just know it."

"That's dark," I tell her. I've been drinking all night, and my speech is starting to slur. I don't care, though. I like when everything is slow and blurry. It makes living easier to deal with.

"Mmhmm ..." she mumbles, her eyes drifting shut. "I have a dark soul. So do you."

Do I?

Time ticks by ...

Eventually, the air settles into a pulse-spiking quiet.

So quiet.

Too quiet.

I fall asleep, and when I wake up, Clover is gone, but her wallet with the daisies on it is on the ground beside me. She always carries it with her, so it's weird that she left it behind.

I reach to pick it up, and something falls out of it. Something sharp—

My mind jolts to consciousness, but my eyes don't open. I've been down this road before. The one where I wake up and all I see is darkness. Not a single drop of color, shape, or emotion consumes my mind. It's empty and bare and, for a faltering second, I bask in the sensation.

But then it comes rushing back to me—the reason why I can't remember anything,

I got so drunk last night that I blacked out. And even though my mind is blank with holes of the events that occurred after Ellis left the bar, the emptiness inside me carries a familiarity, like I've been reunited with an old, toxic friend I didn't really want to see again.

I groan, clutching my head as I stare up at my bedroom ceiling, at the glow-in-the-dark stars, a reminder of my childhood. They're not glowing right now, since sunlight is trickling in through the small window.

Sunlight ...

What time is it?

I roll over and fumble for my phone, crossing my fingers that it's on the nightstand.

Clara is passed out on the trundle bed, snoring softly. She has on her outfit from last night and one shoe. I managed to get my shoes off, but I have on the same clothes I wore to the bar. I can't remember much after I started drinking, including how we got home. Did we call a driving service? Is there even one in town? There didn't used to be.

I marginally relax when I find my phone. I pick it up, roll back over, and search through the calls I made last night. The last one was to a local number, but I don't recognize it, so I look online and discover it belongs to a cab company. Well, at least I learned how we got home, although it's weird Stars Meadow has a cab company.

I didn't make any other phone calls, which is good. The last thing I need is to wake up and realize I drunk-called someone, like Ellis or Jason.

I note the time. It's close to noon, which means I need to get ready to go meet Ellis to talk to him about my father's murder.

Murder.

I still can't fathom it, especially since my mother said he fell off a cliff. Has she not heard about this yet? Because Ellis made it sound like she had. And how did someone even kill him? Did they wrap their hands around his neck and slowly watch the life fade from his eyes? Did he feel fear, like the blinding, uncontrollable fear he forced upon me the day he tried to strangle me?

His hands were so strong. That part is branded into my mind the most. And my throat felt so weak, like a branch about to *snap*. I could almost feel the bones about to break. I had been gasping, trying to get air into my lungs, tears streaming down my eyes as I begged him to stop.

"Dad ... Dad ... please."

He had looked at me with blinding rage. And one thought had flashed through my mind—*He's going to kill me.* It was followed by a brief, *Maybe it's better if he did.*

I was eight years old when that took place, and I had been acting like a brat after having a bad day at school. Kids had picked on me after the teacher had gone around the class and made everyone say what they wanted to be when they grew up. I said a race car driver because I liked cars. My dad had this old Camaro he was fixing up, and I thought it was so cool. He always talked about ways to make it go faster, and I sometimes dreamed of driving one.

When I said this aloud, though, some of the guys in my class laughed at me, and one of them said, "Girls can't be race car drivers. They suck at driving."

Tears had pooled in my eyes. But after arriving home, that sadness had morphed into anger for incomprehensible reasons at the time. Later that day, my father returned from work and told me to go to his room, because he was having some friends over and didn't want me around. I replied with a *no.*

I rarely told him no, since I knew I'd get spanked or

slapped. But I was too angry to care, and my dad must have been furious already, since instead of yelling and smacking me, he grabbed me by the throat and squeezed until I could barely breathe. He only let go when my mom walked into the room.

What haunts me the most about that day is that I'm unsure if he would've stopped had she not walked in.

I gently touch my throat, the memory seared into my mind of what it felt like to be so weak. Sadly, that was not the last time in my life that I'd find myself in that position, and part of me worries it won't be my last.

Another memory prickles against my retinas; one of me from last night in the bar's bathroom, locked in a stall, listening to a voicemail of that day in the woods. Part of me hopes it was a fucking nightmare, but when I check my voice-mail, it's there.

I press my hand to my forehead as my head pulsates. I blame it on the alcohol, but that's not the truth—

"Dude," Clara groans. "Why are you breathing so loudly?"

I suck in a deep inhale before rolling over to my side to peer down at her. "I'm guessing you feel about as shitty as I do."

Her eyes aren't open, and she's clutching her head. "I feel like someone played the bongos on my head."

I snort a laugh, but then wince, the noise amplifying my headache. "We made bad life choices last night."

She shakes her head, her eyelids lifting open. She looks at me with her bloodshot eyes and smiles. "Nah, it was fun. Well, up until this point right now."

"You can remember it was fun?" I question. "Because I can

barely remember anything. I couldn't even remember how we got home until I looked on my phone and saw that I'd dialed a number to a cab company."

"Yeah, the driver was a total perv," she mumbles through a yawn while stretching her arms above her head. "Your mother was pissed off, too."

"*What*? We talked to her last night?"

She bobs her head up and down. "She met us at the front door and gave us this huge lecture for being drunk. I felt like we were sixteen years old and got busted for underage drinking. Sorry to say this, but she's crazy. We're grown-ass women who are old enough to drink and who were responsible enough not to drive drunk."

I don't know what sort of face I pull, but Clara notices something is up.

"What's wrong?" she asks, sitting up.

"It's nothing," I mumble, sitting up as well.

Every part of my body aches, particularly my back.

The room spins like a cracked-out merry-go-round, and I struggle to breathe through the vertigo. "Did she say anything else? Or did I say anything to her?"

She shakes her head. "Not really. You could barely talk." She pauses, assessing me. "When I first met you, I didn't think you'd ever be the kind of person to party that hard." She tucks a strand of hair behind her ear. "I clearly read you wrong."

"I used to get that drunk all the time," I divulge, unsure why I'm offering her a piece of my history, other than maybe I'm too hungover to think clearly. "Back when I was in high school."

She doesn't seem that surprised, but how could she be after last night?

I DREAD GOING UPSTAIRS BUT CAN'T STAY IN THE BASEMENT forever.

After about ten minutes of staring at the glow-in-the-dark stars on my ceiling, Clara falls back asleep, and I drag my ass out of bed to take a shower and get ready to meet Ellis. It's painful to move, but I push through it and step underneath the water.

As I'm scrubbing off the grim of last night, I can't stop thinking about that voicemail. Who left it? What was the point? To scare me? Is it merely coincidental that they started after coming back to Star Meadows? I don't have any answers to these questions, but I don't believe it's a coincidence. No, whoever sent them knew I was coming home, whether they learned it through my mother or because they learned about my father's death and assumed I'd come back for the funeral. One particular person comes to mind. Trystan. I haven't seen him yet, but he still lives here. He moved away for a while to become a doctor, like his father, but then returned home to start his career here. That's all I know, and it's more than I want to know.

I wince as my fingers brush along some sort of wound on my back. What the hell? Did I fall last night or something? Possibly. I'm not a stranger to the blur of alcohol-infused nights where I'd wake up and have a cut or bruise on me with no recollection of how I got it. Frustrated that I've returned to this same place, I hurry up, wash my hair, and get out of the shower. Once I dry off, I angle my back toward the mirror.

And just like that, my problems become much bigger than getting a voicemail on my phone.

Because carved across my lower back is the word *Slut*.

CHAPTER 15

ONLY A FEW PEOPLE KNOW ABOUT THE DAY *"DIE SLUT"* WAS written on my locker in high school. Two people to be exact. One of them couldn't have done this to me, and the other person is Ellis. The probability he would—or even could—shave done this seems unlikely. He's the only sweet guy who's ever made a presence in my life. He's also a detective, but that doesn't necessarily mean he doesn't do shitty things. The issue I'm having that causes a drop of doubt in me is that he was at the bar last night. Maybe it's a coincidence. Or did I even get cut at the bar? Plus, I saw him leave. Not that he couldn't have returned.

There's another option—the person who painted the word on my locker years ago may have done this. But I never figured out who did it. I had my suspicions, but those were based on the assumption that whoever it was was connected to the incident in the woods.

But if my suspicions were right, then that means …

Trystan.

Could he have done this?

I can't recall seeing him at the bar last night. I could've spoken to him last night and wouldn't even be able to drag a sliver of a memory about it.

Fuck, how in the hell can't I remember someone carving a word into my flesh? Yeah, I was wasted and the cut isn't extremely deep, but still …

Why can't I recall even a single detail?

One reason pops into my mind that causes my stomach to lurch.

I run to the toilet and barely make it there before I vomit. My eyes water, and every one of my muscles throb. Once I'm done, I sink to the floor and slump against the wall. The toilet is only inches from me, and the linoleum floor is cold against my sweaty skin.

This isn't the first time I've been in this position where I can't remember much of what happened to me the night before, and I hate it.

Back when I ran out of the woods, my mind was at its worst. Fragments of memories pushed me so far down into the darkness that I was drowning in it. It was all I could think of, feel, breathe—the darkness and those branches, the chill of the snow, and the blood droplets that stained my vision like deeply engraved scars.

I wanted it to stop, but crying did nothing. And sleeping? It fed those memories into my psyche and bled them through my nightmares. I'd wake up screaming and choking on the images.

I tried everything I could to get it to stop, but my small

room that had become my life over the years didn't offer much. Eventually, desperate for silence, I found a bottle of pills and swallowed them. That would've been the end for me, but my mom found me moments later and forced my finger down my throat so I'd vomit up the pills. Once I was done, I sank back against the wall, feeling empty and tired.

My mother crouched down in front of me. "Do you know what happens to people who end their lives, Ava? They go to hell. They don't get to be with their family after they die." She rose to her feet. "You won't do this to me. I won't have a daughter who disgraces their family like this." Then she walked away, leaving me alone.

Always alone ...

The memory evaporates as a tear streams down my cheek. It's been a long time since I cried. Early on, I learned it was difficult to stop if I let myself. So, I found a way to control it, which was easier when I was drunk or stoned. But there were times when I was with Jason that my control over it would slip away. He'd use that against me. I was weak, too emotional and immature, he'd tell me.

I've spent months wondering if it's true, and I still have no damn clue.

But I want it to stop.

I want everything to just *fucking* stop.

I decided months ago that I didn't want to be that broken girl, but I still don't know how not to be.

I swipe the tear from my cheek and stand up. I'm uncertain where to go from here, but I need answers or this will be another thing that eats me alive.

As I'm getting dressed in jeans and a gray top that reaches

just below my stomach, I notice a bruise on the side of my arm, another battle wound from getting blackout drunk last night. This used to happen all the time after a night of partying where I'd wake up and discover a large welt or bruise with no memory of how it got there.

Old patterns really do die hard, I guess.

I quickly brush my hair then return to my bedroom. Clara is still asleep, so I crouch down beside her.

"Clara," I say.

She barely stirs so I lightly shake her.

She rolls over. "Where am I?" she mumbles. She blinks and shakes her head, her confusion dimming. "Oh fuck, I was having a super vivid dream." She yawns and stretches her arms above her head. "How long have I been asleep?"

"About thirty minutes," I respond, eliciting a frown from her.

She groans. "Aves, seriously, you have to let me get more sleep … Wait, unless you need me." She sits up quickly and rubs her eyes. "Did something happen with your mom?"

"No, it's not my mother." Although, depending on how things go when I embark upstairs, it might be. "I have to ask you a question about last night."

"Okay." Her brows furrow. "What's up?"

I plop down on the floor and pick at my chipped fingernail polish. "Did I wander off by myself at any time after I started drinking?"

She shakes her head, the crease between her brows deepening. "No, you were with me the entire time. Why?"

"You can remember that much?" But she said she was pretty drunk last night.

"Yeah, I wasn't blackout drunk, unlike you." She studies me. "What is it? Because I can sense something is up."

I rub my forehead. "Are you positive I didn't go anywhere by myself? Not even to go to the bathroom?"

"Yeah, I'm sure. I kept an eye on you because you were so trashed." She pauses, worry filling her bloodshot eyes. "You don't remember anything at all?"

"No, my mind just sort of blanks out after I took that first shot of vodka."

"You know, it's weird that you can't. Yeah, people get drunk and can't remember things, but normally, that starts to happen after they've drank too much." She hesitates.

"You want to say something else?" I hedge.

"I don't want to freak you out."

"I'm already a little freaked out."

She remains silent before blowing out an exhale. "It's just that there was this one time that I blacked out after one drink, and it's because my drink was drugged." She draws her knees up to her chest. "I still can't remember anything about that night. It was like one second I was in the bar, and the next, I was home, laying in my bed with the worst stomachache I've ever had and no recollection of leaving the bar. I still think about it sometimes—what I could've done during those hours. To be safe I had to ..." She releases a shaky breath. "I got tested for STDs and took the morning-after pill. Better safe than sorry, right?" The most haunting smile I've ever seen forces its way onto her lips.

My next words nearly choke out of me. "When did that happen to you?"

"On my twenty-first birthday." She shrugs like it's no big

deal. But it is a big deal. It's a big fucked-up, screwed-up, horribly big fucking deal that no one can fully grasp unless they've experienced something like it. "Want to know the really fucked up part?"

All I can think is, *You already haven't told me the fucked-up part? Just how bad is what she's about to tell me?*

She doesn't wait for me to answer her question. "I was with friends, and they all left me at the bar. Pretty shitty, right?"

I nod, unsure of what to say. I've had crappy friends before, but none as bad as that.

"It's why I had no friends when I met you," she continues. "I got good vibes from you, and I was right." She smiles again. It's small but genuine. But then it dissolves. "I don't understand. Ever since that fucked-up night happened to me, I'm always so careful to watch my drinks when I go to bars. And I swear I was last night. I thought I was keeping a good eye on you, too. Apparently not. I'm so sorry, Aves."

"It's not your fault," I tell her. "I'm the one who chose to drink. I wasn't your responsibility."

Guilt masks her face. "Yeah, but I kind of pressured you into it."

"No, you didn't," I assure her. "Trust me; I made that choice all on my own."

"Because of what you learned about your dad's death?" she treads cautiously.

I nod, the wound on my back burning.

"There's something else," she assesses. "I can tell."

I could tell her about the wound, but I'm not ready yet.

"It's nothing." I revert to Liar Ava since I'm so damn good

at being her. But maybe this is a step in the right direction, since I sort of opened a door to the truth.

Baby steps, Ava. Baby steps.

"Are you sure?" she asks skeptically. "Because it seems like maybe you're keeping something from me."

"I promise I'm not." I push to my feet, muttering, "I'll be right back. I have to go to the bathroom."

I make a beeline into the bathroom to splash cold water on my face. Then I stare at myself in the mirror. I used to do this a lot when I was younger. Stare in total vanity, wondering if I was pretty.

What I should've wondered is why it mattered so much to me.

I step away from the mirror and sink onto the edge of the tub, lowering my head into my hands. I feel horrible for lying to Clara, but the idea of telling her the truth makes me sick.

How did I come to this? Where lying was comfortable for me and telling the truth made me sick? And how did I become such a good liar anyway? From my father who, to the outside world, was this strong man who took care of his family, who was friendly and had a lot of friends, but behind closed doors was an abusive, raging father and husband? Or was it from my mother, who was always smiling when we were out in public, who could blend in with a crowd no matter what, but when it was just her and I alone in the house, she was cold and cruel?

Or perhaps my lying tongue wasn't inherited at all. I did start lying at a young age to stop myself from getting into trouble. Was that where it began? Out of fear?

I may never figure out the answer, but I want to find out

who carved me up last night after I was drugged. Because if what Clara is saying is true, it leaves the people in this house as suspects. So, basically, Clara and my mother.

I highly doubt Clara did it to me, so that leaves my mother. Unless someone else snuck into the house? That's not totally impossible. But what is the point of all of this—the voicemail, the hang-up calls, the wound on my back? Because I feel like they're all interconnected.

And I think the key to finding out who's doing this to me is: why?

To threaten me? To torment me? To punish me?

If it's the latter, it might be what I deserve.

I probably deserve worse.

CHAPTER 16

THE PAST...

It's been three weeks since I started hanging out with Clover and Ellis. Each weekend, I sneak out and we go to parties. But tonight, it's just Clover and me at her house. Her mom is gone with her boyfriend for the weekend.

Clover lives in this single-wide home located on an older man's property. It sits beside a dilapidated barn filled with hay that feeds all the cows wandering around on the surrounding acres. The owner lives in a single-story 1970s-style home at the front of the property. A dirt driveway is the only exit to and from Clover's house, and it goes right by the owner's house, so he knows when they're home. Clover says the guy is a creep. She told me that, one time while she was outside sun tanning, she caught him gawking at her from across the yard. He was trying to act like he was watering his plants, but it was pretty obvious he was staring at her. She said when she informed her mom of this, she brushed it off and said to let him stare because he was letting them live in his extra house for cheap and she didn't want to risk them getting evicted. She also said men couldn't help but stare at half-naked girls, so it wasn't a big deal anyway.

I've been at her house for about an hour but haven't seen the guy yet. We're sitting in her backyard in camping chairs with the crisp air circling us. I'm looking at hairstyles online, and Clover has her phone out, scrolling through one of her social media accounts.

As I'm searching, I notice movement in my peripheral vision. I turn to see what it is and spot an older man with dark hair standing in the house's backyard. He's holding a garden hose and is spraying water on the dry, yellow grass, but his eyes are locked on us.

His lips spread to a grin when our gazes collide, and I swiftly look away.

"Umm …" I say with wide eyes. "Is that the owner of the house?"

Clover has sunglasses on, her hair is pulled up into a messy bun, and she kicked off her shoes when we arrived. When she glances up from her phone, her gaze drifts over my shoulder, and she frowns.

"Yeah, that's Jerry," she says without taking her eyes off him.

Jerry shamelessly keeps staring at us.

"Why is he still looking at us?" I hiss under my breath while shifting my weight uncomfortably.

"Because he's a douchebag who gets away with everything," she replies then lowers her sunglasses, carrying his gaze. "Yeah, we see you, asshole."

His grin only widens.

"What a fucking asshole," she grumbles, flipping him off.

His smile dissipates as he drops the hose and strides toward us.

"Shit, he's coming over here," I whisper in a panic.

"Good. I'm going to tell him off," she replies, setting her phone down and sitting straighter in her seat.

"Didn't your mom tell you not to?" I chew on my thumbnail. "What if you get evicted?"

She grimaces. "Fuck, I hate being poor."

I feel bad for her. While my family isn't wealthy, we're not poor either. My dad has a steady job that pays enough that we can pay the bills. However, things haven't always been that way. Before we moved to Stars Meadow, my dad would often yell at my mother for spending too much money, that she needed to start budgeting. That's when we started shopping at secondhand stores, and she started carrying around a calculator and a pile of coupons while she grocery shopped.

But once we moved, that seemed to change, at least enough that they stopped yelling about money.

"Hey, girls," Jerry greets us as he slows to a stop about a handful of feet away. "What're you doing out here? Just hanging out or are you waiting for someone?"

"That's none of your fucking business, Jerry," Clover responds while throwing him a dirty look. "And no one invited you over here."

"Hey now, there's no need to be rude." He crosses his arms and smiles at us. It's such a strange thing, the way smiles are supposed to represent friendliness and happiness and yet there have been so many times in my life where they've made me feel unsettled and afraid.

Jerry's is definitely doing the latter. When he directs it at me, I find myself uncomfortably returning it, like I was taught to do. It makes his eyes spark with a fire I desperately want to ignite.

He winks at me before looking back at Clover. "And besides, this is my property, so if I want to come over, I can." His lips crook into a smirk.

My chest constricts and Clover's nostrils are flare. Her lips are smashed together, and she's gripping her phone so tightly that her knuckles have turned white.

"That's what I thought." Tossing one final shit-eating grin at Clover, he turns to leave, but not without saying, "I'm having a party tonight. I've got all kinds of booze and drugs, so stop by if you girls want to party. I promise it could be worth your time." He winks at me again, and I have no damn idea why the hell he keeps doing that. It's getting annoying.

He walks away and up the driveway instead of where the hose is still on.

"He left the hose on," I say, twisting around in my seat.

Clover still has her gaze narrowed on him. "Good. I hope the fucker floods his yard and his house." She tears her eyes off him and twists back around in the seat. Her knee is bouncing up and down as she crosses her arms and grits her teeth. "Can you believe him? Coming over here and inviting us to a party so we can basically be whores to his friends?"

"*What?* I didn't hear him say anything about the whore party." I loathe saying the word aloud. It feels weird and wrong, and it reminds me of the word that was painted on my locker.

"He didn't flat-out say it, but he implied it. By his little not-so-subtle comment at the end of his invite." She makes a face. "'I promise it could be worth your time,' was basically him saying: hey, if you fuck my friends, you can get drunk and stoned for free. Plus, I wouldn't put it past him to drug our drinks." She says it so casually that it throws me off.

Shock whips through me. "Does …? Does that happen?"

"All the damn time. You remember Greg, right?" she asks, and I nod. "Well, there's been rumors that some of his friends have been doing that shit to girls at parties. He denies his part of it—and maybe he's not doing it—but Jane's cousin said that Greg took advantage of her while she was wasted, so fuck him." She reaches for her pack of cigarettes that is on the ground, retrieves one, lights up, and takes a long drag. Smoke circles her face as she exhales. "Fuck all the Jerry's in the world."

The moment is so intense that I almost divulge the secret that's been festering inside me, about the Jerrys I know. My lips are parting, and the words are slipping up my throat, but then she rises to her feet.

"Come on; let's go paint our fingernails or something. I'm tired of this emo-shit mood."

Just like that, I feel the moment fade away like the smoke circling the air.

"Besides, I have to write about this in my diary."

I stand up and brush a piece of dirt off of my shorts. "You keep a diary?" I don't know why that surprises me.

She puts the cigarette to her lips and inhales. "Yeah, it's where I keep all my secrets that I don't tell you, my daisy friend. Mostly the ones I know you'll spill to Ellis because you *so* like him." She flashes me a smirk as she starts toward the house.

I narrow my eyes at her as I follow. "I do not."

"You do, too. Don't worry. I won't tell him." She pulls up the screen door open, and we step inside. "And you can return the favor by not telling him I write in a diary."

"I don't think he'd care. In fact, he probably has one himself."

"Oh, he certainly does, and that's exactly why I don't want him to know I do. The last thing I need is for him to think I'm all deeply emo like he is." She lets the door bang shut behind us. "It'll ruin my façade of indifference." She winks at me.

I can't tell if she's joking or not.

She starts through the house then, and I trail behind her, noting the heavy stench of cigarette smoke and old booze. With all the curtains shut, the room is dark, and the air is musty. It reminds me of some of the places we go to parties at, but this is her home.

Her room is located at the back and is scattered with all sorts of items that remind me of her—a collection of CDs, an array of makeup and clothes, and shoes line the shelf in the small closet, ranging from heels to worn sneakers. Clover walks into the space and begins rummaging for something on the floor.

A smile materializes on my lips at the sight of photos covering the wall, similar to the ones in my room except for hers are real photographs, ones of her standing in a park, hanging out with friends, jumping off a cliff into a lake.

She moves beside me, hugging a small notebook with daisies on it against her chest. "That was a fun day."

"Wasn't it scary?" I ask, thinking about my fear of heights.

She shrugs. "A little. But what would be the point of life if I let my fear own it?"

I nod like I understand, but I don't think I do since I'd never jump off that cliff.

She plops onto the bed and gets situated on her stomach before opening her diary. Then she chews on the end of her pen while contemplating.

I sink into a chair near her bed, grab a throw pillow, and hug it against my chest. "What're you going to write about? Just what happened with Jerry?"

"I'm not sure yet. I'm definitely going to write about him, but I feel like there's more I need to say." She wavers then lowers the pen from her mouth and presses it to the paper. "Sometimes I feel like I need to write every detail about my life in these pages before I fade away."

"Are you …? Are you worried you're going to … die?"

She sweeps a strand of her hair away from her face. "Nah. I'm just worried that … I don't know, I'll fade away into nothingness or something."

"That's … dark."

"I know. Ellis would be so proud." She smiles then returns her attention to the diary, leaving me to wonder what she meant.

How can someone fade into nothingness?

And why do those words feel so … true?

Clover glances over at me, and her brows furrow. "Is everything okay?"

I suddenly find myself longing to tell her everything, like she is to her diary. But then she gives me this funny, puzzled smile, and I bite down on my tongue. If I spill my secrets to her, would she look at me differently? Would she see the scratches in blood across the inside of my flesh?

I honestly don't know.

Fear. It owns me more than anything else does in this world.

"I'm just spacing out. Sorry." I sink back in the seat.

She eyes me over before returning to writing in her diary.

My phone rings then, and I dig it out of my pocket.

"People who call are so weird?" Clover jokes. "Seriously, just send a text."

"I know, right?" I agree as I glance at my phone screen.

Another unknown number. I've been receiving those lately and someone always breathes heavily into the phone. I decide not to answer it and move to put it into my pocket as it stops ringing. But then it pings, announcing that the caller left me a voicemail.

Weird.

I put the phone up to my ear to listen to it.

At first, I hear nothing but profuse breathing. That goes on for a while, and I'm about to hang up when a noise scratches my ears.

A scream.

"Shh … it'll all be over soon," someone whispers.

Someone whimpers.

Then the line clicks dead.

I move the phone away from my ear, my heart racing faster than it did that day in the woods.

Tree branches peel away at my flesh.

I got away.

They're chasing me.

I wasn't supposed to get away.

They're going to kill me if they catch me.

"Aves?" Worry floods Clover's voice.

I blink. "Huh?"

She sits up and scoots to the edge of the bed, watching me with concern. "Who was that on the phone? You look like you're going to be sick?"

My lips part. "I—"

Music abruptly fills the air, booming from somewhere outside. It's loud enough that I can't hear my heart beating anymore.

Clover's gaze darts to the window. "Dammit, Jerry." She storms over to the window, throws it open, and yells, "Turn it down!"

Jerry shouts something foul back, and Clover screeches in frustration.

Me? I can't get my mind off that phone call and how it sounded …

It sounded like what I heard while running for my life in those trees.

CHAPTER 17

Since my car is at the bar, I have to call for a cab. I used the same service from last night. It'll be a bit before one arrives, so I have some time to kill.

I'm avoiding going upstairs. When I do, I'm positive my mother will be waiting to hand me a lecture about coming home wasted last night. I feel like a child, and it's frustrating, but communicating this with her is a hopeless task.

But remaining in the basement forever isn't an option, so after I clean up the cut on my back, I inform Clara where I'm going and ask if she wants to go with me. She tells me she will if I need her to, but she's fine staying here and sleeping. I decide to let her rest and trudge up the stairs.

When I step into the foyer, my back immediately goes rigid.

Voices are drifting from the kitchen. Shit, people are here. I reel around to bolt out of the house and wait outside for the cab, but something snares my attention.

"She's losing her mind," my mother says. "She really is."

"I know." The low voice belongs to my uncle Stephan. "I'm working on it, but she's complicating it."

"She always makes it complicated," my mother replies with a dramatic sigh.

I lean forward to hear better but bump my foot on a shelf.

Shit. I hold my breath—

"Ava?" my mother calls out.

Dammit.

Exhaling unevenly, I enter the dimly lit kitchen.

She's sitting at the table, which is covered with pans, bowls of various food, plates, cups, and utensils. And seated by her are my aunt Marissa and my uncle Stephan.

Uncle Stephan resembles the man he was six years ago, but his dark hair is thinner, he's slightly more overweight, and he's sporting his traditional button-down shirts and jeans. He used to be my doctor when I was younger, but I hated going because of his cold demeanor.

All three of them are staring at me, and I inch back, causing my mother to throw me a sharp look.

"I need to talk to you," she tells me as she pushes a plate out of the way to rest her arms on the table.

Telling myself I can handle this, I step through the doorway. "What's with all the food?"

"Some neighbors brought them by when they came to offer their condolences." She crosses her arms. "What I want to talk about is what happened last night. I thought we were past you drinking. Clearly, nothing has changed. But I'm not surprised. I wish I were, but I'm not." She shifts in her chair.

"What I don't understand is why Jason lets you do this. Or are you keeping it a secret from him?"

My mind soars with things to say to her—excuses, lies. It's what I used to do all the time. But my state of being hungover complicates being able to lie easily.

"What I do isn't your business or Jason's," I mumble. "I'm an adult, and I'll do whatever I want."

Her eyes widen, but she hastily composes herself. "An adult? Look at you. You're hungover and hanging out with a girl who I'm guessing is promiscuous and a partier. It's just like that girl you used to hang out with in high school. And look what happened to her," she says with judgment in her eyes. "And that's how you'll end up if you keep on this path of sin. And what a way to honor your father's memory by getting drunk and disgracing him. You should be ashamed, but I know you aren't. You were always such a selfish brat."

I'm not sure what pushes me over the edge—her insult or the assumption that I need to honor my father's memory, like it was something to honor, or her mention of Clover.

Or maybe it's all the things that make me say what I say next.

"I wasn't a selfish brat. You were just a selfish mother, and a liar," I snap, the wound on my back burning.

Did she do this to me?

Could she do this to me?

Is she that cruel?

The room plummets into silence except for my aunt's gasp.

"Are you going to let her talk to you like that?" my aunt says, gaping at my mother.

"*Let* me?" I question. "I'm twenty-three years old, for fuck's sake. She's not allowed to tell me what to do anymore."

With wide eyes, my aunt's lips part, but my uncle speaks first.

"Your mother is right." He stabs a fork into a slice of cake that's on the plate in front of him. "You are a brat. Your father would be so disappointed in you."

"He was, anyway," I say then turn to leave.

I never should've come back here.

"Ava," my mother shouts after me. "Don't you dare walk away from me until I'm done talking to you about what happened last night."

Shaking my head, I whirl back around. "What happened last night?" I let out a hollow laugh. "Okay, Mother, let's discuss what happened last night." I inch toward her. "I had no plans of getting drunk. In fact, I've been sober for years. But then I ran into an old friend of mine—Ellis. You never did meet him when we were friends in high school, but I'm guessing you met him recently when he informed you that Dad's death is currently under investigation because the police think it's a homicide."

For a flash of an instant, I swear I see worry in her eyes. And surprise, probably over the fact that I know Ellis.

She lifts her chin. "That detective friend of yours is wrong. Your father fell off that cliff."

"Then why did Ellis tell me that they think he was?" I ask with my arms crossed.

"I'm sure he's just inexperienced," she replies while collecting a fork off the table. She cuts into a slice of cake, and for some reason, the movement feels so cold. Here we are, chatting about my father—her husband possibly being murdered—and she decides to eat cake?

"He's young and looking to stir up trouble, probably to cover up their corruption," my uncle assures her around a mouthful of cake. "Remember when the police force had that outsider working for him, and he tried to rule Bill Jenkinford's wife's death a homicide when it was clear the woman overdosed on drugs? Everyone knew she was a closet junkie, but this guy tried to convince people that her death was a murder. He even went after Bill. But the truth came out eventually when the autopsy report came out, and then Frank Mullegans stepped in to confirm it. I saw the body, too, and there were track marks all over her arms. I have no idea how that detective was ever allowed to work the case—or any case, for that matter. Thankfully, they fired him after that."

I vaguely recall what he's talking about. Bill was a friend of my father's and my uncle's. I was about twelve when his wife died, and it was all anyone could talk about. Nadine—that was the name of Bill's wife—was one of those women who was always put together, always smiling and involved in a lot of charity work. And yet, according to the final report, she'd been doing drugs behind the walls of her two-story home for years.

The thing is, either story could be true. Maybe she was living a lie to the public eye and then dying on the inside. I've seen my mother and father be as fake as possible to the outside world, craving to look perfect even though their house is filled with decay. So, maybe Nadine overdosing is a possibility. However, there are people in this world who do terrible things and are pros at concealing them. Jason was a master at that. So was my mother and father. And to be honest, so am I. It's frightening to think about how much easier it is for me to live in a lie than to speak the truth.

"Whatever," I mumble, more than ready to get away from them. I wanted to see if my mother gave off any I-cut-up-my-daughter-last-night vibes, but I won't get anywhere while my aunt and uncle are here.

Honestly, I'll have a hard time ever getting to the bottom of this. My mother is an expert at keeping secrets and locking them away inside her with so many padlocks that I don't even think she knows what key goes to which. It was one of the things she taught me how to do. I'm aware of what hides behind my locks, but what hides behind hers?

"We're not done talking!" my mother yells as I exit the room and rush for the front door. "And don't you dare leave this house!"

I pause in the doorway and glance at her from over my shoulder. "Oh, I am leaving because I have to talk to the police about Dad's death."

She narrows her eyes at me. "You don't have to talk to them about anything. They can't force you."

"They're not going to. I agreed to do it." With that, I leave the house, slamming the door behind me.

But not without catching the worried look on her face.

CHAPTER 18

THE PAST...

WHEN I RAN OUT OF THE WOODS, I WORRIED I'D NEVER BE ABLE to escape the trees. That the memory of the branches would constantly reach for me, not quite touching my flesh, but casting shadows across me. But I was wrong. I can escape. Even with that stupid voicemail I received the other day.

My mind is blissfully sedated. so much that nothing else exists except the fog.

"You're so high right now," Clover remarks as she moves a joint toward her red-stained lips.

We're in Ellis' truck, and the cab is flooded with so much smoke that only glimpses of the parking lot can be seen through the windows. We're parked by a small park near the foothills where hardly anyone comes except to get stoned. This is the third time I've been here with Ellis and Clover and gotten high. And I've gotten drunk a lot over the last two months. The more I do it, the more I crave the silent promises it whispers to me from the cavity of my dark, polluted chest.

"Nah." I let my head fall back against the headrest.

My ass is planted in the passenger seat, Clover is lounging in the back, and Ellis is in the driver's seat. This is our customary setup whenever we hang out. Sometimes Jane comes with us and sits in the back with Clover. And even when Jane or I drive, Ellis sits up front with me.

I try not to think about it, but I overanalyze it all the time. Does he like me? He does hold my hand sometimes, but we've never kissed or anything. I haven't seen him with anyone else, though.

Ellis chuckles, drawing me from my thoughts. He's staring at me with bloodshot eyes and an amused smile.

"You're fucking blazed out of your mind, Aves," he teases me while adjusting the knitted cap he's wearing. "That's okay, though. I am, too."

I giggle, and he echoes my laughter.

"Aren't you two adorable?" Clover's head pops up between us, and she smirks at me then puckers her lips. "Hey, Aves, maybe Ellis can be your first."

The other day, I confessed to her after I'd downed a few shots of tequila that I'd never been kissed. Clearly, that was a mistake.

"Don't you dare," I warn, giving her what I hope is a firm look.

But either I fail miserably or I'm not scary because she laughs, kisses me on the cheek, and says, "Sorry, bestie."

Yeah, her laughter sure seems like an apology. Still, being mad at her is difficult when she's so nice to me.

"Fuck," Clover suddenly mutters. Her attention is on her

phone, and all evidence of her light mood has plunged into grimacing darkness.

"What's wrong?" I ask as Ellis takes a hit from the joint.

"My mom just texted me. Apparently, Jerry told her I was a bitch to him that day you were over, and he's threatening to make us move out." She shakes her head, the muscles in her jaw ticking. "That fucker is just pissed because we didn't attend his pervert party."

"Pervert party?" Ellis blinks at her with the joint resting between his fingers. "What the hell are you talking about?"

"Jerry being Jerry." Clover stares at her phone. "The other weekend, Ava was over at my house and he wandered over and tried to get us to come to this party he was having. He promised us drugs and booze and said it could be worth our while if we showed up."

"What a fucking psycho," Ellis mutters, his anger lacing through the air as potently as the smoke.

I'm not surprised by how upset he is. Not only is Ellis a good guy, but he also has issues with guys trying to give drugs to girls because of what happened to Zoey.

"Do you want me to go beat his ass?" Ellis offers while passing me the joint.

Clover rolls her eyes. "As much as I love the offer and you, you are not the kind of guy that beats other guys up."

"Hey, I could be," he grumbles while pouting.

Clover rolls her eyes again. "You're not a violent person, and I won't let you become one because some old dude wants to get me in trouble. And my mother needs to get her head out of her ass and realize he's taking advantage of our situation."

With that, she types a message. "There. Problem solved."

"What did you tell her?" I wonder, rubbing at one of my eyes that is starting to burn.

"The truth. Not that she'll care, but it needs to be said—"

She's interrupted by her phone buzzing.

Whatever the message is causes her to shake her head and roll her eyes.

"What'd she say?" I ask.

"Nothing really." She reaches across the console, snatches the joint from me, takes a hit, then returns the joint to Ellis. "Let me out. I have to pee."

Suspicion weighs in the air that she wants to get out so we won't ask questions. Still, I climb out and flip the seat forward.

As she's getting out, though, she sneaks me a smile. "Oh, and Ellis? You should ask Ava what she told me the other day about something she's never done."

I glare at her, and she laughs, jogging away in her platform shoes.

I climb back into the car, and Ellis and I sit silently, listening to the angsty song playing. I don't think of much, mostly because I can't. But I'm curious about what Clover's mom said in response to what Jerry said.

"So, what was that about?" Ellis asks as he cranks down the volume.

My head angles to the side. "What was what about?"

He wavers. "What did you tell Clover about never doing?"

Dammit, Clover.

"She was just giving me shit about something," I reply as evasively as possible.

"About what?"

I internally sigh. "I'd rather not tell you."

He juts out his lip. "But you told Clover and feel like I'm just as good of a friend to you as she is."

"You are," I promise him. "But, honestly, I didn't even mean to tell her. I was just drunk."

He maintains his pouting. "Come on, Aves. I don't like being out of the loop. It makes me feel all edgy."

I eye him over. "Is that true?"

He exaggeratedly bobs his head up and down. "Absolutely."

"Oh, fine." I sigh. "I told her I've never been kissed before."

His brows elevate. "Seriously?"

I self-consciously squirm. "I know. It's weird."

"It's not weird," he tells me, resting his arms on the console. "I know a few people who haven't been kissed."

I pick at the cracks in the leather seat. "Is that true?"

He nods. "It's not that big of a deal."

I meet his gaze. "Thanks. For being nice, like all the time."

He lets out a low chuckle. "You're always telling me I'm nice."

"That's because you are."

He rubs his lips together. "Maybe if you knew what I was thinking right now, you wouldn't say that."

I swallow hard, self-doubt creeping up in me. "What do you mean?"

His eyes searched mine. "I mean, I'm thinking I want to be your first ..." He trails off as his phone rings. Sighing, he retrieves it from the cupholder, and when he looks at the screen, he mumbles, "Shit, it's my dad. He never calls me."

I sit up straighter in the seat. "Do you think he knows we're ditching?"

"Probably." He grimaces while staring at the phone as it repeatedly rings. "My bet is the school found out we ditched, and then they called him."

I stiffen. "They do that?"

I've ditched several times with Ellis and Clover and have never been caught. Because of that, I hadn't put too much thought into it. But what if we've been busted? Will my mom get a call from the school, too?

My chest constricts at all the ways I might be punished.

Ellis pales as he answers the phone. "Hey, Dad." His voice carries an unevenness that I've never heard from him before.

Someone starts yelling from the other side of the line, but I can't tell what they're saying. The longer it continues, the more color drains from Ellis's face. His lips are so pressed together that the edges have gone white, and he grips the steering wheel with his free hand.

After a moment, the line grows quiet.

"Shit. Shit. Shit." He hangs up the phone and flops his head back, squeezing his shut. "I'm so damn screwed."

"What happened?" I tread cautiously.

"He found out I was ditching." He exhales loudly. "I'm in so much shit."

"Will you get grounded?" With how he's reacting, I'm betting he'll be in more trouble than that.

He opens his eyes, raises his head, and stares out the window. "You know, he didn't used to be like that. He used to be chill. But then my sister died, and he became angry and bitter." He picks at the leather of the steering wheel. "And I get it. Him and my mother have been through a lot, but I hate being at home anymore. It's just so … tragically and angrily dark everywhere, even when the sun is shining."

"That's poetically dark." I throw a glance at the woods—at my own tragic and angry darkness.

"I know. I can be emo when I want to be." He forces out a laugh, but the noise diminishes as he sighs. "My parents have gotten even worse since those girls went missing recently." He gives a short pause then flicks his gaze to me. "There was a point right before my sister OD'd where she would go missing for days. But she'd always come back … until she didn't. At least, not alive."

I scratch my wrist, uncertain how to reply. He's talked about his sister a few times, but never about the exact details of her death. All I know is that she overdosed, and he partly blames that guy Ben for it.

"It took the police over a week to find her after my parents reported her missing." Anger bleeds into his tone. "They kept insisting she was a runaway and didn't do anything to look for her. And the really fucked-up part is that the autopsy showed that she had been dead for just under a week, which means that if they would've looked for her when my parents first reported her missing, maybe she never would've died." He releases an uneven breath. "Who the fuck knows, though? Maybe it would've just prolonged the inevitable."

"Were you guys close?" I wonder.

"We were up until about six months before she died. Zoey was close with Clover, too." He momentarily dazes.

"I didn't know her and Clover were friends," I say, wondering why she never mentioned it.

"All of us were … It was before Clover and I started doing all this shit that we do now." He almost looks guilty about it. "After my sister became distant, when she was around us, she was mean as hell because she was strung out all the damn time." He stares out the window. "I sometimes wonder why she decided to start doing drugs. I mean, I know she got them from Ben"—he opens and flexes his fingers—"but I just don't understand why she started doing them." He stares down at his hands. "I know Clover and I get high sometimes and drink, but this is different. Zoey," he whispers the name. "My sister, she was really into some heavy drugs. But I don't know … maybe I'm just being hypocritical."

I don't know if he is or not, what the difference between light drugs and hard drugs is. I do wonder why he started doing them. And Clover. Because Zoey died, and they couldn't deal with it?

"Sometimes, when I'm really stoned, I feel close to her," he divulges, his gaze meeting mine. "To the point where I can almost convince myself she never died. How messed up is that?"

"I don't think that's messed up." And I mean the words wholeheartedly. I understand the compulsion to go to that place where my mind is so filled with a haze that nothing is real and nothing is fake.

He assesses me. "Why did you start partying with us? We've gone to school together for years, and you never seemed like a girl who'd want to party. And you've never really talked to us before."

Thump. Thump. Thump. Thump. Thump. Thump.

I can't stop my gaze from traveling to the trees encompassing the area.

"You don't have to tell me if you don't want to," he hurriedly says.

I couldn't tell him if I wanted to, not the entire truth of it anyway. But he's been so open with me that I figure I can give him a small truth, which might be a first for me.

"Clover was the one to talk to me first," I say, lowering my gaze to my lap. "And I didn't have any good friends before that, and Clover was just so nice … And as for the partying thing … my mother's a complicated woman … And my father …" My breath claws at my throat. "He's not a very nice man. But he's only that way behind closed doors. To the public, they're the perfect family." I lift my gaze.

He's looking at me intensely. "Do they … hurt you?"

I shake my head, which is a lie. But I've told all the truths I can for the day. It's too agonizingly unfamiliar, this truth-telling thing.

Doubt fills his eyes, but he doesn't press. "Well, if you need anything at all, you can always call me, okay?" he says, and I nod.

I want to tell him he's nice again but decide against it since I've said it so many times that I probably look like a freak.

He offers me a small smile then reaches over and brushes a strand of my hair out of my eyes. For an instant, my pulse sparks to life but then lulls to sleep again as he withdraws his hand and sighs.

"I should probably go home," he says. "The longer I drag it out and avoid it, the worse my punishment will be. But I need to get out and clear my head for a minute."

I wish I could say the same, but my punishment will be brutal regardless of my choice.

I check my phone to see if my mother has messaged me, and a tiny spark of hope rises when

I see she hasn't.

Maybe Ellis was the only one who got busted.

"I should go back to school"—I pocket my phone—"since it doesn't seem like my mom has found out I ditched."

"Are you sure?" he questions. "You're really stoned."

"I know." I blink a few times. "I'll have to manage."

"I can give you eye drops," he offers, tracing his fingers along the top of the steering wheel. "And I have some cologne you can spray all over you."

"Thanks." My gaze travels to the restroom. "Is it just me or has she been in there for a while?"

He checks the time on his phone. "Honestly, I can't fucking remember." He shoves the door open. "I'm going to get out and get some fresh air."

"I'll go check on Clover." I open the passenger door.

Then we both hop out, and he stretches his arms above his head, causing his shirt to ride up. I stare, thinking of the moment before he got the phone call from his dad. I think he was going to tell me he wanted to kiss me, but I could be wrong.

When he lowers his arms, his gaze finds mine, and question marks fill his eyes. I quickly look away, my cheeks flooding with warmth despite the frigid fall breeze. Without glancing back at him, I dash toward the restroom. The women's entrance is on the opposite side of where the truck is parked, so I can no longer see Ellis as I enter the restroom, shivering from the cold.

"Cloves?" I call out, wrapping my arms around myself.

It doesn't look like anyone is in here.

So weird.

I check under the stalls anyway, but my original assumption is correct. I turn toward the entrance, totally perplexed. Where the hell would she have gone?

Digging my phone out of my pocket, I exit the restroom and begin to send her a text. As I glance up, I notice a blue car parked out by the tree line, and exhaust fumes are funneling out of the exhaust.

When did it pull into the park? Or was it here before we got here? It's hard to know for sure since I'm high.

Me: Where are you?

I send the text as I head back to Ellis, but then the passenger door flies open and Clover hops out.

"Hey Aves, wait up." She ducks her head into the cab of the car and either grabs something or says something to the driver before slamming the door. Then she hikes across the parking lot toward me. "Hey bestie," she says as she tugs down the hem of her black dress.

What the hell is going on? And who the hell was in that car?

The answer arrives as the driver's side door opens and Ben climbs out.

Irritation rolls off him as he holds up something and shouts, "You forgot you're fucking wallet!"

Clover whirls around and hisses, "Stop fucking yelling." She stumbles back toward him and reaches for her wallet.

But he moves it out of her reach. "You owe me," he says in a low tone.

Glaring at him, she sticks out her hand. "Give me my wallet, Ben."

"I will when you promise you'll pay me back." He grazes the thumb over her bottom lip. "Say it."

I expect Clover to tell him to fuck off because she's feisty and doesn't take shit from anyone. So when she gives an unsteady nod, I feel stunned, perplexed, and uneasy.

Why would she just agree? What will she owe him? And why the hell is she hanging out with Ben?

Ben hands her the wallet, and Clover reels around and begins making her way back to me. Ben watches her walk for a beat before his gaze trains on me and a smile curls at his lips.

"And you?" he calls out. "Call me if you ever need a hookup. You and I, we could have a lot of fun." With that, he ducks back into his car.

By the time Clover reaches me, my head is so jammed with questions that I feel vertiginous.

"Sorry about that." She tucks her wallet into the pocket of her leather jacket. "He can be a real asshole sometimes."

"Yeah, he seems that way," I note how messy her hair is and her red lipstick is smeared. "I thought Ellis hated Ben."

She sinks her teeth into her bottom lip. "He does, so I'd really, *really* appreciate it if you didn't tell him what just happened. Please, Aves. Can you do that for me?"

I wrap my arms around myself as the cold air seeps into my skin. "I don't know ..." I hate the idea of lying to Ellis. It's a new feeling—this urge not to lie.

"Hey, I know you like him, and trust me, I get it. Ellis is such a great guy. Probably one of the nicest guys I've ever met," she says then drags her thumb across her lip, cleaning up the smudged lipstick. "But I've known him for longer than you have and, trust me, telling him would hurt him more than keeping the truth from him would."

Is she right? I have no damn clue. She has known Ellis longer than I have, but it still feels wrong.

"Come on, Aves, it's just one little, tiny lie, and it's to protect someone from getting hurt." Clover clasps her hands in front of her. "Please, just do this for me. I mean, you've told a lie before, right?"

God, if she knew how right she was.

"And besides," she continues, "we're supposed to be daisy friends, remember? And this can be our first real secret." She pats her pocket where her daisy wallet is.

Something tugs inside me, like I'm about to be ripped in two pieces.

"Fine," I agree quietly, and I swear I feel myself slowly starting to wilt.

"Thanks, Aves." She gives me a quick hug. "You're seriously the most loyal friend I've ever had."

My smile is forced, but she doesn't seem to notice.

We start making our way back to the truck then. It's quiet, and part of me thinks I should just let it be that way, but the other part needs to know why I'll keep another secret locked inside me.

"Why were you with Ben, anyway?" The temperature is so low now that my breath is fogging in front of me.

She lifts a shoulder. "We just hang out sometimes and get stoned."

That doesn't make sense since … "But we were already getting stoned."

"Yeah, but Ben and I …" She dithers as we near the side of the restroom. She stops there and looks at me. "We hook up sometimes for fun." She tugs at the sleeve of her jacket. "It's not a big deal. I don't have feelings for Ben or anything. It's just something I do sometimes."

My mind wanders back to when I saw Camilla at the party with Ben and what Ellis told me about him then. I also think about how he said Clover and Zoey were friends. So shouldn't Clover hate Ben?

"But Ellis said he likes to get girls addicted to drugs," I point out. "He did that to Zoey."

"I know. But Zoey … what happened to her was partly her fault." She combs her fingers through her tangled locks. "No one can make you do drugs. It's a choice, unlike some shit in our lives." Her expression briefly darkens, and then she starts walking again.

I follow her, guilt eating away at me as I prepare to lie to Ellis. Can I do it with a straight face? I usually can, but Ellis is … well, Ellis.

As I'm about to step around the corner of the restroom, my phone rings. My fingers shake as I fish it out of my pocket. It has to be my mother calling to me know she found out I ditched school.

But it's from an unknown number.

"Hello?" I answer as I hike around the restroom.

Heavy breathing fills the line, just like it did that morning of the party.

"Who is this?" I press as I start toward Ellis's car.

Clover is standing beside the passenger door and is texting someone while holding a lit cigarette, and Ellis is sitting on the hood of his truck with his attention fixed on me.

More breathing floods the line as I make my way over to them.

Ellis slides off the hood as I near him. "Everything okay?"

I nod, moving the phone away from my ear. "Yeah, I think it's just a spam call." My thumb hovers over the *end* button.

"You look cold." A voice rises through the line.

I freeze before moving the phone back to my ear. "What?"

"You look cold," they repeat. "Standing out there by those trees."

I frantically scan the tree line. "Who is this?"

"If you know what's good for you, you'll keep your mouth shut." The line clicks dead.

The sound of my unsteady heart fills up my eardrums. Are they talking about the woods? Is this call from someone who was there that day? Were they the ones who left me that voicemail the other day? It's hard to tell for sure.

"Who the hell was that?" Ellis asks with concern. When I don't respond, he hooks a finger underneath my chin and angles my head up to look at him. "Talk to me, Aves."

As I stare into his eyes, I ponder the idea of confessing. I could tell him. He'd probably be supportive. But that'd evolve into more questions I'm unprepared to answer.

"It was just some creep prank calling me." I slip the phone back into my pocket. "I was worried it was my mom, but thankfully it wasn't." I step back from him, and his finger falls from my chin. "I should get back to school, so I hopefully won't get caught."

His gaze searches mine for a painful amount of time before he nods. "All right, let's get you back to school." He steps away from me.

"You didn't tell him, did you?" Clover whispers as I open the passenger side door.

I shake my head. "No." But I kind of wish I did.

"Good." She drops her cigarette to the ground and stomps on it. "Thanks. I owe you big time." She ducks her head to get in, leaving me with a haunting thought.

If I'm doing the right thing by not telling Ellis, then why does she owe me?

Once we're in the truck, silence falls over us. Ellis backs up out of the parking spot, and as we drive toward the gated section of the park, I peer over my shoulder at where Ben's car is, and a thought strikes me hard.

What if the prank call had nothing to do with what happened in the woods? What if it was Ben? After all, I was standing out in the cold, enclosed by the forest, and Clover told me to keep quiet about her and Ben spending time with each other. Maybe it was Ben calling to make sure I did that. But why would Ben want me to keep my mouth shut?

I'm not sure about anything right now, and that may be as frightening as knowing what happens in the shelter of the trees.

CHAPTER 19

WHILE WAITING FOR THE CAR, I FEED BAILEY AND PLAY A quick game of fetch with him. The trees are lazily swaying, but the air is warm. Since moving around makes me feel like I'm going to puke again, I don't spend as much time with Bailey as I'd like. Tomorrow, though, I'll take him for a run.

My mother doesn't come outside, which is suspicious and out of character for her.

My thoughts wander to the wound on my back. Could she have done it? It's strange to think about my mother tiptoeing into my room to cut up my back, especially when she was aware of the risk of Clara or me waking up and catching her. Unless she knew I was drugged.

But how the hell would she?

The headache consuming me leaves little room to come up with any answers. One thought manages to pierce through, though. That call I overheard my mother making right before

Clara and I left for the bar yesterday evening. She seemed so cagey, like she was agitated and afraid.

Just what secrets is she hiding?

I could find out if I can get a hold of her phone. It wouldn't be the first time I've stolen her phone. When I was younger and had been grounded for coming home so damn high I thought I was a ghost—and told her that—she grounded me and revoked my phone privileges, going as far as locking my phone in the safe.

So, I stole her phone to call Clover. I was terrified the entire time, but I did it anyway since I didn't want Clover to think I was ignoring her.

I chew on my bottom lip as I consider doing sneaking into her room while she's taking a shower or something and going through the call logs. The sad part is that, even now, I tremble at the thought of her catching me.

That doesn't mean I won't. I want—need—to know who she was talking to me about. Maybe she wasn't even the one who cut me up. Maybe it was the person she was speaking to. Like say, Trystan.

I shiver at the idea of him slipping into my room while I'm practically unconscious, lifting my shirt, and cutting up my back.

My stomach lurches, and I end up dry heaving in the bushes until the cab arrives.

The driver is a middle-aged man with dark hair and a beard. He barely speaks to me as I climb in. Maybe I'm being self-conscious, but every so often, he trows me dirty glance in the rearview mirror.

I remain quiet for the drive, watching the trees blur by

while trying to dig up memories of last night. By the time we arrive at my car, nothing significant has come to me, so I pay the driver then open the door to get out but pause.

"Were you the driver that drove me home from the bar last night?" I ask as I pocket my phone.

He nods, adjusting the air conditioning knob. "Yep, I'm the only driver that works the late shift around here."

"Was I …? Did I seem weird at all?" I wonder if I sound crazy.

He twists around in the seat. "You were wasted, if that's what you mean. I had to pull over on one of the turnouts so you could vomit, and you fell on your face. And you got a little bit of puke in my back seat." He seems annoyed.

"Sorry," I mumble as I slide to the edge of the seat. "That was all that happened, though? I just puked, and then you let me out at my house."

"All that happened?" He glares at me. "You stunk up my car. I spent an hour cleaning the smell out of the seats."

I cringe. "Sorry again." I hurry to get out, shutting the door behind me. Then I start walking toward my car.

"Oh, for fuck's sake. There is one more thing," the driver calls out as I'm walking around the front of the car. He sticks his head out the window. "You kept insisting we were being followed. You were so freaked out about it that you were crying."

I put my hand to my forehead to shield my eyes from the sunlight. "Why would I think that?"

"I'm not positive, but you kept mumbling about someone harassing you in the bar, and I think you thought they followed you out. But as far as I could tell, no one was following us. Like I said, you were pretty wasted, so you could've just thought someone was." With that, he rolls up his window and drives away.

I stand in the parking lot, again trying to unravel memories of last night. Was I actually being harassed? Or did I say that to the driver because of the voicemail?

Or was it merely the drugs in my system?

It's difficult to say since my mind, drugged or not, has always been a bit unreliable.

* * *

I arrive at the diner ten minutes early, so I message Ellis.

Me: I'm here. Should I meet you inside?

Ellis: I'm here already. I got us a table.

Dammit, I was hoping I had gotten here first so I could prepare myself for this conversation, but I guess I'll go in blind.

Besides, I'm not a suspect. I *know* I'm not.

Yes, keep saying that, and maybe you can finally convince yourself that the lie is true.

My body is humming with anxiety as I enter the café. The place is packed, the atmosphere buzzing with clinking glasses and light chatter, and the air is heavy with the scent of greasy French fries and burgers. It makes my head and stomach hurt. I wish I'd popped a few painkillers before I left.

I probably look as hungover as I feel.

Grimacing, I scan the tables and booths for Ellis.

"Can I help you?" A woman a few years older than me with red hair pulled up into a bun steps in front of me. She's wearing a pale blue apron over her slacks and a T-shirt, and her nametag reads, "*Tessa*."

I went to high school with her, only she was a few grades above, so she wasn't at the school during my downfall. But I'm crossing my fingers that she won't recognize me. I don't want to trip down memory lane right now.

"I'm just looking for someone I'm supposed to be meeting," I inform her. A second later, my gaze falls on Ellis in one of the corner booths. "And there he is." I start to walk off.

"You're Ava, right?" Tessa says, causing me to wince.

Why did she have to recognize me?

And how did she even recognize me?

I slowly rotate back around. "Yeah, why?"

She adjusts her glasses. "They're having a memorial for him, right? Your dad, I mean."

I nod. "My mother's holding one so people can pay their respects."

"Well, I wonder if she'll be okay with people coming and saying their two cents about what a piece of shit your father was." With that, she grabs some menus from the counter. "You can go ahead and have a seat. A waitress will be with you shortly." She glowers at me before striding off toward a table.

What in the hell just happened? From what I was aware of, people in the community spoke about my father as if he was a wonderful man. So, what the fuck did he do to Tessa? Or maybe he did something to someone she cared about?

A few ideas come to mind, all based on what he did to me while I was growing up. But would he have done that to someone outside of the house?

As a group of people wander into the diner, I snap out of my trance and make my way to the booth where Ellis is seated. He has a cup of coffee in front of him, his phone is out, and he's reading something on the screen.

"Hey," I greet him as I reach the table.

He startles, his gaze snapping up. "Shit, you scared the hell of me."

"I can tell." I lower myself into the leather seat and tuck my hands underneath the table to hide how fidgety I am.

"I was getting ready to text you again." He puts his phone into his pocket. "It took you a while to get inside. I thought maybe you went to the wrong diner."

"One of the waitresses knew me." I leave it at that, hoping he doesn't press further.

"Anyone I know?" he asks, cupping his hand around the mug.

I lift a shoulder. "Do you remember Tessa? She was a few grades above us?"

Recognition registers in his expression. "Yeah, vaguely. I didn't realize you were ever friends with her."

"I wasn't. She just stopped me to say something about my father." I pick at a loose thread hanging off the side of my jeans.

His full attention is on me, and it's a lot to endure. "What exactly did she say?"

"She was just asking about his memorial." I can't read him, and I don't like it. I was never fantastic at reading people, but I thought I'd improved. But I was wrong.

"Actually, I'm glad you brought that up." He picks up the cup of coffee and takes a sip. "Do you want a cup before we start with this? It might help with your hangover."

I crinkle my nose. "How can you tell?"

"That you're hungover?" he checks, and I nod. "Aves, I spent how many days with you the day after we went to a party?"

"Right." My shoulders slump as I recline back in the booth. "This isn't normal for me. I mean, getting drunk. Last night was an exception."

Guilt floods his eyes as he rests his arms on the table. "Shit, I feel like that might've been my fault after I just dumped that information on you about your dad's death."

"It wasn't that," I lie, not wanting him to feel guilty.

I hate this about myself; that this need to please sometimes still manifests. I've been doing better, but this is Ellis and while I may not know him anymore, he'll never be someone I want to put blame on.

He sighs. "I can tell when you're lying."

It's annoying that he can still read me, and yet I can't read him.

"Fine, I am. But it still doesn't mean it was your fault. I chose to drink. It's not a big deal. I feel like shit and have no desire to do it again." Not an entire lie. A sliver of me craves a bottle of vodka so I can forget about everything. But a much more significant part of me can't stop focusing on the burning sensation on my back, a reminder of what happened when I got drunk.

"You know what? A cup of coffee would be great." I try to collect myself, sitting up straighter. My nervousness is ridiculous. I didn't do anything wrong.

The corners of his lips tug upward. "Great, let me flag down the waitress."

He does so within seconds. Fortunately, the waitress isn't

Tessa but an older woman with gray hair and freckles. I order a coffee and a bagel, and Ellis gets a sandwich and some fries. Once she takes our order and walks off, Ellis focuses on me again.

"How have you been really?" he asks. "I know I asked you last night, but I didn't have much time to give you the attention you deserve."

God, I forgot how he constantly focused on me, how he smiled, and how kind he was—still seems to be. Nice Nice. Nice. If only I'd ended up with him. If I had to end up with someone, anyway. Looking back, I wasn't ready to be in a relationship with anyone. I was too confused, too lost, too broken. Even now, I'm unsure what effort needs to be put into a committed relationship, even with myself.

"I'm fine." It's a placeholder word I regularly use.

He must recollect that about me since he says, "Is that the truth?"

"No." I sigh in annoyance, mostly at myself for telling the truth. "I don't know." I reach for a saltshaker to busy my fidgeting hands. "I'm getting divorced, I live alone, and I work at a coffee shop." I pause, unable to keep my gaze on him. "But even though that all sounds sucky, my life is better than it was before the divorce." I shrug like what I'm saying is no big deal.

It is, though, a huge deal because it's the fucking truth.

He hesitates. "You married that guy Jason, right? The guy that was like seven years older than us?"

I nod. By the time I met Jason, Ellis and I had stopped talking, and I was barely attending school anymore. Occasionally, we'd see each other around town, but when my gaze would even so much as slide over him, I'd be thrown back to that night that was one of the worst moments of my life, the one that sits up there in the dark, stormy clouds with the day in the woods. Only this one is surrounded with less haziness, all the images sharp and bright like a bolt of lightning.

"Were you happy at all while you were married to him?" he cautiously asks.

I shake my head. "Sometimes I wish—" I bite down on my tongue. No, I won't air out my dirty laundry to him. I hardly know him anymore.

"No, go ahead and say it. Whatever you say here can stay here."

"It's not a big deal," I mutter. "I was just going to say that sometimes I wish I wouldn't have married him. You know, because I was so young."

"You were young," he agrees, his eyes boring into me as he lifts the coffee mug to his lips. He takes a drink then sets the mug down. "I remember when I heard that you were marrying him. I thought it was odd. Not just because you were seventeen and he was like what? Twenty-four or something. Plus, we'd never hung out with him. It just seemed"—he scratches his neck—"odd."

Why do I get the feeling that he's using odd as a placement word?

"He was visiting here for the summer after our junior year ended," I explain. "He used to live here with his family, but he left for college and returned for the summer. We crossed paths at this party. Not like the kind of parties you and I went to, but this community party my parents made me go to."

I was so damn pissed off that my parents had forced me to go. It was only months after losing Clover, and I was so …

shattered. Plus, I'd gotten so high the night before and was still feeling the aftermath of it, so I was too exhausted to fight with my mother about going. For a while, I sat at our family's table they'd purchased for the event, feeling out of it and refusing to get up and mingle no matter how hard my mother pushed me to do so. She was infuriated with me and grabbed my leg, right above my knee, hiding it underneath the table. Then she dug her fingernails into my flesh and hissed, "If you don't get up and put a smile on your face, you're going to regret it, Ava."

I already regretted many things in my life, so what was one more?

I didn't get up.

Eventually, my aunt came over and distracted my mother, but she tossed me a look that warned this wasn't over.

As I sat there, picking at the cake on my plate, a guy with dark hair and green eyes approached me. At the time, I guessed he was three or four years older than me, but later I discovered he just looked young for his age.

"So, did your parents make you come to this thing, too?" he asked as he took a seat at the table.

I nodded. "Yeah."

"Yeah, mine are a real pain in the ass. You'd think after becoming an adult, they'd stop telling me what to do."

I felt like he was giving me a glimpse into my future, that my mom would continuously try to tell me what to do. Clover and I had had plans to leave this town, but she was gone, and I was alone. And those plans faded with her.

"That sucks," I replied. "And now I'm worried my parents will be the same way."

"More than likely, they will." He dragged out a pause. "Your name's Ava, right?"

I nodded. "How did you know?"

He wavered. "Don't hold this against me, but your mother is friends with my mother, and they both convinced me to come over and talk to you."

I kind of wanted to hold it against him, simply because it felt like my mother was setting me up.

Was I? I couldn't tell.

"My name's Jason, by the way." His lips spread into a smile.

It felt different than what Ellis used to give me, but I couldn't decipher the difference. Later on—too much later—I realized that his smile looked different because Jason was an expert at faking them. He rarely genuinely gave one. He also had this particular grin that would appear right before he talked down to me and made me feel so small that I felt as if I could seep into the floor's cracks and disappear. For years, I bought into his plastic smiles and believed I was the one who was messed up— not him. And I am. But so is he. He just hides it better than I do.

The thing is, whenever I look back, I still question if my mother set me up with him. It was never clarified, and while I didn't care much back then since I was drifting into a vastness of nothingness, part of me wants to know. Did she do it to get rid of me? To hand me off to someone else who had to take care of me and my problems? Someone who was considered a good guy in our town? Didn't it bother her that I was so young and he was older? Did she even think of me at all?

"Did your parents ever have an issue with him being older?" Ellis asks me, yanking me from my thoughts.

It takes me a moment to catch on to what he asked. "No. My mom liked his mother a lot, and my dad hunted with his father sometimes, so there were no issues." I pause. "I think they were relieved to get me off their hands." I cross my arms and shrug. "I was so messed up back then, and I was heading nowhere, except maybe in the direction of all those girls that went missing."

His expression fleetingly falters, but he promptly composes himself. "What you went through back then ... you had every right to struggle."

I think it's the first time someone has said something like that to me, and it makes my breath lodge in my throat.

"Maybe," I utter. "But my parents were never very good at understanding."

"I know. I remember." He rotates his coffee cup around in his hand. "You're okay now, though, right? I mean, with the divorce? Considering what happened to your father, I know everything can't be okay, but are you doing better with everything else?"

I don't know how to answer that. Better isn't the word I'd used, but I'm definitely not in as dark of a place as I used to be, walking in the shadows all the time, trying to chase the sunlight but never succeeding in catching it.

"Things are getting better, for the most part. I still need to figure out some stuff." I give a short, considering pause. "What about you? You're a detective now." I force a smile onto my face. "Seriously, how the hell did that happen?"

He chuckles softly while dragging his hand across his mouth. "I know. It's crazy, right? And kind of unbelievable."

"A little bit," I admit. "I always thought you'd end up doing something with art."

"I still paint and draw sometimes." He taps his fingers against the table. "I took a few art classes in college but couldn't envision a future with it. It was always more of a hobby and, truthfully, once I started to outgrow my angsty teenager phase, my art wasn't as cool."

"Oh, come on; your art was always cool."

He laughs, his eyes crinkling around the corners. "Some of it was, but a few months ago, I was going through my old artwork and, man, did I have an obsession with drawing graveyards and dead trees."

"You were just trying to show the world you were truly emo."

"I really was. Now my paintings and drawings are more of landscapes and places I've seen."

"Those sound nice."

"They are."

The waitress interrupts us then, setting our food and my coffee on the table.

Once she's gone, Ellis reaches for the bottle of ketchup. "But to answer your question about why I became a detective, it's a bit complicated. I'm unsure if you want to hear the answer."

I'm about to bite into my bagel, but pause. I stare at him and, for once, he doesn't make eye contact with me as he squirts a glob of ketchup onto his plate.

Suddenly, I fear the worst. Perhaps he somehow discovered my secret that lies dying in the trees near my house. What would he do about it, though, other than think I'm a disgusting human? That idea makes me feel sick to my stomach.

I set the bagel back down as he puts the ketchup bottle in the tray. Then he meets my gaze.

"It … It has to do with Clover," he says then quickly adds, "But if you don't think you can hear about her, I understand and we can change the subject."

That wasn't what I was expecting at all.

"Clover? I don't understand. Unless you're working on some drug case?"

"I'm not." He picks up a fry. "And like I said, we don't have to talk about this if you don't want to."

Do I want to talk about *her*?

Can I handle talking about *her*?

Every time I even think about her, guilt slices through me.

But I want to know what's going on.

"You can tell me." My voice doesn't convey much confidence.

Still, he drop the fry back onto the plate and leans forward. Maybe he didn't ever care what I wanted. Perhaps he would've told me regardless. Because he seems almost desperate to have this conversation with me, as if he's about to tell me some devastating secret he's kept trapped inside him for years.

"I became a detective because I don't think she overdosed," he reveals, opening and flexing his hands. "I think she was murdered."

Am I hallucinating, like that time when I was strung out for days on end without any sleep and started thinking that I heard frogs croaking inside my television? I freaked out and started ripping the house apart, thinking there were some inside the house. I tipped over my bookshelves and threw my blankets onto the floor. My mom returned home in the middle of my fit and yelled at me. When she looked at me with my eyes all bloodshot and my pupils dilated, I wondered if she saw what was actually going on beneath my withering flesh.

"Aves … are you okay?" Ellis asks. When I say nothing, he slowly reaches across the table and places his hand over mine. "I know this is probably hard to process. And trust me, I get it. I spent years feeling the guilt over her death—"

I yank my hand away from his. "She wasn't murdered. She overdosed. I saw it with my own eyes," I snap.

I can remember it so vividly that it hurts, like staring at the sunlight for too long. I found her only a few seconds before she took her last breath. She died in my fucking arms. And I have refused to think about it ever since it happened because I can't think about it without the weight of guilt crushing the air from my lungs.

I can't breathe.

The walls are closing in, about to crush me.

I jump up and stumble past the tables, heading for the front doors of the diner. Ellis calls out my name, but I quicken my pace, slam my hands against the glass doors, and burst outside. Then I sprint down the sidewalk and toward my car.

I don't know if Ellis follows me. I never look back to see. I have to keep my gaze ahead, because if I don't—if I don't focus on the present—the past will eat away at me until nothing is left but cold, dead limbs and hollow eyes.

I don't go home. With the frazzled condition I'm in, I can't. If I did and my mother even so much as tried to push me to talk about anything, I'd lose any amount of control I have and the aftermath would be brutal and ugly.

So, instead, I drive. I drive for a while, just like Clover and I used to do whenever we ditched school. Ultimately, I end up at a place minutes from the diner—the park, the one where I saw Clover climbing out of Ben's car. She had her daisy wallet with her—she always had it. And yet, the night she overdosed, she didn't. And it was strange, but I forgot about it relatively quickly in the fog of misery that constantly clouded me after I lost my best friend.

But now … it's all I think about.

Did anyone ever find it? Why didn't she have it with her?

I park my car near the bathrooms and stare at the entrance. It looks dark inside, like the lights are off. Maybe the town closed up the place. Considering how many teenagers used to come here to do drugs and sell their bodies, they should. I didn't realize that for a while. Call me naïve, but the day I saw Clover getting out of Ben's car, I assumed we were the only ones here getting high. Later, after Clover died, rumors would slowly brew about Clover selling herself for drugs. I didn't want to believe it, but I had seen the needle in her arm that night I found her. I also knew she didn't have a job, so where did she get the cash for the heroin? I never really thought about it since it hurts to think about her. This is why I should leave this place. I'm overthinking. It'll consume me if I allow it, and I might do something stupid.

Don't go in there, Ava. The last thing you need to do right now is dance with ghosts.

I reach for the shifter to back up and leave this place, but Ellis's words are stuck in my brain like a fucking sliver. Grimacing, I push the door open and get out of the vehicle.

The air is warm with a light breeze as the trees gently rock from side to side. I haven't been this close to the forest in Starr Meadows in a long time. After all these years, I hoped I wouldn't feel that shiver creeping up my spine, but the bastard makes a grand appearance, as prominent as it was my junior year.

Blowing out a shaky exhale, I turn away from the woods and hike toward the bathroom. My boots crunch against the gravel with each step, and the noise causes images to wince through my mind, ones of that night, when I found Clover on the floor, the girl who had once been so full of energy, dulled into nothing.

That night, it wasn't as silent as it is now. That night, the air was filled with laughter, drunken stupor, and car engines roaring. Maybe that's why it took me so long to find her.

Because her silence got smothered by all the noise.

But maybe that was happening for longer than anyone ever realized.

CHAPTER 20

THE PAST...

Clover is turning into one of my favorite people to spend time with. She's so much fun and typically keeps the mood light. She'll say things like, "And where the party goes, so shall we!"

And she has this way about her; this cease to exist with the moment and rarely drowns in the past. But occasionally, our conversations drift toward the edge of darkness. Like when we're smoking and drinking by ourselves.

But it's okay. I like the balance of light and dark she brings to my life. It makes things feel more real.

I never realized how much fakeness encompassed my life until I met Clover.

Where would I be if I hadn't met her?

This thought is heavy in my mind during last period as my teacher drones on and on about equations. I used to be decent at math, but when we moved to Star Meadows, the classes I needed to take didn't line up with the ones I was taking at my old school, so I ended up spending the last semester of that year confused and barely passing most of my classes. Due to Mr. Davis' monotonous voice, math class feels even worse now. Plus, I didn't sleep much last night because of a storm and the havoc it rained against my window, causing the tree branches to scratch across the side of the house. The noise burrowed into my nightmares.

Thankfully, the teacher hands out an assignment and the classroom falls silent. Instead of working on it, I scratch the pen across the paper, sketching shadows of thorny vines and rotting tree branches as my eyelids become heavier and heavier.

Eventually, the teacher exits the classroom to do who knows what and people start whispering and taking out their phones. Livia is in this class with me. She's sitting up front with Evelyn and Sofia, her two new friends. They're laughing about something, but Livia's is sharp and uneven, like broken plastic.

As I'm sitting at my desk, wishing I took my medication today, something I'm forgetting to do lately, Livia glances in my direction. When our eyes lock, she doesn't look away. Neither do I. I wonder if she misses me. Does she ever miss hanging out with me? Does she ever miss laughing for reals?

"Who are you staring at?" Evelyn asks her while rotating around in her chair to track her gaze.

"No one." Livia quickly diverts her gaze, but not fast enough, and Evelyn's eyes fall on me.

She stares at me for an uneasy amount of time before leaning across the aisle and whispering something to Livia.

Livia stiffens and looks at me one final time before directing her attention back to the assignment.

My anxiety bursts to the surface. What did Evelyn say about me? Does she somehow know the truth about me? Is she making up lies?

"Aves," someone hisses.

I startle and drop my pen. As I lean over to pick up off the floor, I look around for who called out to me. But I can't figure it out.

Confused, I sit up straight in the seat. Then my phone buzzes from inside my pocket.

I dig it out and read the message.

Clover: Yo! I'm standing outside the door. Come on. Let's ditch, Daisy friend. Let's add another secret to our friendship. School sucks ass!

My gaze travels to the doorway where Clover is peeking her head in. A smirk plays on her lips as she quickly motions me over.

Nervousness bubbles inside me. Do I dare walk out? No one appears to be paying attention to me, and I'm at the back of the classroom. Plus, it's the last class of the day, and I've already been marked as being here.

Pressing my lips together, I collect my books, stand up, and quickly cross the classroom. As I'm hurrying out, Livia watches me with a frown.

But I ignore her, and rush out of the classroom where Clover is waiting for me. Her hair is down and wavy today, and she's wearing a pair of torn jeans, a baggy dark blue shirt, and a mini backpack.

She snorts a laugh when I dash out of the classroom like a

lunatic. Then she snags my hand and pulls me down the empty hallway. "Come on; let's get the hell out of this prison."

"Wait—my backpack is in my locker." My thick-soled boots squeak against the scuffed-up linoleum floor as I jog beside her.

She slows down. "Do you need it?"

"Well, my car keys and all my cash are in it."

"All right, to your locker we go." She loops her arm through mine, and we veer off in the other direction.

We pass by a few students but, fortunately, no teachers. When we reach my locker, I hurry and open it up, grab my bag, and then slam the locker shut.

"Okay, let's get the hell out of here," I tell Clover.

She has her phone out and is frowning at the screen.

I adjust my backpack onto my back, looping my arms through the straps. "Is everything okay?"

She nods and then slips her phone into her back pocket. "My mom is just being a beotch, but that's normal for her."

We start wandering toward the entrance doors. As we're crossing through the quad, I spot someone that could ruin my attempt at ditching without getting caught.

Trystan is sitting on one of the benches with some of his friends. They have textbooks scattered around them like they're working on an assignment, but they're mostly just throwing balled-up papers at each other.

I start to duck my head, but his eyes find me before I can. A crease briefly appears between his brows before his lips spread into a grin. His eyes continue to track me as we make our way across the brightly lit room.

Breathe, Ava. Just breathe.

The exhale rushes out of my lips the moment Clover and I shove the glass doors open and burst outside. The noise is loud enough to capture Clover's attention.

Her gaze sweeps across my face. "You okay, bestie?"

I nod, tucking a strand of my hair behind my ear. "Yeah, I'm just worried we might get caught."

"We're fine." She nudges me with my elbow. "Just chill, okay?" She pauses as we reach the parking lot. "Hold on. I gotta go to the bathroom before we leave." She spins around and pulls open the door to head back inside.

I grab the door handle before it slams shut. "Can't you just go after we leave?" I ask.

She flits a glance at me from over her shoulder and smirks. "Well, I think I just started my period, so unless you want me to bleed all over the seat of your car, I should probably take care of it here."

I wrinkle my nose. "No, dude, go take care of it now."

She laughs then urges, "Just wait in the car for me so you won't have to stress about being caught," before taking off down the hallway.

I let the door shut and start across the parking lot with the sunlight beaming down on me.

"Hey, little Aves, you ditchin'?" Trystan's voice bites at my heels, rusty and jagged.

I freeze at the sound.

Tree branches clawing at my face ...

Snow crunching underneath my shoes ...

Smoke funnels through the air ...

I just need to make it to the gate ...

A red ribbon bleeds across my vision ...

I slam to a halt as disoriented memories bleed across my vision, one of them throwing me off balance.

What fucking gate?

There is no gate up in the trails, is there?

"Ava." Laughter chases after me.

I snap out of my trance. *Stop thinking about it!* my brain screams.

I take off in a sprint, running toward my car as Trystan calls out to me again.

"Ava, don't run!" Laughter echoes around me. "Or I'll have to chase you!"

"Don't you dare move," he whispers. "Or I'll cut your throat."

My mind wrestles with reality and with my past.

"Oh, come on; you're being ridiculous," Trystan says, his footsteps growing louder. "I'm not going to do anything to you."

Like I believe that bullshit.

Why the hell is he chasing after me now when he's left me alone for months?

Although, this is the first time he's seen me alone.

I arrive at my car about a second later, unlock the door, and yank it open. My hands and legs tremble as I slide in and move to shut the door, but it stops before clicking shut.

"Why are you running?" Trystan is gripping my car door.

The sunlight casts against his back, causing his features to be shadowed enough that his expression is unreadable, but his tone carries a taunt.

"L-let go of my door." I cringe at the unevenness of my voice.

"Will you chill?" he scoffs. "I just wanted to see where

you're going. I didn't realize you were into ditching school." He drags out a pause. "Doesn't seem like the Ava I remember. She was always such a good girl."

"Be a good girl and stay fucking still," someone whispers.

"Shh ... Behave and this will be over quicker."

I stare at the shadow of Trystan, frantically trying to connect the voice to his.

They sound so similar. It had to be him that day, whispering in my ear.

"Let go of her fucking door." Clover's voice is the sweetest sound ever to grace my ears.

Trystan's attention snaps to the roof of my car, and then he releases a hollow laugh. "What? Are you like her protector now?"

"No, I'm the girl who's going to turn your pencil-sized dick into a punching bag if he doesn't get the hell out of here," Clover informs him boldly.

I envy her so badly at that moment as she says the words to him. I wish I could be that bold.

Silence stretches by, the air congesting with tension.

"Whatever," Trystan sneers as he steps back and lets go of my door. "Fucking crazy bitch."

"Yeah, I'm the fucking crazy bitch," Clover calls out as she yanks the passenger door open. "You're the one standing here, bullying your cousin, you sick fuck."

She slides into the seat, slams the door, then turns to me. "You okay?"

I nod, my gaze flicking out the window to where Trystan's walking away. Occasionally, he throws a glare at my car.

"I'm fine," I lie.

Disbelief flashes across her face. "You're not fine, bestie. I can see it all over your face."

A slow breath eases from my lips. "I'm just worried he'll tell on me for ditching."

She meticulously studies me, a frown tugging at the corners of her lips. "He won't tell. I can promise you that."

I'm not positive if she believes my lie or simply lets me off the hook. Still … "How can you be so sure?"

"Because he's scared of me."

"Really? Why?"

She crosses her arms as she slants back in the seat, the muscle in her jaw ticking as she stares out the window, unblinking. The way the sun reflects in her eyes has to be painful, yet she doesn't look away as she says, "Because if he tattles on you, it'll ruin his reputation around here, and no one will trust him anymore."

"You think so?"

"I know so." She props her feet up onto the dash. "I'll let you in on a little secret. Almost everyone in this damn town is hiding who they really are and they're afraid of someone finding that out. Me included."

I open my mouth to ask what she's hiding, but then I stop myself.

If I ask, will she ask me the same question?

Will I end up telling her the truth?

Can I trust her with the truth?

We are supposed to be Daisy friends … and she's given me some of her secrets. But the idea of doing it scares the hell out of me.

No, I can't do it.

So, I smash my lips together and swallow down the words that fester and feed in my stomach like a weed.

* * *

After peeling out of the school parking lot, we drive around town for a bit. Clover informs me that Ellis had a dentist appointment today, and that's why he isn't with us right now. And Jane had a math test during final period. So, it's just her and me. I don't mind that. I like spending time with Ellis, but sometimes when I spend time with him sober, I get so caught up in his hand-holding and soft smiles that my anxiety becomes almost to much.

Clover rolls the window down and lets a breeze in. "I do hate it here, but I love the smell of the air." She sticks her head out and shuts her eyes, breathing in the crisp air, the sunlight gleaming across her face.

"You look like a dog," I inform her as I slow down for a stop sign.

She chuckles then plops down in the seat again. "Do you have a dog?"

"No. My mom never let me get one."

"My mother never let me either. I want one, though. Maybe a lab or a retriever, and I'd name it Bailey."

"Why Bailey?"

"It was my little sister's name."

I start to pull forward but pause. "You ... you had a little sister?"

She nods, flipping down the visor. "She died when I was young. I barely remember her, but it broke my mother and turned her into a ghost of herself. And my father left because he couldn't deal." She sinks back in the seat and fiddles with a worn leather bracelet she always has on. "He gave me this before he took off and told me to remember him every time I look at it. And I do. Every damn day I look at it and remember how he packed up his shit and left me with my mother, who couldn't even take care of herself."

"Cloves," I start, unsure of what to say. All I know is that my heart hurts. Hurts for her. Her mom. Even her father a little bit.

Plus, she told me something personal while I haven't offered her much of anything.

"You don't have to say anything," she interrupts. "In fact, let's change the subject. Ditching school shouldn't feel so depressing." She plasters on a smile.

And at that moment, I become aware that Clover might be equally as good at pretending everything is okay as I am.

"Are you sure?" I question carefully. "We can talk about it if you want to."

She dismissively flicks her wrist. "Nah, I'm good." She tilts her head and then perks up as she points at the grocery store parking lot across the street from us. "I see Noah over there. Let's go get him to buy us some beer."

I consider telling her no. It doesn't feel right, the way she brought it up, like she's avoiding her pain. But isn't that what I'm always doing?

Thirty minutes later, we're heading toward Star Meadows Lake with a six-pack in the trunk of my car. When we arrive at the sandy shoreline, we're relieved to find no one else parked there. So, we get out, settle on the hood of my car, and pop the caps off our beers. Then we sit in silence, watching the waves of the lake gently lull.

The trees encompassing the shore are dead and rotting due to a fire that occurred a few years ago. They offer a drop of serenity to the usual nagging phobia I have at the sight of branches and tree trunks.

"I don't even know him," Clover abruptly says while setting her beer down on the front end of the car.

I pause mid-sip and lower the beer from my mouth. "Know who?"

She draws her knees to her chest while staring at the lake. "My father."

"How …? How old were you when he left?"

"I was six … Bailey was three when she died. She got cancer."

I have to remind myself to breathe. What do I say to her? Is there anything I can say? "I'm sorry, Cloves. I really am."

She shrugs. "It's not your fault. And besides, my father was never a good parent. How could he be with how easily he left us?"

"My father's a shitty father, too." The truth falls off my tongue and freely floats in the air across the lake,

Clover's gaze skates to me, her brows rising. "Really?"

I nod, picking up the beer bottle that's perched on the bumper beside my feet. "He stuck around and everything, but so many times I wished he would leave." I take a long sip of my beer. It's warm and stale, but I don't care. "He's always been an angry, mean person.

She squints her eyes against the sunlight as she studies me. "Has he …? Has he ever hit you?"

I blink. "What?"

"Has he ever hit you?" she repeats, watching me intently. "Because mine did all the time."

I swallow hard. "I …" I can't get the lie to leave my lips. Why, when it's always been so easy for me?

"It's okay if you don't want to say it aloud," she assures me. "I get it."

I swallow thickly. "Get what?"

"That fear of speaking the truth."

All I can do is nod.

I feel woozy, lightheaded, and terrified, like my mother will find out about what I just confessed to Clover. But how could she know? She's not here.

"Did your mom ever do anything about it?" Clovers wonders, reaching for her beer bottle.

I shake my head. My throat feels dry, so I take another swallow of my beer.

"Neither did mine." She directs her attention back to the water and slips on her sunglasses. "I want to hate her for that—I really do—but I guess she was a victim in her own way."

"Did he hit her, too?" I finally find my voice again.

She nods, strands of her hair dancing in the breeze. "All the damn time. In fact, I sometimes fell asleep to their shouting. And when he left, the quietness of the house made it harder to sleep. How fucked up is that? Especially because that's all Bailey got to see. Me? I'll probably get to leave it, if I'm lucky. But that's all she knew." She yanks her fingers through her hair. "Sometimes, I fucking hate my parents. How fucked up does that make me?"

The air grows quiet as I think about her and Bailey. Then my thoughts drift to my own life and how yelling is constant weeping out of the walls of my home. If it left, would I feel unsettled by the silence? I honestly don't know.

And do I even deserve anything better?

Clover does.

"You're not fucked up." I pick at the label of my beer. "I am."

She shakes her hand. "You're not fucked up, Aves. You're like the most un-fucked up person I know."

I want to tell her how wrong she is.

Just fucking say it, Ava. Tell the damn truth for once. After everything she's just told you, she deserves it.

But what if she hates me?

"Ellis's parents fight a lot, too," she informs me. "He's told you that, right?"

I nod. "He's told me a little bit."

She reclines back, resting on her hands, and angles her head toward the sky. "Did he tell you how it wasn't always that way? That his family used to be normal—whatever that means. But they were nice, and his parents didn't yell at their kids. They went on trips, had dinner together, and I saw them laugh a lot." She briefly pauses. "Before Zoey died, I spent a lot of time over there, partly because Ellis and Zoey were my friends. But I also liked not being at my house. I still don't, but mostly because of Creepy Jerry. And my mom's rarely home..." She gives a short pause. "But anyway, back in the day, before everything went to shit, I had a lot of fun at Zoey and Ellis's house. I liked being around their mom. She was really funny. And their dad was always baking stuff. He seriously made the best chocolate chip cookies. I'd never even had homemade ones until I went over there." She scratches her wrist. "I was like eight or something." She smiles genuinely, and I long to join her, to have a good memory I can latch on to. But as quickly as the moment comes, it dissolves, as her smile fades.

"Everything changed when Zoey died. Death does that to people. It breaks their souls. But it was worse after Zoey died because of how she did. There was no closure, Just questions. So many damn questions."

My brain rewinds to the day I saw her getting out of the car with Ben and how she acted like it wasn't a big deal. It was the complete opposite of how she's behaving now. It doesn't make sense.

She suddenly sits up and slides off the hood. "You know what? I think I'm going to go for a swim," she announces as she sets her beer bottle down on the ground.

Her change of topic knocks me with a burst of whiplash. "Wait … What? You can't do that." I jump off the hood and follow after her. "The water's too cold."

"Maybe. Maybe not." She kicks off her shoes and shucks off her hoodie. "Maybe I'm just as cold as the water." Then she jogs down the rocky shore, straight for the lake.

I watch, partly in horror and partly in awe of how easily she runs into the water. She doesn't scream out against the frigid chill that is for sure creeping through her legs right now. She doesn't make a sound as she wades forward until the water reaches her chest.

"Are you okay?" I call out as I skid down the hill.

She silently inches forward until the water rises to the top of her neck.

A gust of worry rises inside me, like a warning that a storm is coming. "What are you doing?"

She wades out farther until only the top of her head is showing.

Panic bursts through me, and I run down the hillside, tripping over rocks.

"Clover!" I yell as I halt on the shore. "Just get out, please!"

She angles her head back. "I'm fine, Aves. Just chill." Then she ducks underneath, submerging her entire body.

I don't think. I walk right into the lake, the chilly water seeping through my shoes. I'm a terrible swimmer, so if I have to go get her, I might not be able to get us both out.

I keep my eyes trained on the spot she went under. Time stretches by. It feels like an eternity.

"Come on," I mumble as I scan the water. "Come on, Clover. Come back up."

I wait for a breath longer then wade in further until the water touches my waist. A shiver rolls through my body, and my muscles hiss in protest as the cold water seeps through the fabric of my jeans, flesh, and bones. My body convulses, and I start chattering uncontrollably. But I push forward, preparing to dive in and battle the instinct inside me telling me— begging me—to go back.

Tree branches claw at my flesh as I sprint through the snow.

I'm terrified and bleeding, and every part of my body desperately screams to escape. But in the back of my mind, guilt whispers to me.

Go back for her!

Help her!

Save her!

Red bleeds across my vision.

Blood ...

No, not blood ...

Red hair ...

Where did that come from?

Camilla has blonde hair ...

I suck in a breath and lower myself—

Clover bursts from the lake a few feet to my side, the water rippling around her. She coughs, water sputtering from her lips as she blinks.

"Holy shit, that was insane," she breathes out. She's shivering, chattering, and water drips down her face. "D-Dude, you g-got in." Her blue-tinted lips curve up into a grin.

Usually, I'm all about trying to play it cool, but something inside me snaps.

"Why d-did you do th-that!" I shout with my hands balled at my sides. "I th-thought you w-were g-going to drown!" I spin around, disregarding the ache in my muscles as I inch my way back through the water and toward the shore.

"Ava!" she yells after me.

Ignoring her, I continue moving until I'm out of the water. Then I stomp back up the hill. My clothes are soaked and shivers rack through my body. I barely acknowledge any of this, though, as I stumble for my car, climb into the driver's seat, and turn on the engine. Then I crank up the heater and lower my head onto the steering wheel, breathing in and out.

"Help me!" she screams. "Please, someone help me!"

Turn back around, Ava! Help her!

I keep running, my fear so potent that it screams louder than the cries plaguing the woods.

I can see a gate. I run for it. I'm unsure why the gate is there, but it has to be the way out. I throw one final glance over my shoulder.

Red hair blows in the distance.

No, not red hair …

A girl with red hair …

I shake my head from side to side. What the hell is that? Someone else was there?

"Sometimes when something bad happens to us, Ava, our mind plays tricks on us because it can't cope with reality," my mother said.

But which way is the trick?

I barely register the door opening and don't lift my head.

Clover is chattering as she drops down onto the passenger seat. Then she closes the door and sinks into silence.

I want to be so angry with her, but worry tiptoes through my anger.

Why did she do that?

"A-are … Are you o-okay?" she hesitantly asks.

Clover is typically blunt, loud, and a confident person. She doesn't waste time worrying about others often, so hearing the worry in her tone right now is strange.

"I-I'm f-fine," I lie. "A-are you?" I ask, turning my head toward her.

Her hair is drenched, her skin is pale, and her arms are wrapped around herself.

She nods, meeting my gaze. "I'm fine. I'm more worried about you."

I lift my head off the steering wheel. "Me? You're the one that just dunked yourself in a freezing lake."

"I know. And I'm sorry. It seemed like a good idea when I

did it. But now"—she wavers—"I'm regretting my poor life choices." She offers me a weak smile.

I don't believe her at all. She's not sorry. And she might do it again.

She smashes her lips together as she hunches forward. "Why did you just freak out on me?"

I shrug, looking away from her and out at the water, willing that guilt to stay put. I buried it so well. At least, I thought I did. Yet I make one dive into a cold lake, and that guilt desperately tries to resurface.

"Because I thought you drowned," I mutter, which isn't a complete lie.

It's not the entire truth either.

"I really am okay," she attempts to reassure me. "I'm sorry if I scared you."

I nod, trying to untangle myself from the branches of my past, but they're thriving by slowly drinking the life from me. "I'm sorry for yelling at you."

She smiles. This time it's real. "You don't need to apologize. I probably deserve it."

I don't nod or shake my head. I'm unsure what sort of reaction would've been the correct one.

What was the real reason she went into that water? Was it just for fun? Clover does like to do wild, crazy stuff a lot. I have this unsettling feeling about it, though; one connected to the silence that hedged the air right before she sank underwater. If she was having fun, then why didn't she laugh?

What caused the silence?

Because we were talking about our parents? Her sister? Death?

Zoey?

I want to ask her, but bringing it up again could cause her to run back into the water. So, I let the silence choke the air.

Silence. It's such an odd thing. Because, while known for being completely lacking in everything, it can still say so many things, sometimes even more than a piercing scream.

CHAPTER 21

When Ellis enters the bathroom, my surprise level is zero. I'm unsure why I'm not caught off guard, other than checking on me seems so Ellis-like.

I'm sitting on the dirty, concrete floor when he enters, like a replica of how I was that night when I found Clover lying lifeless on the concrete floor.

Ellis doesn't speak as he moves past the sinks and toward me. His boots appear in my line of vision, but I merely hug my legs tighter against my chest and stare at the crack in the wall that's by the dingy sink.

He steps to the side. Is he leaving? He should.

But he sinks onto the floor beside me instead and stretches his legs out in front of him.

Quietness settles between us. I get the impression he's waiting for me to speak first. What the hell does he want me to say? Does he want me to talk about what happened that night? Does he want me to tell him what I saw? Does he need me to give him clues to support his theory that Clover was murdered?

How could she be? I saw the needle sticking out of her arm …

But does that mean she put it there herself?

Fuck, what if she didn't?

What if someone killed her?

"I miss her," I whisper, sucking back the tears threatening to pour out.

"Me, too." He reclines against the wall. "She was one of the few constants in my life. Like she was always just there, you know? And I think I took that for granted."

I rub my lips together. The truth is I don't know since Clover and I were only friends for a few months. And yet, during those months, her presence was sunlight in the darkness that had overtaken my life.

"She thought of you as her best friend," he adds.

I arch my brow. "She told you that?"

"She didn't have to. I could tell." He fiddles with the band of his watch. "She never stayed still very much, you know. Even though I knew her for a long time, she kind of floated in and out of my life, especially after Zoey died. Even before that, though, she … well, Clover was kind of like how autumn leaves, but always returns. Clover was autumn. But when she became friends with you, it felt like she was trying to stay still." His throat muscles work as he swallows audibly.

"Maybe." But I'm not entirely convinced. "But maybe there just wasn't enough time for her to float in and out of my life."

While Clover and I were close, sometimes she'd become restless, like she was waiting for a snowstorm to blow in and sweep the autumn leaves away. And eventually, it did. But when that change occurred remains a mystery. Was it the night she died? Or the day she swam into the lake? Or was much sooner than that, like the day I witnessed her getting out of Ben's car at this same park?

Why the hell were you in his car, Clover? Just to get drugs?

I've never told Ellis about that, but I never had the opportunity since before Clover died, I felt obligated to keep her secret. And after, the knowledge got lost in a sea of drugs and alcohol. Ellis was lost, too. But we were being pushed in separate directions—him toward the shore and me floating toward the horizon.

"Yeah, maybe." He drags his teeth along his bottom lip. He used to do that when we were younger as he was pondering a complex theory in his head. I spent so much time analyzing what he was thinking, but I never figured it out.

"Why do you think Clover was murdered?" I ask as I criss-cross my legs.

He bends his knee and rests his arm on top of his leg. "It's because of a few things." He takes a deep breath. "Like the way the needle looked in her skin when I walked in here … It was like it had been shoved in there, not slid in by her. And from everything I saw back then—and from what I've seen in the police report—they never found anything she could've heated the drugs with." He starts chewing on his lip again. "Something's missing, Aves. And I think you know enough about drugs to know I'm right about that."

I despise talking about the days I tried to replace my trauma by self-medicating. The sad reality is that I got clean only because after I married Jason, and moved to a town where I didn't know anyone who could get me a hit. But in Star Meadows, I had enough connections that I could numb myself whenever I wanted.

And fuck, I wanted to a lot.

But there's another reason why I got clean. Because Jason told me I couldn't get high anymore. It was probably the one thing he did for me that was helpful. Although, the way he did it wasn't the best …

His hands are wrapped around my throat. "If I ever catch you getting high again, I'll fucking lock you in this room forever. If you want to be a prisoner to drugs, you can be mine, too." He squeezes tighter. "Don't fucking embarrass me, Ava. No one wants to be married to a junkie."

I was so terrified he'd make good on his threat that I stopped. And it hurt badly, the way my body cleansed itself and let all the other toxins back in.

"I get that it's weird—I do"—I inhale and exhale—"but that doesn't mean she was murdered."

He thrums his fingers on the side of his leg. "There's more than that. Her autopsy report shows she had bruises on her wrists and arms, but the coroner listed them as normal bumps and bruising from injections. But I've seen injection bruising before, and the photos of Clover's arms in the autopsy report did not look like that."

I imagine him sitting at a table with photos of Clover's decomposing body scattered in front of him. Images of how she looked that night, all lifeless and fake, like that smile she gave me the day at the lake.

"Did she look like she was beaten up?" I ask once I can find my voice again. "Or maybe it was because she bumped into something? She did do that a lot, especially when she was drunk."

He shakes his head. "This was far worse bruising than her bumping into things while intoxicated." He stares off at the wall across from us. "It looked like right before she died, someone violently grabbed her." He gives a short pause. "Or maybe someone tied her up."

From what I can recall about that night, I barely saw Clover and spent most of it with Ellis, wandering around at the party together. But not seeing Clover wasn't entirely odd. She tended to go off and do her own thing. But she'd find us by the end of the night.

That night, though, she didn't. I found her.

Dead on this floor ...

No, don't think about it.

I shift my weight. "Why has no one ever looked into this before? And the cops ruled her death an accidental overdose."

Although, some rumors whirled around of Clover OD'ing on purpose. I even punched someone at a party because they said that, which was out of character for me, but I was high on who knows what and was in the middle of refusing to mourn.

Looking back, part of me questions if she could have.

That day at the lake, when she went under the water, it felt like she wouldn't come up for air ever again. We had been talking about such depressing things—her family, her sister ... Zoey.

Ellis yanks his fingers through his hair and then looks at me. "Honestly, Aves, I don't have an answer for you. I've seen autopsy reports like this before, and Clover's death should've been investigated more thoroughly. And while that could be just due to the fact that she was a drug addict and the cops let that blind their judgment, I can't shake this feeling that maybe it's a coverup. This town has too many teenage girls that overdose or that just go missing, and I've always thought it was fucking weird." He cracks his knuckles against the side of his legs. "Clover, Zoey, those three girls that went missing that summer …" The muscle in his jaw ticks. "How can such a small town have so much dark shit going on?"

Tree branches claw at my face as I run through the trees. A gate is ahead. It's green and metal and leads to a path. If I can just get to it, I can get home. I know I can.

"Help!" a scream shatters the air.

I keep running but throw a glance over my shoulder.

A girl with blonde hair is crawling across the ground, trying to get away, too.

Camilla.

I want to go back to help her—I almost do—but then he *appears in the trees, faceless and just a shadow. But I swear I know him.*

He steps out and strides toward another person stumbling just behind Camilla.

Red bleeds my vision …

Red hair …

No, not red hair … Hair soaked in blood.

"Aves." Ellis's voice tears through the memory.

He has a hand on my cheek, and I jerk away, disoriented.

He quickly withdraws his hand. "I'm sorry. You were zoned out, and I couldn't get you to snap out of it." Worry creases his brow. "I'm sorry. I shouldn't have touched you like that."

As I regain control of my breathing, reality slowly creeps back to me. "You're fine," I tell him. "I just …" I touch the cheek that he touched. *I'm not used to being touched so softly like that*, I want to say.

But I can't get the words to leave my mouth.

"You're fine. You don't have to explain," he tells me, carrying my gaze. And I get the feeling that he may already have an idea of what I was about to say.

I nod, fiddling with a loose thread on the hem of my shirt. My head is throbbing, and confusion is dancing through the pain.

I knew Camilla was with me that day, but someone else was there. I saw a brief glimpse of it years ago when I was at the lake, but somehow, I forgot. On purpose maybe?

What happened to her?

Did she run out of the woods and was too scared to speak about it, like Camilla and me?

Or did she never leave those woods?

"Do you …? Do you think the girls that went missing, and Clover and Zoey's overdose, are all connected?" I ask.

He studies me before nodding. "I've wondered it, yeah."

"Oh." I think about the calls I received that summer and the calls I've received over the last few days. I need to tell him. It's on the tip of my tongue, but fear wraps around my throat.

"There's something else, too." His gaze is fixed on the floor. "It's something that's been bothering me for a while, but it took me a few years to remember it because I was too consumed with guilt and couldn't think about it … about Clover, I mean. It was something Clover said to me a few days before the night she died when we were hanging out in her room. We were listening to records, and then, suddenly, she said that if anything ever happened to her, that she wanted me to know she loved me, and for me to tell you that she loved you, too. She also had me promise to take care of you." He lifts his gaze to mine. "I failed her on that one."

"*What?* No, you're not responsible for me," I assure him. "Everything I did after she died was *my* choice." Well, some of my choices anyway. It's something I've struggled with for a while because, while I chose to numb my mind and body with drugs and drinking, my marriage to Jason felt forced on me by my parents.

When I said I'd marry him, I felt as if I was standing on the ledge of a cliff, and my mother was telling me I could either jump, she would push me, or I could choose to let Jason pull me back. Only, he never entirely pulled me back. He simply stood there behind me, threatening to push me for years.

"No, it was my fault. I abandoned you." Ellis carries my gaze unwaveringly. "I left you all alone in that shitty house where I knew your mother would eat you alive. And I did nothing. I just walked away. And I did it because I was selfish. Because—" His voice cracks. "Because being around you reminded me too much of Clover, and that reminded me too much of the guilt I felt about her death."

"You're not responsible for me," I repeat firmly. "Even if Clover told you to take care of me, it wasn't her place to do that." I stare at my hands because looking into his intense gaze complicates breathing. "I understand feeling guilty about her death, though. I feel it even now."

He remains quiet for a slamming heartbeat, but I can feel his gaze on me.

"I want to make this right," he finally says. "I want to find out how she really died. I owe her at least that . . . I should've seen that day she said she loved me and to take care of you if anything happened to her for what it was instead of assuming it was Clover being dramatic."

"There's no way you could've known. She did and said many things that felt like she was saying goodbye."

"I know, but looking back, this felt different. I was just too caught in my own shit that I wasn't paying enough attention."

"Yeah, I get that." I pick at my chipped fingernail polish. "I'm always remembering these moments and questioning everything that happened."

He hesitates. "Did you ever think she was killed?"

I shake my head. "Not by someone else anyway. But I sometimes wonder if . . . she may have taken her own life."

"I've thought about that sometimes, too. But even if she did, with there still being a drop of suspicion that someone did this to her, I have to look into it."

I lift my gaze to him. "How are you going to do that?"

"I'm trying to get approval to reopen the case. If I can, I'll have full access to her records, including her toxicology report, which I'm having a tough time getting my hands on." He restlessly bounces the leg his arm is resting on.

My brows pull together. "That's weird, right? Especially since her cause of death was an overdose?"

"It's beyond weird. And it's just another suspicion to add to my growing list." He sighs heavily. "I have to ask you for a favor. Well, a few actually."

"Okay," I say warily. "What are they?"

Apprehension masks his expression. "Well, until I get

approval, I want to know you'll keep this conversation between us."

"Of course." Who would I tell anyway? Well, maybe Clara, but I won't if he doesn't want me to. I haven't even told her about the cuts on my back that I got last night.

"Also," he continues, "if you can try to think of everything you remember about what happened the night Clover died, and the few days leading up to it, it'd really help. You were with her so much, and you may have knowledge that could help me prove she didn't overdose that night, even if you might not realize it."

Think about that night? The one I've spent years trying to burn from my memory with every shot of vodka I drank and every line I snorted? How the fuck am I supposed to do that sober?

But don't I owe Clover that?

If someone killed her …

Fuck, what if someone took her from me when all this time I thought she just left me?

My daisy friend and all our secrets may have been *stolen* from this world, not just floated away.

Breathe in. Breathe out.

"I can try," I tell him, scratching my arm. "I struggle, though … thinking about past things."

He places a hand on mine. "I get that. And I don't want you to try to push yourself too hard. Just … if you think of anything at all that you think is odd, let me know."

I stare at his hand on mine. Why does he keep touching me like this? It makes me feel … disoriented.

I'm so fucked up in the head.

"Sorry," he says apologetically as he draws his hand back.

"You're fine," I mumble, feeling like an idiot.

He stands then and offers me his hand with a warm smile. "How about we get off this dirty bathroom floor before we end up with hepatitis or something?"

"Good idea." I place my hand in his, and he helps me to my feet. Then he releases my hand and dusts off some dirt from his pants.

"I have one more thing I want to say before we go," he tells me. "It's about your father's death."

"Okay." Throughout the discussion about Clover, I'd forgotten why I met with Ellis today.

My father was murdered.

"You're familiar with the woods just outside your house, right? And the paths that cut through Star Meadows Canyon?" he asks. "I think if I'm remembering right, you once told me that you used to love going up there alone."

My hangover suddenly becomes more prominent, and I have to swallow down the compulsion to vomit all over the gross floor. "I used to when I was younger, but I stopped."

He sticks his hands into his pockets. "But you knew the trails well? And the ones your dad liked to hike on?"

I have no idea where he's going with this, but I answer anyway and truthfully this time. "I did."

He bobs his head up and down. "I know you said you stopped going into the woods because you started hating them, so I hate to ask you this, but I kind of have to." He sucks in a breath then lets it out. "I'd like to look around in the area where your father fell, and I want to go there with someone familiar with the place."

Fuck. What the hell am I supposed to say to that?

No?

Fuck no?

I'd rather eat my own tongue.

Yeah, that wouldn't make me look like a freak at all.

"I don't know … I don't know if I can. I have this … phobia of the woods now."

"I remember you telling me that, too," he treads cautiously. "And if you don't want to go there, I can find someone else. But I think you'll be the most helpful person because you know all the trails your father liked to hike on, right?"

Yes, but only because I heard him talk about them. And sometimes, my mother and I would go on hikes with him. My aunt, uncle, and cousins would be with us. And there'd be moments where I'd almost get a taste of normalcy. But in the end, we'd always return home.

I should say no.

I should refuse.

But wouldn't that make me look suspicious? Shouldn't I want to do everything I can to help solve my father's death?

A normal person would.

"Okay, I'll try." The sad truth is I don't agree because I want to help solve my father's murder. I do it because I don't want to appear suspicious.

Sometimes I question if I am dead inside, just a decaying tree trying to thrive without sunlight or water.

Before we leave, Ellis and I plan to meet tomorrow morning to go into the woods. Then we get into our cars and drive away. He waits for me to leave first, which is something he did when we were younger. I used to convince myself that he did it because he was making sure I left safely. But I wonder if he did it now to observe me because he knows I'm a liar and wants to dig through my lies and find the truth.

I struggle not to focus on that as I drive back into town, and my chest keeps getting tighter and tighter as if a rubber band is being wrapped around it repeatedly. I keep thinking about Clover. And Zoey. And all those girls who went missing. Most of all, I think of the girl in the woods with blood in her hair.

The bands get tighter. I can barely breathe.

I need to lie down.

My gas tank is nearing empty, so I pull into a gas station to fill it up. It's midday, and tourists are filling the area, so I wait in line to get to the pump.

About ten minutes later, I'm swiping my card and digging out my phone while I wait for the tank to fill up.

Clara hasn't messaged me, so she must still be asleep. But my mother has.

Mom: The way you left the house was extremely disrespectful. And I can't believe you're speaking to that detective. You should've listened to your uncle.

Mom: When will you be home? We have a dinner to go to tonight and you need to be present for it.

Mom: You've been gone way too long just to be speaking to the police. What are you doing? Drinking again? I can't

believe you. You're such a disappointment. I'm going to call Jason and tell him what's going on.

I startle as the pump clicks, announcing that my tank is full, and I nearly drop my phone. I scramble to open the messages to see if she followed through with her threat.

"Please say she didn't," I mumble as my chest constricts even more. "I can't handle this right now."

But she didn't send another message after that. Did she call and talk to him? Did he not answer? Or is she trying to scare me into obeying her?

Any three could be true.

I put the gas nozzle back into the pump, then grab my receipt and move to duck into my car again. As I'm about to slide in, though, something captures my attention.

Camilla is exiting the gas station. She's carrying a brown paper bag, her hair is pulled up into a messy bun, and she has an oversized hoodie, torn jeans, and worn sneakers. She walks toward a beat-up blue car parked near the entrance doors and yanks the passenger side door open to get in.

But then she spots me and freezes.

So do I.

And I swear the scent of crisp snow mixed with rust washes over me.

The wound on my back throbs.

Red hair ...

Blood everywhere ...

Who the fuck was the other girl that day?

I think about Ellis and his need for answers. Then I think about myself and my existence in the unknown, my lack of need to seek out anything, and my ability to hide in my lies.

For the first time in my life, I think I might need answers. I want to ask her what she remembers about that day and if she recalls someone else being there.

Who was she?

The girl with blood in her hair?

Fear lashes inside me as I step forward.

I've never felt this way before.

I take another step—

Honk! Honk! Honk!

"Move the hell out of the way if you're done, honey," a guy yells. "I don't have all goddamn day!"

I spin around.

The guy in the car behind me has his head out the window, glaring at me. But then his lips kick up into a smirk as he eyes me over. I suddenly have this compulsion to stride up to him and punch that smirk right off his face.

"As cute as you are, I need to fill up my car," he says with a cocky grin.

I curl my fingers inward and stab my nails into my palm. I want to hit him. Smack that shit-eating grin off his face.

I don't know where this feeling stems from, but I may be losing it.

After seconds of me merely staring at him, his grin fades. "Fine, just move your ass out of the way!" He throws his hands up in the air. "Dumb female drivers."

I should get back in the car, and cower away, but my feet won't budge.

"What is wrong with you?" the guy repeats, his brows knitting.

"What's wrong with her?" my father says. "She can be so damn stupid sometimes."

"I really think you shouldn't take the test, Ava," Jason says with a condescending smile. "You'll just end up failing and feeling like shit about yourself. Do you want that? To fail at something else."

"Goddammit, Ava!" my mother screams. "Why can't you just behave!"

"I really hate that fucking guy," Clover says as she glares at Jerry from across the yard. "He's always smirking at me in this disgusting way."

Camilla's sobs echoing through the canyon.

Blood splatters across the snow.

Another girl cries out in pain.

A hand slaps over my mouth. "Just lay still like a good girl, and it'll be over soon."

Another girl missing.

Another girl overdosed.

Death.

Pain.

Silence.

Shut the fuck up and be a good girl—

"Shut the hell up!" A scream tears from my chest as I march forward and kick the front bumper of the guy's car.

He hurriedly backs up, his tires skidding against the asphalt. "Crazy bitch!" he shouts out of the window before peeling out of the parking lot.

The haze of rage that veiled me slowly lifts. Everyone is staring at me, and panic clips through my anger.

Looking away, I climb into the car and shut the door. Then I lower my head onto the steering wheel.

Coming back here was a mistake. I feel like I'm losing my mind again. I feel like I'm falling back into the past.

I should go home. Who cares if I'm here for my father's funeral? But if I leave, I won't be here to help Ellis figure out what happened to Clover. Could I do that? Bail on him?

Bail on her?

No, I can't even if I may want to.

I lift my head from the steering wheel, start the engine, then reach for the shifter, but something on the passenger seat snags my attention—a small envelope.

When did that get there? Did Camilla do this?

I frantically peer around, but I can't see her anywhere.

I nervously pick up the envelope and dump the contents out—a piece of paper and an old Polaroid are in it. I pick up the piece of paper first and unfold it.

Written on it are the words: *We need to talk. Meet me at the Star Meadows Bar at noon on Monday. Don't be late.*

Smashing my lips together, I move to the photo. Then my insides wind into tight, nauseating knots.

It's of the green metal gate from my memories. In the background is a field lined with towering trees and overgrown bushes.

My breath rushes out of me, and I can see it, the smoke circling my face as I gasped for air while running through those trees.

Someone is messing with me. Someone from the woods that day?

My fingers quiver as I flip the photo over.

Written on the back, in different handwriting than the letter, are the words:

Do you remember the things that happened in the woods?

I remember the girl now.

The blood in her hair.

And how I don't think she made it out of there.

Yes, it's coming back to me again in pieces.

I can't escape it.

And this time, part of me doesn't want to.

I set the photo and note down on the seat then pick up my phone, noting the cuts on my palms from where my fingernails dug into the flesh when I yelled at that man.

Unhinged is what my mother would say about me losing my cool. She might be correct, but maybe not. Maybe the cuts on my palms are bleeding the fear out of me.

"What would be the point in life if I let my fear own it?" Clover said that to me once.

I didn't understand what she meant then. In fact, I did the exact opposite every day of my life, except for a few moments when I was friends with her. She gave me glimpses of being fearless. And she gave me glimpses of the truth, even if I didn't pick up on them at the moment.

I dial his number, and he answers after three rings.

"Is everything okay?" Of course, Ellis would answer his phone like this.

"Yeah." Not the entire truth, but I'm making progress. "I thought of something, though."

"About your father's case."

"No, about Clover's death."

"Really?" he asks, surprised. "Did you remember something about that night?"

"No, but she had a diary, and she once told me she kept all her secrets in it. Ones that I didn't even know."

"Shit, I didn't know about it. She didn't seem like the kind of person to keep a diary."

"I know. And she made me promise not to tell you about it; she said you'd get all excited and think she was deeper than she wanted people to believe she was." I fall silent for a moment, recalling exactly what she said. "But she also said something else that was weird … That she wanted to write everything down because she felt like she would fade into nothing one day. I thought she meant she was going to die, but …" A memory is tugging at my mind, one that seemed so insignificant at the time, but looking back … "What if she thought she was going to disappear like those other girls?"

CHAPTER 22

I TUCK THE PHOTO AND NOTE INTO MY BAG, UNSURE WHAT TO do with it—if I'll meet the person. It seems dangerous as hell, but what if I could get answers? Perhaps I could hide and see who shows up. Do I dare?

Just thinking about it sends fear snaking around my throat.

I have a few days to attempt to conquer my fear. Maybe I'll become upset enough that I'll snap and meet them, like I snapped when I kicked the hell out of that man's car.

Once I leave the gas station, I drive home. When I arrive, cars are parked around the circle driveway. One of the vehicles belongs to my aunt and uncle, but I don't recognize one of them.

I hate this—the unknowing—and I want to turn around and leave. But I'm not about to do that to Clara, so I parked near the front door and get out. Before I head inside, I wander down the shallow hill to check on Bailey. He seems happy, running around in circles while wagging his tail. I check his water, give him food, and play fetch with him for a few minutes. It's peaceful out here with only the light breeze, the lull of the river, and Bailey's occasional bark to fill up the silence.

"I think I'm regretting coming here," I say to no one in particular as I take the stick from Bailey. I crouch down in front of him and scratch his ear. "I'd probably go home, but I feel like I need to help Ellis figure out what happened to Clover. I owe her that much."

Bailey barks, and then his attention darts over my shoulder. The hairs on his back rise as he bares his teeth and growls. He's never been aggressive, not even toward Jason, but mostly because he feared him.

Confused, I start to twist around, but then a voice that's haunted my nightmares for years stabs at my eardrums.

"Well, well, well, if it isn't little Ava, all grown up," Trystan says with that stupid taunt I always loathed.

I freeze, returning my attention to Bailey. I don't want to look at him, and yet every one of my senses is screaming for me to keep an eye on him.

Pressing my lips together, I ignore him, hoping he'll go away.

"What? No, *hello, Trystan, long time, no see?*" he taunts me.

Biting down on my tongue, I latch onto Bailey's collar as he tries to sprint toward where Trystan's voice is drifting from.

"Your dog seems like a psycho," he continues. "He needs to chill the fuck out or I'll make him."

Before I can grasp what I'm doing, I rise to my feet and face him. "Touch my dog, and you'll fucking regret it."

His arms are resting on top of the fence, and a smile is on his face, like he thinks he's the funniest person in the world. He was always like this, able to easily keep a smile on his face as he whispered cruel words.

He's similar to how he looked when I left this town—tall with blond hair—but now he has a scruffy beard, wrinkles crease the corners of his eyes, and a fresh cut runs down his cheek.

I wonder where he got that from?

"Oh, relax," he says. "I won't hurt your dog. I just came to say *hi*. It's been a long time since we've seen each other."

Not long enough.

If I had my way, I'd never see him again.

So many words are burning at the tip of my tongue. I want to tell him how much I despise him. I want to say that I remember. I want to shout that I'll tell the entire world what he's done.

But I can't. My mind is still like a fucking cave—full of holes and tunnels that lead to who the hell knows where.

"Still as quiet as ever, huh?" He smirks as he backs away. "Glad to see some things never change." With that, he walks up the hill and goes into the house.

I want to scream that I'm not the little Ava he can torment. But the words get gobbled up by the fear feeding inside me.

Maybe Trystan is right.

Maybe I can change in some ways.

But perhaps some things will never change.

* * *

I remain outside for a while. Bailey attempts to console me, but even he can't bring me out of my plummeting state mood. I may have remained outside until the sun set behind the hills until the town was asleep, but eventually, Clara messages me.

Clara: Where are you? I think there's like a bunch of people at the house.

Me: I'm heading into the house now. Sorry this thing with Ellis took so long.

I pocket my phone and, with a deep breath, head inside. When I enter, chatter is flowing from the living room. A wall blocks my view from the area, and while I'm curious to see who's in there, I'd rather gouge my eye out than see Trystan and my mother. So, I move to sneak downstairs.

"Ava," my mom calls out and I tense. "Is that you?" A second later, she appears in the doorway.

I assess her, attempting to measure her vibe on whether or not she's still upset with me for how I left.

"Come say hi to everyone." She grabs my hand then tows me with her as she strolls into the living room where my aunt and uncle are sitting on the sofa, and so is Trystan. Sitting beside him is a woman who looks around our age. She has long, blond hair, and she's wearing jeans and a gray shirt. I have no clue who she is, but with how close she's sitting to him, she's probably his girlfriend.

Does she know what kind of man he might be?

Does she know his dark secrets like my mom knew of all of my dad's?

Another couple is seated in the room; an older man and woman—the mayor and his wife. My father and the mayor sometimes went hunting together, so his presence isn't too strange. What I don't understand, though, is why everyone is here.

"Ava, you remember Mayor Fellford." My mother gestures at the mayor while continuing to grip my arm.

I force a smile. "Yeah." I'm unsure what the fuck she wants me to say.

He's a heavier-set man with a thinning hairline, and he's donning a button-down shirt and slacks. He has a cup in his hand but sets it down and smiles at me as he reclines back in the sofa.

"Ava, it's so good to see you again," he says. "The last time I saw you, you were at that community event where you met Jason."

Thump, thump. Thump, thump.

"Mmhmm ..." My throat feels tight, and my vision is spotty.

"He's such a nice young man. A good hunter, too. Although, I don't think there's a lot of that over in Boise, is there?" He chuckles like he's said the funniest thing in the world.

I can feel my fingers curling inward again, and my fingernails split open the wounds on my palms.

"Jason's probably too busy to hunt nowadays," my mom tells him. "He works for an important law firm."

That's a stretch by a lot. While I was married to him, he worked as an assistant for a lawyer, but I heard that changed within the last month or so. I'm not exactly sure how, and I don't care—can't care. I don't want to know anything about him or his new life.

"I'm not surprised," the mayor replies, rolling up his sleeves. "He was always such an overachiever, even when he was younger. Everyone knew he'd achieve greatness, just like his father."

My fingernails burrow deeper. On paper, Jason's father seems like the perfect man. A hard worker who owns several businesses in this town, he's been married to the same woman for thirty years, donates to charities, goes to church, smiles and chats with everyone. However, early on in our relationship, when Jason hadn't revealed the corrosion under his flesh, he confided in me, particularly about his childhood, and gave me glimpses of who his father truly is.

"Does it make me a bad person if I hate him?" he asked me once. He was driving me home after hanging out at his parents' house.

As we were leaving, his father pulled him aside and said something that pissed Jason off. I had a feeling it was about me, since it was clear from the beginning that his parents weren't fans of him dating me because of the rumors of my drug use.

"I sometimes hate my father, too," I admitted.

"Your father's a great man," Ellis snapped so abruptly that I thought I'd misheard him. "God, you're ungrateful. Seriously, what the hell is wrong with you?"

His unexpected rage had thrown me off so much that I remained quiet the rest of the drive.

"Hey, I'm sorry," he apologized when we arrived at my house. "I shouldn't have snapped at you like that."

It was the first time anyone had ever apologized for getting angry at me, and it was part of why I fell for him. But he didn't mean the apology, not really. It was a manipulation tactic. That's what I learned later on—that he liked to play tug-o-war with my emotions. Hot and cold, light and dark, sugary sweet or blinding with rage—he could be any of those at any time and the abrupt shift happened so frequently and swiftly that it left my head spinning and made me doubt everything about my own thoughts. It was like walking around in a maze blind.

But I finally got out.

And yet, I still feel so lost.

And sometimes it feels like I didn't entirely escape. Like right now.

Instead of commenting on the mayor's remark about Jason, I wiggle my arm from my mother.

"I'm going downstairs to check on Clara," I say calmly.

She narrows her eyes at me like *how dare you be so rude as to just walk away from this conversation?*

But that's precisely what I do.

She follows me and catches up in the foyer where she grabs my arm again to stop me.

"What on earth is wrong with you?" she hisses. "That was so rude."

"No, it wasn't." I jerk my arm from her grip. "I said I was going to check on Clara, you know, my friend who was nice enough to come here with me. That's not rude. That's a nice thing to do."

She makes a judging sound in the back of her throat. "You and your friends. You always pick the worst ones."

"I'm going downstairs." I start to move, but she grabs my arm again.

"You're going to dinner with us tonight. Be ready in thirty minutes. We're going to that café on Third and Main, the one your father loved. If your friend is going, please drive yourself." She releases me and strides away before I can argue.

I won't go. I'm exhausted and hungover, and I have no desire to hang out with anyone in that living room. That's why I lock the door behind me after I enter my bedroom.

Clara is up, lounging in bed and messing around on her phone. She's changed into a pair of shorts and a tank top and has pulled her hair into a ponytail. She eyes the door after I lock it then looks back at me.

"What the hell is that about?" She nods at the locked door.

I kick off my shoes, cross my room, and flop down on my back, staring at the ceiling. "My mother wants us to go to dinner with my relatives and the mayor."

She sets her phone down. "Let me guess, you told her no, and she refused to accept that as an answer."

"You're catching onto her tricks."

"Yep." She briefly pauses. "I hate to say this, but your mother is basically one big walking toxic behavior."

I let out a shaky breath. "Yeah, she is."

It feels so damn good to speak about this aloud, to have someone who will listen to me. In ways, Clara reminds me of Clover, only she's not quite as wild. But maybe that's because we're older than when Clara and I were friends.

"Okay, enough about your mother." She leads me away from my thoughts as she sits at the bottom of the bed with her legs crisscrossed. "What did the sexy-as-hell detective want to talk to you about?"

A heaviness crashes on my chest at the reminder of everything Ellis told me. "He thinks my father's death may have been a murder."

Her lips part in shock. "*What?*"

I sit up and pull my knees to my chest. "He also believes that our old friend, who overdosed our junior year, may have been murdered, too. That she never really OD'd, but that someone made it look like she did."

Her eyes widen. "You had a friend that OD'd when you were in high school?"

That wasn't what I was expecting her to fixate on.

I nod, my chest constricting. "Yeah ... I was only friends with her for a few months, but she was my best friend back then."

"Oh, Aves, I wish you would've told me about this," she says. "You shouldn't have to just silently carry this stuff."

"I talk to my therapist about it." *Once.* "I don't like to talk about it because I don't like remembering her ... like that."

Her brows knit. "Wait ... Did you find her after she ...?"

I nod shakily, my throat crammed with words I can't seem to get out.

"I'm sorry that you had to go through that." She scoots up beside me and wraps her arm around my shoulders. "My dad's brother overdosed. I know it's not the same, but I understand how hard it is on someone to lose someone that way."

All I can do is nod.

Her words don't make me feel better. Well, they would have if Ellis hadn't just altered how I saw Clover's death. Now I question the memories I have.

What did I see that night?

I'm not so sure anymore.

I'm not sure about anything anymore.

That seems to be the walking story of my life.

I used to latch on to that—my brain's ability to cover up the dark spaces in it. But perhaps I should dig deeper. Because if I had, I may have wondered more about Clover's death instead of just falling into acceptance.

And if Clover was murdered, and I was the first to find her that night, answers to the truth may be buried in my fucked-up brain.

CHAPTER 23

ABOUT FIVE MINUTES LATER, MY MOTHER KNOCKS ON THE door. "Are you ready to go?" she asks, jiggling the doorknob.

Clara mouths, *"Dude, did you not tell her we're not going?"*

I shake my head and say, "Yeah, we're getting ready." Then I whisper to Clara, "This way is better."

Clara throws me a questioning look. "Why?"

I shrug, hugging my knees tighter against my chest. "Because this way she'll leave us alone for now."

She frowns but doesn't remark. She clearly disagrees with me and wants me to be honest with my mother, but this is all I can do right now.

Baby steps, my therapist is constantly telling me. This is my baby step toward standing up to her, and it's all I can handle now. Hopefully, one day, I'll be able to tell her how I feel, but it seems improbable at this instant.

"You know where the place is, right?" my mother asks.

"Yes," I tell her.

"Good."

The air falls into silence.

Thinking she left, I look at Clara while opening my mouth. "I—"

"Make sure you dress appropriately," my mother says curtly. "And by appropriate, I mean in nice clothes that don't make you look like a slut."

My heart stops beating for a second at her choice of word.

I've never heard her say *slut* before. What an odd coincidence she chose to use it the night after someone carved my skin with that precise word.

Or maybe it isn't a coincidence ...

Clara's eyes go huge and reflect her surprise.

Silence ticks by, and then a door slams from somewhere.

"She is so intense," Clara mumbles with a shake of her head. Then she picks up a pillow and hugs it against her chest. "And she treats you like a child."

"Sort of, I guess." I scoot to the edge of the bed and lower my feet to the floor.

"Not sort of." She slides to the edge of the bed, too. "She one hundred percent does. And what the hell was up with her saying slut? Because that doesn't seem like a word she ever says."

"That's the first time I've ever heard her use it." I stand up, nervousness webbing through me at what I'm about to do. "And she doesn't necessarily treat me like a child. She only does it when I'm not obeying. If I am, then I become nonexistent."

I begin pacing across the small space of room that the trundle bed doesn't cover up. I pick at my fingernails. I gnaw at them. And the entire time, Clara tracks my movements but never utters a word.

Can she can sense I'm on the verge of a breakdown, like an impending storm brewing in the sky, about to rain havoc down on the land?

But I want to know what my mother's secrets are. I want to know what she's hiding.

If she cut me up last night.

If she had something to do with my father's death.

"I need to do something," I finally say, stopping and facing her. "And it might make me a horrible person, but I need to do it."

She cracks her knuckles. "Okay … What is it? 'Cause you're kind of freaking me out right now."

"Sorry." I tuck a strand of hair behind my ear. "My mom has been acting weird ever since she told me my father died."

"Is that why she's been such a bitch?"

"No, that's normal for her. It's those brief glimpses of when she's upbeat that are weird." I lower my hands to my sides and open and flex my fingers. "Like when she told me my father was dead, she sounded perfectly okay. And I know people deal with grief differently, but I saw her after her mother died, and she was hysterical. Plus, she and my uncle and aunt were acting strange when I said I was going to talk to a detective about my father's death possibly being a murder."

A crease forms between her brows as she grips the edge of the mattress. "I'm a little confused what you're getting at, babe."

"I'm not even really sure what I'm getting at." Or maybe I

do, and I'm too afraid to utter the words aloud. "But I think I want to search my mom's room."

Her confusion increases. "Wait … Do you think your mom murdered your dad?"

Apparently, Clara isn't afraid to speak the words aloud.

"I don't know." I meant to lie, but the truth crashes against the air.

We stare at each other. I can't read her, but the fear that she thinks I'm a lunatic is gnawing at me.

"We should be careful." She stands up. "Like, if she comes back and catches us …" She visibly shudders. "I should play lookout, right?"

"You're … You're okay with doing this?" I ask, rubbing my hands up and down my arms as goosebumps sprout across my flesh. I'm unsure why they're there since I'm not cold. Perhaps it's from the worry of getting caught. Or maybe it's the terror of taking a step forward and seeking answers to questions I've been terrified to ask.

Deep down, I'm aware that if I do this—take this step—it may start to unravel this mess of a web I've created around myself.

She nods, pulling the elastic out of her hair so she can pile the strands into a messy bun on top of her head. "Yeah, let's do it. I'll keep a lookout through the window while you go look."

My nerves are thick as fog as we leave the room, the quietness bringing me no sense of comfort. When I reach the top of the stairs, I peek out the window at the top of the front door to ensure everyone's vehicles are gone. They are, so I turn to Clara.

"Stay low when you're looking out the window, okay? You can see right into the house when you pull into the driveway."

"Should I look out this window?"

Shaking my head, I signal her to follow me as I enter the living room. "Look out this one." I point to the large picture window. Darkness has consumed the land, except for a few porch lights. "You can see headlights coming up the road from a mile away, so it'll give us some time."

"Okay. Yeah." She anxiously uncrosses and crosses her arms.

"Hey, if you don't want to do this, we don't have to." I feel awful. "In fact, we can just go home if you want. This has to be scary."

"Aves, stop," she cuts me off, facing me. A light is on in the kitchen, but the lamp in the living room is turned off, making her face just a shadow. But her tone is firm. "I'm not going to lie to you, okay? This is fucking scary, but I get why we need to do it. I'm just hoping that you don't find anything."

"Me, too," I agree.

And I probably won't.

My mother can be ruthless, but mainly toward certain people. She was mostly submissive and agreeable with my father, but perhaps that's what pushed her over the edge.

"Thanks. I'll be right back. And yell if you see a car." I wait for her to nod then hurry to my parents' bedroom.

But the door locked.

"Shit," I curse in frustration.

"What's wrong?" Clara calls out.

"The door's locked."

"Hold on. Let me see." She walks up beside me and assesses the doorknob. "You have a hairpin?"

"My mom might. Hold on." I dash into the bathroom and ransack through the drawers until I find one. Then I return to Clara and hand it to her.

She crouches down, sticks it into the hole in the knob and, a second later, there's a soft click.

"Easy-peasy." She offers me a smile as she stands up, twists the knob, shoves open the door, and hands me back the hairpin.

"Thanks." I pocket the hairpin.

"No problem. I'll go back to keeping an eye out." She rushes back to the living room.

Facing the doorway, I suck in a deep breath and then enter. The lights are off, and I'm about to turn them on, but decide against it and instead take out my phone and use the light on it.

Everything appears to be in place—the bed is made, the floor is clear, and most of her clothes have been put away except for a folded-up pile of shirts at the foot of the bed. A few books are piled on the nightstand, along with an iPad.

"What am I even looking for in here?" I mumble as I scan the light around the room.

I notice the closet door is shut, so I open it. My dad's gun safe is tucked in the corner, and the door is cracked open, which means it's unlocked.

A memory tugs at my brain.

My mother is crying ...

Photos surround her ...

A red ribbon floats in front of my face ...

No, not a red ribbon ...

A red streak of light. It's mixed with blue—police lights.

A knock sounds on the door, and my mother glances at me. Tears stain her face, but rage flares in her eyes.

"Get out of here," she hisses as she jumps to her feet and rushes toward me with her hand raised, about to strike.

Someone knocks on the front door again, and she freezes, her eyes snapping toward the hallway behind me. Red and blue lights flash across her face, illuminating her pupils.

She lowers her hand. "Go to your room, Ava." She sounds eerily calm.

"Why? What's happening?" I wrap my arms around myself as the knocking on the front door grows louder.

"Go to your room," she repeats. "Don't make me ask again."

Swallowing down a shaky breath, I turn to go to my room, right as someone shouts—

I jerk from the memory as I bump into a box that's on the floor.

"Are you okay?" Clara calls out.

Am I? I'm not so sure. That memory ... I've dreamed about it before but never saw past the point of finding my mother until now. Why were the cops at our house that day? And why did I forget it ever happened? Because I was so young?

I exhale to steady my voice. "Yeah, I just ran into a box."

I carefully move around the box, open the safe door the rest of the way, and shine the light inside. My dad's guns, crossbow and arrows, and a series of knives are lined up. My fingers drift to my back across the wound hidden underneath my shirt. Could one of these have been used to slice my flesh open? Is that why the safe is open? Because my mother forgot to lock it back up after she was finished?

The way she said "slut" was such a red flag, but that still leaves me questioning how the hell my drinks were drugged. It seems ludicrous that my mother snuck into the bar to do it. Plus, what was the point?

But if she didn't do it, who did? The person who's sending me these voicemails? Camilla? And what about that note I found in my car today?

Maybe everything is connected.

"How the hell am I going to figure this out?" I mumble as I stare at the knives.

That's when I notice a smudge on one of the blades. I lean forward to get a closer look. The spot is dark and resembles dried blood, but I'm not positive that's what it is.

I take a photo of it and then move on from the safe, peering around at the shelves lining the small space. Most are holding stacks of clothes, and clothes are also hanging up. A few boxes line the top shelf, so I set my phone down with the light pointing upward, then stand on my tiptoes and grab one.

Inside are stacks of papers, a few envelopes, and a few books … No, not books. They appear to be journals.

I skim-read through a few pages.

I DON'T WANT TO FEEL THIS WAY ANYMORE. EVERYTHING ALWAYS feels so heavy with anger, and I worry I might burst and do something I'll regret.

. . .

I TURN TO ANOTHER PAGE.

I HATE HIM. I DO. AND I LOATHE HER, AS WELL. I KNOW I shouldn't. That's not how I was raised to be. But I can't stop myself from wanting to ruin them.

IS THIS MY MOTHER'S JOURNAL? IS SHE TALKING ABOUT MY father and me?

My heart pounds as I set the journal down and then rummage through the box more. Inside one of the envelopes is a stack of photos of various parts of the woods. They look like scenic photos, but words are written on the back.

LOW TRAFFIC, BUT THE TREES ARE THIN.

Saw campers in the area.

Very thick with trees. Low traffic area. Very well hidden. L.T. said the trail that leads to the site isn't on any maps. The top spot so far.

I'M UNFAMILIAR WITH MY FATHER'S WRITING, BUT THIS HAS TO be his. Wanting to check, I dig through the stack of papers in the box, which are primarily financial statements. His signature is on a few, along with dates and addresses. The handwriting on those and the photos appear to be a match. But I still have no clue what the photos mean or who *L.T.* is.

I reread the words on the back of the photos. That's when

it clicks. The handwriting on these matches the note left in my car.

What the shit is going on?

I stare at the photos for a while then start putting everything the way I found them. I snap a few pictures with my phone before I do so I can look at them later.

I'm about to head back out of the room when I spot a shiny, silver object sticking out from underneath one of the boxes.

My mother is sitting in front of some photos and is holding something shiny and silver in her hand. Red and blue lights flash everywhere, and her attention darts to me ...

"Look at what I found," Clover says as she bends down and scoops up something small and silver off the parking lot at school. We're heading inside late after spending way too much time eating lunch.

I step up beside her. "What is it?"

She holds it up. "A key."

"Um ... cool?" I'm so perplexed. "Are you planning on turning it into the lost and found?"

She laughs as she pockets the key. "Nah, I'm going to keep it."

"Why?"

"Because it's the kind of key that goes to a chest or safe or something, which means it's probably the key to someone's secrets." She grins. "Which means I now hold their secret in my pocket." She loops her arm through mine. "Want to know one of my secrets, Daisy friend?"

I nod. I love hearing her secrets.

"I'm dating someone," she whispers scandalously.

"Really? Who?"

"I can't tell you."

"Why not?"

"Because it has to stay a secret for now, but maybe I'll tell you one day."

For a horrible moment, I think she's dating Ellis.

She must read my expression because she says, "Oh, get that look off your face. It's not Ellis." She tows me forward with her. "I'd never go there, not only because we're not into each other, but because he's so in love with you."

Love? I shake my head. "No way."

*"Yes way." She winks at me as we head into the school ...*As the memory fades, on pure instinct, I scoop up the key and pocket it. I'm not sure what it goes to, but it feels like I have one of my mother's secrets in my pocket.

Now I just need to figure out what it is.

Clara turns away from the window as I enter the living room.

"Did you find anything?" she asks.

"I'm not sure," I answer truthfully, thinking about how the photos and the note tucked away in my bag resembles the handwriting on it. "But something odd is definitely going on."

CHAPTER 24

Clara and I grab a bite to eat before returning to my room. We're both pretty exhausted due to the lingering hangovers, so we decide to get some sleep.

I wake up the following day, feeling oddly blank inside after a seemingly dreamless sleep. Plus, I can't remember my mother coming and banging on my door when she returned home from the dinner. Was I simply too tired and slept through it? Or did she not knock? The latter seems implausible.

My arm is throbbing, too, and the bruise on it has worsened overnight.

Clara is asleep when I sit up, massaging my aching shoulder. I rake my fingers through my hair as I struggle to grasp my bearings. Exhaustion weighs down on me, but I'm unsure if it's from remnants of a long-ass hangover or something else. Maybe depression?

"Fuck, I hate this place," I mutter as I scoot out of bed.

The air is soundless as I wander into the bathroom, and it's more unsettling than anything else.

Where the hell is my mother?

When I return to my room, I rummage around in my bag for some clothes and stumble across the note left on my car seat. I double-check if the handwriting matches.

It's close, for sure, but I can't be positive it's the same. Besides, it'd make zero sense for it to be my father's. No, someone had to have forged his handwriting.

"You okay over there?" She's lying on her back with her arm draped over her forehead. "Because you're sighing a lot."

"I'm fine. I'm just tired of being here. Part of me wants to leave, but I think I need to stay here and help Ellis figure some stuff out." I waver, bending the corner of the note. "Maybe you should go back, though. You can take my car."

She flips over onto her stomach, pushing up onto her elbows, and blinks her eyes open. "Then how will you get home?"

"I can rent a car. There's also an airport about an hour away."

"That sounds like money you don't have." Yawning, she sits up. "Maybe we can find someplace else to stay."

"That sounds expensive." I stuff the note bag. "And since it's tourist season, the hotels are booked up."

She pulls her hair tie out of her hair. "I might be able to borrow some cash from my mother so we can book a rental house for a few weeks."

I promptly shake my head. "No way am I letting you do that."

"You're not letting me do anything." She rises to her feet

and pulls her hair into a ponytail. "I don't want to stay here as much as you do. Plus, my mom owes me."

I can't tell if she's lying or not. "Why?"

She shrugs. "Don't worry about that. I'll let you know what I can pull off. I have to pee, though." With that, she walks out of the room.

And once again, I feel like the world's worst friend.

But I become distracted when I receive a call from Ellis.

"Hey," I answer, crossing my fingers that he has some news about the diary.

"You sound tired," he notes. "Did you get enough sleep last night?"

"I'm fine. I'm just suffering from tired-of-my-mom syndrome." I balance the phone between my ear and shoulder as I dig around in my bag for some clothes.

"I'm sure I added to your stress after what I told you yesterday," he says apologetically.

"No, it's fine." A total lie since I kicked the shit out of the man's car right after he told me his theory about Clover being murdered.

He sighs, like he's aware I'm full of shit. "Well, I might have some good news. Apparently, Clover's mom doesn't live in town anymore, but the man who owns the trailer they used to live in told me that she left a lot of her belongings behind, and we can go look through them."

"Clover's mom just left her stuff behind?" I question. "That seems odd."

"It does," he agrees. "But I'm putting a pin in that right now because I really want to look through the stuff."

I frown. "Is Jerry still the owner?"

"Yeah, but he's being cooperative."

"That seems weird to me, considering how he used to be."

"I know. But like I said, right now, my main focus is looking through her stuff. And I know I said I wanted to go up to the cliff today, but I was wondering if you'd be okay with us going to Jerry's first. And if it takes too long, we can go to the cliff tomorrow."

I stand up with my clothes in my hand. "You want me to go with you to look through Clover's old belongings?"

"I do. I'm not working on this as an official case, so I'm not breaking protocol. And you were closer to Clover than anyone I know, so I think you should be there."

Did I know her better than anyone? Because sometimes it doesn't feel that way. Sometimes it felt like I only knew the parts of her she wanted me to see.

Still … I want to try to help her like I didn't while she was alive.

"All right, yeah, I'll go." I sound more confident in my ability to handle this than I might be.

* * *

I agree to meet Ellis at Jerry's place in about an hour.

After getting dressed in a tank top, jean shorts, and sandals, I head upstairs while Clara remains downstairs, making coffee with the new machine she picked up before we came here. She's going with me to meet Ellis. If Ellis doesn't want her there, I'll give her my car keys and she can drive around town for a bit, but leaving her here isn't an option.

The kitchen is empty when I walk in. Assuming my mother is still asleep, I tiptoe around while searching for something to eat.

The pantry and fridge are running low on food, so I make some toast. If we're still hungry later, we can get lunch later.

The entire time I'm doing this, the house remains quiet. Even when I drop a plate on the floor, my mother doesn't make a grand appearance.

Is she not here?

As I wait for the toast to be done, I scroll through my messages to see if I have any from my mother, but I don't. Setting my phone down on the counter, I approach the window and peer outside at the driveway. My confusion doubles at the sight of the empty driveway. Did she even come home last night?

Perplexed, I wander over to her bedroom door and, with a breath, gently check the knob. It's locked.

Rubbing my sore arm, I return to the living room again, and search for signs that she's been home. The cups that were on the coffee table last night are gone, so she has been home. But why didn't she bother me? Has she finally given up?

My thoughts laugh at me. *Yeah, right, Ava, that'll never happen.*

Shaking my head, I go back into the kitchen where Clara is waiting for me with two steel mugs of coffee in her hands. I quickly butter the toast and exchange two pieces for a cup of coffee. Then we embark outside.

I decide to take Bailey with me, and since he's a bit muddy, I run in and grab a towel to spread across the back seat.

Then we hit the road.

The sky is cloudy today, the air is nipping, and the grass is dewy as if it rained last night. The leaves that cover the tree branches are dripping with remnants of that, and the grass fields are greener than usual.

"I know you don't like this place," Clara tells me as she balances a piece of toast on her leg so she can roll down the window, "but the air smells so good." She breathes in the breeze.

I don't remark, my thoughts centered on what I'm about to do.

What will we find in Clover's stuff? Something useful? Will I be able to handle it?

"You're nervous about this," Clara says as she takes a bite of toast.

I thrum my fingers on top of the steering wheel. "I have issues dealing with my past."

"That's understandable." She dithers, picking at the crust on her toast. "This girl that you were friends with—Clover, was that her name?" she asks, and I nod. "Do you know if ...? Did you know she was into drugs while you were friends?" She pauses then quickly adds, "You don't have to answer if you don't want to."

Do I want to?

No really.

But Clara is here with me, and that means something to me. "Not hard drugs. We used to smoke weed a lot and get drunk, but that was pretty much the extent of it until ...￼" Until she overdosed. Then I learned Clover had a whole other side to her.

But didn't I suspect that after that day I saw her leaving Ben's car?

Why didn't I say something about it?

Because I promised Clover, which meant everything to me then.

"It's okay. We don't have to talk about it if you don't want to." She stuffs a broken-off piece of toast into her mouth. "Have you thought about calling your therapist, though? Just to talk about it a bit."

"I might. She's out of town until Monday, though." I could call her, and say it's an emergency, but is it one yet?

Silence settles between us for the next ten minutes of the drive, but I get the impression Clara wants to say more.

Finally, I can't take it anymore and crank down the music. "What?"

She wipes her hands off on a napkin. "What, what?"

I give her a look. "I can tell you want to say something."

She balls the napkin up as she lets out a breath. "Fine, but first, I didn't mean to look. I was standing by it when it flashed and accidentally saw it."

My brows pull together. "Saw what?"

"That call you missed from Jason." She picks up the mug of coffee. "I … I didn't realize you were still talking to him."

I nearly run off the road, the tires scuffing against the gravel. "*What?*"

"Jesus, Aves." Clover grips the mug. "Do you need me to drive?"

"No." I grip the wheel so tightly that my knuckles turn white. "I'm not talking to Jason. And he hasn't called me in months."

"Oh." She frowns. "Well, maybe he called because he heard about your dad."

"Maybe." I want to pick up my phone and look at it, but not while I'm driving. "Did he leave a message?"

She shakes her head. "I don't think so."

Great. Why did he call? Just because he heard about my father? That doesn't seem like something Jason would do. Did my mother fucking call him?

I proceed to strangle the steering wheel as I drive, eventually making a right turn onto the dirt driveway that leads to Jerry's house. The moment I see the property, the air gets knocked out of me.

The scene is like a frozen memory slowly thawing; from Jerry's single-story house to the bushes out front, to the trailer home where Clover lived. Even the lawn chairs are still outside, the ones she and I used to sit in while we smoked and talked. The only difference now is that Ellis's SUV is parked in the driveway.

I don't know if I can handle this.

I may have bailed out and peeled out of the driveway, but Ellis hops out of his car and waves at me. He has a cup of coffee in each hand, and he's wearing dark jeans and a T-shirt, along with Converse sneakers that remind me of the ones he used to wear when we were younger.

"You're smiling," Clara remarks with amusement.

"What?" I throw her a dirty look. "I am not."

Pressing back a grin, she lifts her mug of coffee toward her lips. "My bad." She takes a swallow of the coffee.

Shaking my head, I shove the door open and climb out. Bailey barks as I bump the door shut, and I tell him, "I'll be back in a few."

Then I start toward Ellis, who's already walking toward me, his gaze roving over to the side where Clara is sitting.

A crease forms between his brows. "You brought your friend with you?"

"Sorry," I apologize as I reach him. "I didn't want to leave her at the house with my mom. She'll stay in the car, if that's okay? And if not, I can have her drive around town for a bit. Or she can take my dog for a walk."

"She doesn't have to leave," he assures me as he eyes the car. "You have a dog?"

"Yeah." I slip my hand into the back pockets of my shorts. "His name is … Bailey, after … well, you know."

He meets my gaze, his expression softening. "That's nice, Aves."

We start to get lost in memories of the past, but then the door to Jerry's house swings open, and he steps out.

"Are you sure you're ready to deal with this?" Ellis asks me as Jerry approaches us with a lit cigarette in his hand.

"No, but I'm going to." My straightforward words surprise us both.

He hands me one of the cups of coffee. "It'll help you get through this."

I've already had coffee, but this smells like … "Is this a vanilla latte?"

He nods, then takes a sip of his.

I inhale the top of the cup. "Where the heck did you get this?"

"I have my ways." When I give him a confused look, he chuckles. "I got it from the café in my hotel. It has decent coffee. Not great, but decent."

"Well, thanks," I tell him then take a sip.

Jerry reaches us then. He looks over a decade older, his skin leathery and his face covered in wrinkles. His shirt has a stain on it, his hair has thinned, and he reeks of beer and cigarettes.

"Hey," he greets Ellis then looks at me. A slow smile curls at his lips. "And who is this lovely thing?"

Some things never fucking change.

I open my mouth to say … well, I'm not sure, but all that comes out is, "I'm Ava."

"She's my partner," Ellis adds, sneaking me a look.

What the hell? Partner?

Jerry's demeanor changes, the smile fading from his lips. "Oh, right. Nice to meet you, Ava." He takes a drag from his cigarette then directs his attention back to Ellis. "So, like I said on the phone, I have somewhere to be in about an hour, but you can go ahead and look around in the trailer until then. I've left it basically the same as when Hazel left."

Hazel is Clover's mother, and again, I wonder why Jerry kept all of their stuff.

"When did she leave?" I find myself asking.

Jerry calculates this for a second as he ashes his cigarette. "I think about six months ago, if I'm remembering right. She just took off one night, and I never saw her again. It fucked me over financially, too, since she didn't leave rent money."

"And yet you kept all her stuff?" I say, glancing at the trailer down the road.

Ellis glances at me with curiosity, and I worry I'm crossing a line by talking so much.

"What else am I supposed to do with it?" Jerry replies with

a tick in his jaw. He takes another inhale from his cigarette then smoke circles his face. "Throw it away? Besides, I'm planning on seeing if anything valuable is in there. I just haven't gotten around to it because I've been working double shifts to compensate for losing rent money." He flicks his cigarette onto the dirt and stomps it with his boot. "I need to go inside and take care of some stuff, but the door to the trailer is unlocked, so feel free to look around. Just don't damage my trailer."

What does he think we're going to do? Punch holes in the wall or something?

"We won't," Ellis assures him with a formal smile. "I'll let you know when we're done. And thanks for letting us look around."

"No problem," Jerry mumbles. He scowls at me before walking back toward his house.

He casts another glance at me right before he walks in.

"I forgot how annoying he is," I mumble.

"He's hiding something," Ellis says as we walk toward the trailer.

I take a drink of my latte. "How do you know?"

He checks the time on his watch. "Because of how twitchy he's being. And he was overly agreeable when I asked him if I could come here. I think he was trying not to look suspicious, but he came off the opposite." He slides me a glance. "You surprised the hell out of me, though?"

I point at myself. "I did?"

He nods. "You were pretty blunt back there. You didn't use to be like that."

"I'm not normally like that. Jerry just gets under my skin.

The stuff he used to say to Clover and me..." I shudder. "It was gross."

"That's another reason why I don't trust him," Ellis says as we reach the steps that lead up to the front door of the trailer. "He's had a thing for underage girls in the past. And with how many have disappeared around here ..." He steps onto the stairs, and they wobble underneath his weight.

"Wait—do you think Jerry had something to do with that?" Something else suddenly dawns on me. "Do you think he had something to do with Clover's death?"

"I'm not sure." He reaches for the handle of the screen door. "But let's go see if we can figure it out." He pulls the creaking door open as he remarks, "Partner."

"Yeah, what was that about?" I ask as I follow him inside.

The space is dark due to blankets covering every window, and the air reeks of dust and what I think is rotting food.

"I didn't like how he was looking at you. So, since he's been pretty intimidated by the fact that I'm a detective, I thought I'd make sure he was scared of you, too." He tries to flip on the light, but the power's been turned off.

My chest squeezes, but in a different way than it normally does. "You're kind of the same."

The dim light flowing through the open front door casts across his curious expression. "From when I was a teenager?"

I nod. "You were nice then, and you're nice now."

"Aw ... the nice thing again. You used to say that to me all the time," he says with an amused grin.

"Oh, shut up." I playfully shove him.

He stumbles an inch and chuckles.

Shaking my head, I amble further into the house and yank one of the blankets off of a window.

Dust scatters everywhere, and I start hacking. "Shit, I didn't think that through very well."

I step back by Ellis, waving my hand in front of my face. Dust is billowing in the air, but so is sunlight now.

"Jesus, it smells in here," Ellis mumbles as he draws his shirt over his nose.

"I think it might be some old food."

He treads across the shaggy carpet of the living and into the kitchen, where he opens up the stained door of the fridge. "God, yep, there's some old milk and what might have been leftover spaghetti at one point." He closes the door and starts opening the cupboards and doors that line the narrow kitchen.

I roam around, observing the outdated television and the worn flower sofa that always reminded me of the one my parents had when I was a kid.

I trace my fingers along the dusty fabric, and on one of the cushions with a stain that looks like blue punch or something.

"Get your ass up and go to your room!" my dad shouts at me. "You're spilling your drink all over the goddamn sofa!"

"Aves." Ellis's voice pulls me back.

"Hmm?" I turn to him.

A look of concern flashes across his face. "Are you okay?"

"Yeah, it's just weird being back in here, especially since everything looks the same."

"I know." He reclines back against the Formica counter with his arms crossed. "I just can't figure out why she didn't take any of her stuff."

"Unless she didn't leave voluntarily, or she was running from something," I absentmindedly say, thinking about the handful of times I considered running away from my parent's house and also from Jason. I would envision taking off in the middle of the night, which meant packing light.

Ellis pushes away from the counter, crosses the room, and stops in front of me. "You're not okay. I can tell."

He probably can. He's a detective after all and is trained to read when people are lying.

I rotate the cup of coffee in my hand. "Okay, maybe I'm not. But I want to do this."

He studies me intently. "If you want to leave at any time, it's perfectly okay."

"I know."

He gives a bob of his head then says, "Let's go look in Clover's room so we can get out of here. The smell is giving me a headache."

"Me, too." And so are the memories.

As we start down the narrow hallway, we carefully pull down the blankets covering the windows. Dust is littering the air when we arrive at Clover's room, and my eyes are watering.

Seeing her unmade bed, the chair in the corner where I used to sit, the photos on the paneled walls, and the clothes and shoes spilling out of the closet cause my eyes to water for another reason.

Shit, I think I'm about to cry. And if Ellis sees, he'll undoubtedly make me step outside.

Discreetly sucking them back, I pull myself together and start searching through her stuff.

"Do you remember exactly where she kept it?" he asks as he opens the top drawer to her dresser.

I shake my head. "I only saw her take it out once, and I was distracted by the photos on the wall, but ..." I face the closet. "It kind of seemed like she got it from out of there."

He steps up beside me with his arms crossed. "It's a mess in there."

I sweep a strand of my hair out of my eyes. "I know. But she was always messy."

"True. She used to throw her garbage on my floor, even when she was sitting close to the trash bin."

A smile touches my lips. "I think the most disgusting thing she ever did was stick a half-eaten sandwich underneath my car seat. It took me a week to figure out where the smell was coming from."

He starts moving her clothes out of the way. "I have that topped. She once left a condom in the back of my car, and it was used." He pauses then adds, "And it wasn't from me. Clover and I never hooked up. You know that, right?"

I eye him over. "Not even like one time when you guys were drunk?"

He shakes his head as he drags a box off the top shelf of the closet. "Clover was like a sister to me. I never would've gone there with her."

"Oh." Why am I so relieved? I'm not seventeen years old anymore. None of this is relevant. Then again, I'm basically back in the same life I was in then, minus the drug use, which is depressing.

"Sorry I said that. It's just that a few weeks before she died, she mentioned she was seeing someone, but she wouldn't tell me who it was. And a tiny part of me sort of thought it was you, and that's why she wouldn't tell me." I cringe as I realize what I said.

A weird look crosses Ellis's face. "I …" he starts to say when the bottom of the box breaks open and all the items in it scatter across the floor. "Shit." He crouches down to start picking everything up.

I bend down to help him but pause, my focus drifting to the closest floor.

I'm staring at the photos on Clover's wall …

I can see Clover out of the corner of my eye …

She's rummaging around on the shelves …

No … She's crouched down and digging around on the floor …

I blink from the faded memory then crawl over to the closet.

"Aves?" Ellis asks worriedly, probably because I'm crawling across a dirty-ass floor like a deranged creature.

"Just a second." I shove clothes out of the way and feel around on the carpet … around the edges …

Jackpot.

I peel the corner of the carpet back and, sure enough, a notebook with daisies is tucked underneath it. It's such a Clover-like thing to do—hide her secrets in an odd place, like underneath the carpet.

"You found it?" Ellis asks as I stand up, clutching the diary.

I nod, smoothing my hand over the hard, dusty cover. "I suddenly remembered the day she brought me here and wrote in it. I didn't really see her take it out, but I remembered her digging around on the floor. It seemed like something she'd do."

He moves up in front of me. "She did have really good hiding spaces for our drugs and alcohol, didn't she?"

"She really did." I smash my lips together, considering something. "Do you ever wonder what she had in that wallet she always carried around with her? The one with the daisies on it?"

He nods. "I do now, but not at the time. And I only do now because it wasn't with her that night."

Silence consumes the air, and I question what to do next. Will he take the diary and read it himself? Or does he want me to look through it with him?

He places his hand on top of the diary, lightly touching it, before withdrawing. Does it hurt him, too, whenever he thinks about her?

"Should we read it now?" I dare ask, part of me desperate to while the other part wants to run away.

"I'd rather go somewhere we can go through it page by page," he informs me. "Let me look around a bit more, take some photos, and then we can head back to my hotel room and look through it. The place is by the park, and some restaurants are there, so your friend—her name's Clara, right?" he asks, and I nod. "She can get something to eat and maybe take Bailey for a walk?"

"Okay, yeah, that sounds good."

"Good. Let me take some photos of Clover's room, and then I'll move on to her mother's." He fishes his phone out of his pocket. "And I'd like to look into where she may have gone because not only is it odd that she just took off, but I'd like to talk to her about Clover." He raises his phone and begins taking pictures.

I roam around so he doesn't get me in the photos. Every spot takes me down memory lane, from the necklace on top of Clover's dresser to the shoe collection she was so fond of.

"I get them at secondhand stores," she told me once. "You can get some super cheap but awesome stuff there."

I wondered where she got her money, since her and her mother were so poor. But I never thought to ask. Now I wish I had.

I wish I learned more about her. I could've been more helpful now.

By the time I turn away from her shoe collection, Ellis has left the room. Instead of following him, I sit down on the edge of Clover's bed and, with trembling fingers, open up her diary. The first page was dated a few years before I met her, during the summer.

Dear diary,

Ha, how cliché is this starting, which is so not like me. Don't worry, I'll get better. I promise.

I started writing this because I need to vent, and I don't have another way to do that. My mom is high or drunk all the time, I haven't seen my deadbeat dad in years, and all of my friends think I'm this lighthearted, loves-life kind of girl. I don't feel light at all, though. I feel dark all the time, like I'm trapped in a basement and can't get out. Not even my best friend, Zoey, knows this about me, but her life is good. Her parents are amazing, and her brother's nice, and I hate it. I know it makes me such a bad person. I mean, how can I hate Zoey's life when it's so perfect? But I do because I'm jealous.

I hate that about myself.

I hate myself sometimes, too.

But anyway, that's my venting for today. Sorry for being so depressing.

XOXO (again, another cliché I'll work on),

Clover

MY EYES ARE BURNING AS I FINISH READING THE FIRST PAGE.

She was so worn down with sadness, even back then. I wish I could've known her. I wish I could've told her she wasn't alone. But I could barely tell her that later on.

I flip toward the back to see if things improved for her. I note that, in the middle, some of the pages have been torn out, which seems odd. There also appears to be some missing from the very back. Did Clover do this?

Chewing on my bottom lip, I decide to read the final entry, at least the remaining one.

I'M SKIPPING THE INTRODUCTIONS TODAY AND GETTING STRAIGHT to the point, because I'm fucking terrified that if I don't, shit will get really bad, really quick.

But anyway, you remember that thing I told you I was doing (refer to page 28), well, anyway, I think I might be on to something, and I'm pretty sure that this something means that you-know-who's death wasn't an accident. I haven't told Ellis yet, because I don't want to get his hopes up until I'm certain who did it to her. I'm getting nervous, though, that they're catching on to me with how much time I spend asking them questions while we're hanging out.

But that might be paranoia. Plus, all the drugs I'm taking are starting to fuck with my head to the point where I've been losing my grasp on reality. Like the other day when I was with Ava, who BTW is turning out to be a fantastic friend who I can sometimes share my darkness with. But she doesn't know the truth, and I can't tell her even if I want to.

But the want is becoming less the more I numb my pain. I wonder if this is how she felt right before the lights turned out.

At least I have him, though. He may be all darkness inside, but his darkness matches mine. He's my darkness in this blinding light trying to swallow me all the time. He knows everything.

Until next time,

Clover.

MY HEART IS HAMMERING IN MY CHEST AS I FLIP TO PAGE 28.

"Fuck." It's one of the pages that's been torn out.

But while the page may be missing, I may have an idea of what Clover was doing right before she died.

My initial instinct is to seal my lips shut and keep it to myself.

Shut your fucking mouth ...

Shut the fuck up, or I'll slit your throat ...

"*You* shut the fuck up," I mutter to myself. Then I rush out of the room and find Ellis in the living room with his phone in hand.

"I think I know what Clover was doing right before she died," I sputter before I can chicken out. "I think she believed Zoey was murdered, and she was looking into it. Like she was actually spending time with the people she thought killed her.

And it said something about this guy she was dating … I don't know who he is, but one time I saw her getting out of the car with Ben, and she made me promise not to tell you …" I trail off when I note how quiet Ellis is, his face visibly pale. "I'm sorry for piling all of this on you, but I think it might be important."

"I …" He blinks at me. "Clover thought Zoey didn't die by accident?" he asks slowly, and I nod. "I …" He swiftly shakes his head. "I have to go." He strides for the door.

I rush after him. "What? Where?"

He yanks open the door. "I just got a call. A body was found near the woods. I need to be there."

I follow him down the front porch steps and nearly eat shit as I trip over my feet. He catches me, though, and then places a hand on my waist to steady me. The second I get my balance, I step back, shaking for various reasons.

"What part of the woods?" I sputter.

Branches claw at my flesh …

"Help me!" Camilla shouts.

The girl with blood-soaked hair stares blankly at me, the light in her hazel eyes going out—

"The ones near the park." He jogs down the driveway, only slowing down when he reaches his SUV. He yanks the door open but doesn't climb in. Instead, he grabs something from inside and hands it to me.

A keycard.

"Can you wait for me in my hotel room?" he asks. "It's room 309 at the Stars Meadow Inn. I don't know how long I'll be, so I understand if you can't, but I …" He wavers, and fear flashes across his features. "I'd feel safer if you were there."

What is he keeping from me? Because I can tell something has him spooked. Is it that they found a body near the woods? Why would this make him want me to wait at his hotel room?

I clutch the card in my hand. "I can go there. I'd rather not be at my house anyway."

A drop of relief washes over him, but then it dwindles as his phone buzzes.

"I have to go." He jumps into the driver's seat, and then his attention travels toward Jerry's house. I track his gaze to a window and catch the briefest glimpse of Jerry peeking out before he steps away and lets the curtain fall shut.

The guy is suspicious, but of being a creeper or something else?

"I want to make sure you're gone before I back out," Ellis tells me, meaning *hurry and go so I can.*

Still clutching the diary, I jog toward my car and hop in. Bailey is bouncing around wildly in the back seat, and Clara has her phone out, but her attention is fixed on me.

"Is everything okay?" she asks, her gaze lowering to the diary. "Oh, you found it."

"Yeah, we did." I reluctantly set the diary down and back out onto the road. Then I drive away, heading toward the central part of town where the inn is located.

"Where are we going?" Clara asks. "And why are you being so quiet? Because I'm getting a vibe."

I need to tell her about the body that was found, but I worry I'll scare her. Plus, I'm still processing what Ellis told me.

They found a body in the woods?

Was it from a long time ago? Back when the woods tried to eat me alive?

Or is it from now?

Is it starting again?

I need to fucking know.

I change directions, making a sharp turn down a side road and driving toward the park.

"I have to tell you something," I say as I drive faster than I should. "And it's bad."

She grips the handle above the door. "What?"

I shift gears. "Ellis just got a call, and a… body was found near the woods by the park."

Her wide eyes slide to me. "*What?*"

I shift gears again. "And I … I need to see who it is."

She gapes at me in horror. "You want to go look at a dead body? Because you know you can't just walk up to a crime scene."

"I know. But there will be bystanders gawking." Just like when Clover died.

I can remember so many eyes on her … on me …

I had dirt all over my hands …

Why did I have dirt all over my hands?

I speed up, my pulse pounding.

"Ava, you're scaring the shit out of me," Clara whispers. "You're driving so fast."

"Sorry." I slow down a bit.

"Thanks," she mumbles.

I expect her to beg me not to go to the park, but she doesn't.

"Was this person … murdered?" she asks.

"I'm not sure. Ellis couldn't give me any details."

She nods, letting out a slow breath.

We remain silent for the next few minutes as I steer toward the park's foothills. I keep thinking about Clover and wondering if she thought Ben killed Zoey. She was hanging out with him and wanted to keep it a secret from Ellis. And Ellis blamed Ben for Zoey's overdose.

Fuck! Clover really could've been murdered.

Camilla cries for help ...

The girl in the distance is bleeding red. So much blood ... everywhere ...

My distorted memories continue to haunt me until we're near the park. Red and blue flashing lights illuminate the air, and like I expected, bystanders have swarmed the place. I have to park a ways away due to the line of cars and the area being taped off.

I unbuckle my seat belt and move to climb out.

"Wait ..." Clara says, unbuckling her seat belt. "I'll go with you."

I pause. "Are you sure?"

"No, but I'm doing it anyway." She shoves her door open.

I leave the windows halfway down for Bailey, then I get out and lock the car. We start the short hike down the road and toward the group of people crowding the entrance. So many people; some I recognize, and some I don't.

Clara stays behind me as I push through the mob and toward the front where I can see into the park. Officers are wandering around, but I can't see anything else ...

Until I spot the body bag being hauled out of the trees.

She rolls over onto her side and stares at me blankly, blood trickling from her lips.

"Help me," she gurgles. "Please."

She reaches for me, but her arm falls limply between us. Her skin looks odd, as pale as the snow except for a blooming bruise on her upper arm—

"I heard she overdosed," a woman says from the crowd.

"How would you know that?" another woman asks. "They haven't told the public any information yet. It's so annoying. We deserve to know."

"No one owes you anything, Anne," a man from the crowd says. "Jesus, get a life."

"I have a life," Anne snaps. "And I was just asking because I want to know if I should be worried that a killer is on the loose."

"It's not a murder. It's an overdose. And I know this because Arnold was the one who found the body," the first woman says. "He said there were bruises all over her upper arms. And the poor girl must have had a cutting problem because she had cut the word"—she lowers her voice—"*whore* into her arm with a knife."

They keep prattling on, but my mind tunes out as my gaze travels to the bruise on my upper arm. Then my fingers travel to my lower back where the word *slut* is carved.

She lies in the snow, blood trickling from her nose and lips, her bruised arm stretched toward me, the word liar *bleeding out from the wound on her wrist.*

"Oh, my hell." I spin around and hurry back toward my car, leaving Clara in the crowd as I stumble until I can't move anymore.

Then I collapse to my knees and puke out the coffee and toast I ate this morning.

Fuck. Fuck. Fuck!

Reality violently presses down on me.

Whoever was in those woods that day with me might have killed whoever they just found, and the person was at the bar the night I got drunk.

My thoughts drift to Trystan. When I was younger, I was almost convinced he was in the woods that day. But I was never certain. Plus, it was more than one person.

Why is this starting up again? And why did it start up right after my father died?

"You shouldn't have come back here," someone says from behind me.

I gradually rotate around and then push to my feet.

Camilla is standing there. She has prominent dark circles underneath her bloodshot eyes, and her tank top has a few holes in the fabric.

I wipe my mouth with the back of my hand. "Why would you say that?"

"Because it's true," she replies, crossing her arms. "This is all starting because you came back, and you're talking to him."

I'm taken aback. "To whom?"

"To the cop." She lifts her shirt.

Across her stomach is an old scar in the shape of four letters.

Vain.

"You're marked now, too, aren't you?" She smirks as she lowers her shirt. "They finally got you."

How does she know that unless … "What—did you cut me?" I ask, my sandals scuffing the dirt as I inch toward her.

She shuffles back. "Why would I do that?"

My fingers curl into fists as that rage I felt at the gas station pounds through me.

Her gaze falls to my balled fist. Her pupils are so massive that I'm sure she's high, so is this really her or the drugs talking?

"I'd be careful if I were you," she says. "Coming unhinged around here usually leads to death. Just ask your father. Oh, wait, you can't."

My blood runs ice-cold. "What the fuck do you know about that?" Another thought slams against me. "It was you, wasn't it? You're the one who put that note and photo in my car.

Her lips curl as her mouth opens. "I don't know what the hell you're talking about. You're the one who put one in my—"

"Ava!" My mother's voice shatters through the air more piercingly than the sirens.

My gaze snaps to the right, and what I see makes me wish I could go back to being fifteen again, back to when I was invisible, back before the woods, back to when I was just a lonely, depressed, bored girl.

Because not only is my mother walking down the road toward me, but Jason is beside her.

I blink, thinking I'm hallucinating, but I'm not. He's really here.

He's dressed in a T-shirt and jeans, and his brown hair blows in the wind. On the outside, he looks like a regular guy.

But he's not at all.

And why the hell is he here?

I could ask, but I don't want to be near him.

"No." I step back. "No, no, no." I glance back toward Camilla, but she vanished into thin air.

"What the heck is going on?" my mother asks as she stops in front of me. She's dressed in khaki shorts and a button-up tank top, and her hair is curled. "I heard a rumor that they found a body where that friend of yours overdosed, and I was worried it might be …."

She what?

Thought it was me?

Why the hell would she think that?

Jason says nothing, remaining behind her with his hands in his pockets. While he is silent, the irritation in his eyes says it all.

He's upset with something.

Because he has to be here?

Why the fuck is he here?

"I have to go." I sidestep, taking the longest way around them to get to my car—

But shit, Clara is in the crowd somewhere.

"Dammit." I reel back around and stride back down the road.

"Ava, don't walk away from your mother." Jason follows after me, his footsteps like thorns stabbing my ears. "Stop being such a little brat. Jesus, you haven't changed at all."

I focus on my footsteps, on my breathing, on getting my heart rate to slow down before I end up blacking out. I've had it happen a few times, where a panic attack consumes me to the point where my mind gives out from the overload.

I can't let that happen now.

I can't—

"What the hell is he doing here?" Clara's voice is like a warm summer day to this hailstorm slamming down on me.

She's heading toward me, fury flowing off her like the clouds rolling in.

"I have no idea, but let's get out of here." I still have Ellis's keycard. I can go to his hotel until I figure out what to do next.

I could run. Go home and pretend none of this ever happened. I ran that day in the woods. Why not do it again?

Clover's voice whispers through my mind …

"Do you ever get tired of it?" she asks me as we lie on our backs, staring at the stars. We're outside of her house, lying on a blanket spread out on the ground. We're high, and I feel like I could maybe touch the stars tonight.

I lazily turn my head toward her. "Tired of what?"

Her gaze remains fixed on the stars. "Of running from everything."

"Is …? Is that what we're doing."

"That's what everyone does when you really think about it. They run from their problems. Run from life. Run from the brutal reality of the world. I'm getting so tired of it." She drapes her arm across her stomach. "I'm not sure I want to run anymore. I want to stand still so I can find answers."

I roll to my side. "The answers to what?"

"Answers to the truth—to her death."

"Whose death?"

She looks at me, her lips parting, but everything becomes hazy, foggy, and confusing.

"Mine," she whispers.

But I can't be sure if it's real.

"Let's get out of here," Clara says as she reaches me. She glares at Jason from over my shoulder. "And you can get the fuck away from us."

"Who the hell are you?" Jason asks, slowing to a stop beside me.

The smell of his cologne makes me want to vomit again, but I swallow down the urge and turn around, refusing to look at him. Because if I do, I might lose it.

"Ava." He strides after me. "Seriously, what the hell are you doing? I flew out here because your mother calls me and says you need me, and this is how you repay me?"

"I don't need you—she lied," I mumble, focusing on moving one foot in front of the other.

Just get to your car, Ava. You can do this.

He releases a condescending laugh. "Yeah, right? Look at you. You're practically in the same position you were in only months before I fucking saved you. Same park, cops everywhere, and some dead girl getting taken out of the woods."

Blinding, uncontrollable rage lashes through me.

I slam to a stop, and even though it aches so severely in my chest that my ribcage might crack open, I look him dead in the eye.

"When you saved me? You mean, when you slowly started to break me?" My breath rushes in and out. In and out.

His nostrils flare, and his fingers fold inward. It's a look

I've seen him frequently wear as he reaches the point where he's inching toward the cliff ledge I'm standing near.

"And how the fuck do you know the body they found belonged to a girl?" I'm not even positive why I say it.

He leans in, his voice low. "Just what are you implying?"

Truthfully, I don't know. The words spilled out of my mouth before I could process them. But Clover used to say those were the truest words, the ones that didn't have any forethought to them. We actually used to play a game sometimes while we were high where we'd ask questions and have to answer without thinking.

It was where I learned Ellis wanted to kiss me.

It was also where I discovered that Clover had once been sexually assaulted, but she refused to discuss it further. I didn't press that hard. But I should have.

And looking at this moment now, it's odd that Jason is here, at this very park, where a body was found, and somehow he knows the victim is a woman.

It makes no sense, though, that he could've done anything to her when he only arrived here.

But I can't get past this icky sensation twisting in my stomach, warning me that something isn't right.

He holds me down …

Ties up my arms …

Covers my mouth …

"Shut your fucking mouth, or I'll slit your throat," Jason *whispers.*

"Stay away from me," I tell him in a shaky tone. Then I storm away with Clara at my side, and Jason doesn't utter a word.

But that means nothing, since Jason's silence can say as much as if he were yelling. And I know he won't stay away from me.

My mom tries to talk to me as I pass by, but I pretend she isn't there. Then I get into my car and roll up the windows. I'm furious that she brought him here. And why did he even come? Didn't he tell her we were divorcing?

"I can't believe he's here," Clara mutters as she extends her hand for her seat belt. "Seriously, what an asshole. And your mom is a psycho for bringing him here."

"I know," I agree as I start the engine and drive onto the road.

Her seat belt clicks into place. "Please tell me we're not going back to your house."

"No, we're going to Ellis's hotel."

"Good. I'm glad." She rubs her lips together. "It was a girl they found in the woods. She was like seventeen or something." She looks at me. "Didn't you mention once that this happened before in your town? That girls were dying or something?"

"No, they mostly went missing …" I swallow hard. "Some overdosed, though … At least, that's how the police ruled it."

"You don't think they did?"

"I'm not sure what to believe anymore."

I'm not sure I ever did.

I'm not certain I've ever lived in a truthful world.

That thought plagues me during the drive to the hotel. When we arrive, I put Bailey on a leash to take him for a quick walk, partly because he needs it, and partly because I need to clear my head.

"I'm going to go grab something to eat from that diner next door," Clara informs me as I lock up the car. "Do you want anything?"

I shake my head. "I don't think I can eat anything right now."

"You have to eat. I'll see if they have any soup or something." She gives me no time to protest before she walks off.

I wander in the other direction toward a field that borderlines the inn's property. Bailey is tugging at his leash, probably restless from sitting in the car for half the day.

"I'm sorry, buddy," I say as I walk quickly.

But I don't want to walk too far.

Not with so many ghosts haunting the town today.

As we make a path across the grass, my mind replays over everything that's happened over only a few days, and I can't help questioning if it's all connected.

My mother has been acting so odd, even for her.

Then Jason shows up.

And I learned that my father was allegedly murdered.

Clover also may have been murdered, perhaps because she was looking into Zoey's death.

And what about those photos I found in my mother's closet? Places in the forest, ones just like where this body was found.

Places where Camilla and I were ripped apart.

And what the hell is up with Camilla? Why did she say all that shit to me? I have no idea, but I'm fairly certain she didn't leave me that photo.

That note is in my dad's handwriting.

The cut on my back.

The cut on the dead girl's arm in the woods.

The scar on Camilla.

Jason.

Jason.

Jason.

"Why do you have so many knives?" I ask him as I examine the collection hanging on his bedroom wall.

"Because I used to hunt all the time," Jason replies as he sits on his bed and sorts through photos of what appear to be places in fields and trees.

"My dad's a hunter," I tell him, running my fingers along the collection of knives.

Something about how they look seems familiar to me, but that might be because my dad has a lot of knives.

"I know, Ava." He speaks to me in that tolerant tone he uses whenever he thinks I'm acting stupid. "I know your father well. So does my father. Most of this town does."

"Right." I face him with my arms folded around myself, wincing when I bump the bruise on my upper arm that always seems to be present.

My mother says it's because my iron is too low and my body refuses to heal. She says this is because of all the drugs I did, that I rotted my body and mind. I wanted to tell her that happened a long time ago, even before I did drugs.

He looks at another photo, barely acknowledging my presence.

I feel stupid being here with him, like I'm trying to play a role I don't fit into. But if I don't fill that role, then what? I go back to being alone, just an echo in the vast wilderness that I feel like I never escaped.

"Do you ever miss it?" I ask, trying to shove myself into the role. "Hunting, I mean?"

He pauses, thinks about it, then looks at me. "Sometimes. I liked the chase anyway. I was never a fan of the actual kill."

"Oh." I have no idea what to say to that. My father says the opposite. But I guess this is better, right?

Like maybe he doesn't like to kill.

He returns to sorting through his photos while I continue looking at the stuff in his room—photos of him and his friends, trophies he won playing football, and a crossbow on his wall.

He also has a vase filled with dried-up daisies.

My heart tugs at the sight of it.

"Who gave you these?" I ask as I stare at the wilting petals.

"Those flowers?" he asks, and I nod. "I don't know. Some girl ... I can't remember her name. Why?"

"I don't know ..." Tears well in my eyes, but I suck them back. "They're just ... Daisies are pretty flowers."

"They're lame, if you ask me. They're plain as hell." He pauses. "And those are dead—I should've thrown them out a long time ago."

As my eyes water over, I rub at the bruise on my arm, trying to focus on the physical pain instead of the emotion currently ripping through me.

"You really need to stop doing this shit, too." He appears beside me and grabs my arm. "Seriously, you're starting to look like a fucking junkie." He stabs his finger against the bruise.

I wince. "That's not a track mark ... That's just a bruise. I don't do that shit."

"Bullshit." He pushes me away. "You better stop doing it, or I'll leave you."

But I'm not doing it, *I want to say.*

I wince from the memory, the bruise on my arm throbbing. My head is spinning at the buried memory that clawed to the surface.

Something is happening to me. Something is digging up memories that I thought I long forgot, and I want to know why.

I try to delve deeper, and see things inside my head that might be hiding. But then my phone rings.

I dig it out with the assumption that it's either from my mother, Jason, or Ellis, but when *unknown* flashes across the screen, I stop dead in my tracks.

I almost let it go to voicemail, but I'm learning that running away from the known doesn't do anything but create a pile-up of problems later on.

And in holes that plague my mind, the ones where all the secrets are hidden, I realize that I'll eventually have to dig them out and hand them over to Ellis, if I ever want to escape this forest I've been lost in for years.

With trembling fingers, I answer the phone. "Hello?"

The line clicks, and then a recording plays.

"Shut the fuck up, or I'll slit your throat," someone whispers. *"Goddammit, where did they go?"*

"Oh, Ava, where are you?" another singsongs. *"Come out, come out, wherever you are. I want to play."*

"Help me," a frail voice whispers.

"Zoey, be quiet," Camilla hisses. *"If you don't shut up, they'll find us."*

Click—

"Have you told him yet?" an unrecognizable voice flows through the line, but it sounds like they might be using a device that alters how they sound. "That you saw his sister die that day. That you let her die."

I sprint across the snowy field, barreling for the gate.

"Help me!" A scream shatters through the air and birds scatter from the trees. "Help me, Ava, please!"

I look frantically over my shoulder at the girl with blood-soaked hair. Zoey. I can't leave her behind, but if I go back, they'll capture me again.

"Ava," she stumbles from the trees, blood trickling from her outstretched hand. "Please." She collapses to her knees in the snow.

A figure emerges from the shadows of the trees right behind her.

I turn around and run, running away from the blood and screams.

"If you don't leave this town, I'll tell him for you. I mean it, Ava," they say. "Get out of Stars Meadow or all your secrets will be unburied."

The line clicks.

I stand in the middle of it with the forest in the distance and one guilty thought infecting my mind.

Should I run away again?

Or should I, after all these years, try to figure out what the hell happened to me?

Is it time for me to stop running?

CHAPTER 25

Darkness is swallowing me, but this time I allow it. I can't get up yet, even if the sight of the trees in the distance is taunting me with the reminder of what I've done and what I'm about to do.

The sky is beginning to darken, and between all of this and the fact that only hours ago, a girl was found dead in the park miles from here, I should be in Ellis' hotel room with Clara and Bailey.

But if I move—if I run from the darkness *again*—I won't go through with this.

So instead, I sit on the cold ground, leaning against the brick wall of the building, smoking a cigarette and holding the bottle of vodka, which I've been drinking from for the last hour. I should regret doing it, but I can't feel anything other than crushing guilt.

Ellis' sister was there in the woods with me.

I let her die.

Just like I let Clover die.

And I kept quiet.

I locked the secret away and let it rot while the two of them rot in their graves, and the people responsible keep living in the light of day.

It. Is. Time.

It has to be.

It will be horrible to do it. Ellis will probably hate me. Maybe Clara will hate me too. But I have to finally escape those damn trees I've tried to convince myself I ran out of but never really did. Not mentally, anyway.

"Sometimes, when something bad happens to us, Ava, our mind plays tricks on us because it can't cope with reality," my mother once told me.

She was right. My mind tricked me into doubting everything that happened. It made me believe that perhaps I didn't see what I thought I saw. It tricked me into keeping my lips sealed.

It lied to me, and I let it.

But no fucking more.

I have to be strong.

Because that's the thing. I did survive, even if I sometimes don't see that. I survived all the scraping of branches, the blooming of bruises, and the scars, both visible and hidden inside my heart. I survived all the slices of words, the brutal punches, and the soul-crushing insults.

I survived. And that has to mean something.

I'll make sure it does.

I take another drag of my cigarette as I stare at the ground, waiting for him to show up—

"Aves?" Ellis's voice drifts toward me.

I glance up and find him walking toward me.

I stand to my feet. Or, well, stumble. He rushes to catch me before I fall, but I hold out my hand to stop him while bracing my other hand on the wall.

"Don't say anything," I tell him, knowing if I don't do this now, I'll descend back into those branches again.

I summon a deep breath, and then another, and my lungs ache from all the smoking I've been doing.

It's fitting.

Because this will be the third most painful thing I've ever had to do, the most being seeing Clover dead and the middle being the day I ran out of the woods and everything that happened after.

"What's wrong?" Ellis asks as he slows to a stop in front of me.

The lampposts highlight the puzzlement creasing his forehead, but he waits for me to speak next.

I don't take a breath—I don't want to spook the words away.

"I have to tell you about something important," I tell him. "It's about something awful that happened to me and other girls in the woods years ago."

CHAPTER 26

CLOVER... THE PAST

Sometimes, when I'm not too high, I can see her in my dreams.

Zoey.

We first met when we were in grade school. My life was such shit compared to hers, but she was so nice to me, despite me being from a broken home. She befriended me, took me to her house, and showed me what family could be when death hadn't broken them.

But then Zoey died, and her family withered into a state I was familiar with.

Before she died, she had been slowly fading. Everyone noticed, and I knew the truth of why she was.

She made me promise, though, never to tell.

"Daisy swear on it," she told me with her pinkie hitched in front of her.

We'd done it since we were kids and started calling

ourselves Daisy friends. We promise to keep each other's secrets, even in death.

That time, though, I didn't want to make that promise.

That time, the secret felt too big to keep locked inside me.

But I did it anyway, and it's been growing for months, the roots sprouting and feeding at my insides to the point where I can feel myself withering.

Her death is all my fault, and the only person who can do anything about it is me.

I can't go to the police because if what Zoey told me that day is true, the police are part of it.

And I can't tell Ellis because not only will it break him, but he'll do something that'll probably end up getting him killed. Plus, I'm not even sure I'm right about this.

I'm going to find out, though. I'm in too deep now to back out.

"Are you sure you want to do this?" he asks me as we drive up the dirt road into the forest. "Because I can always turn around."

I clutch my daisy wallet that has my phone inside it. It's recording every moment of this. All I need is definite proof of what they really did to Zoey.

"You've seen where I live," I tell him with a shake of my head. "I need the money."

The car bumps and jolts as we drive farther into the woods.

He stretches out his hand and brushes it across my cheek. He can be so light sometimes, but darkness lives inside him. I've seen it when we're behind closed doors and he can no longer keep it in, leaving bruises on my wrists and legs.

But it's not the first time I've been hurt. My father used to hit me all the time. My mother still does. And the guy who owns our property has torn me apart.

Deep down, it's what I deserve. I'm a piece of shit. Everyone knows it, no matter how hard I pretend to be something else. A slut. The girl from a broken home. The girl even her father didn't want. A punching bag. A blowup doll. The only time I could convince myself otherwise was while I was friends with Zoey.

Although, my new friend Ava is coming close to bringing me out of this bottom abyss I keep falling into like a goddamn rabbit hole. But she's got her own abyss—I can tell. Plus, I'm beyond saving at this point.

So, I might as well keep falling until I hit the bottom.

"Well, if you change your mind, let me know. I'll turn this car around in a heartbeat," he tells me as he returns his hand to the wheel.

I wonder if he means it. If I said I didn't want to do this anymore, he'd let me leave. It'd be risky with everything I know, including where this place is, so I'm not confident he would. Would he be the light I get glimpses of? Or the darkness that creeps out when we're in the shelter of his room?

I shake my head. "I'm good." Then I stare out the window and pretend I'm on a drive with my boyfriend.

That's not what this is, though. The only reason I ever started dating him was to obtain access to this place to prove that Zoey didn't really overdose. I knew he was my in because Zoey told me about him.

"He's a little bit older," she confesses. "But he's so hot and intense.

And I like how I feel whenever I'm around him, like I could fall off a cliff at any moment and it wouldn't even matter."

"That sounds ... I don't know, kind of dangerous."

"So? It's better than living my old, boring life. Besides, he's helping me get some money so I can leave this damn town, which is what we want, right?"

I nod. I don't want to, but I do it anyway because I don't want to lose her as a friend, and it sometimes feels like that's already happening. And I want to get the hell out of this town with her ...

As the car slows to a stop, I blink from the memory. Just in front of us is a green gate that leads to a field surrounded by woods.

"We have to walk from here," he informs me as he opens the car door.

Uneasiness stirs inside me as I climb out, too. The air is chilly, and goosebumps sprout across my flesh as I meet him in front of the car.

"I should've brought a jacket," I mumble as I rub my palms across my arms.

His gaze drags up and down me. "Nah, you look perfect."

I only do because I was instructed on what to wear—something short, like a dress or skirt that barely covers anything, and heels.

Without saying another word, he goes over, unlocks the gate, and opens it.

He nods for me to follow as he walks through the open gate.

My feet feel weighed down.

I can't do this ...

I can't do this ...

I can't breathe ...

"Hey, Jason," I call out as I start to back out.

He rotates around, and he's no longer warm and smiling, but looks as cold as the air wrapping around me. "Yeah?"

Just say it.

Turn back.

Run.

But fear pulses through me.

"Nothing. Never mind," I say quietly.

"Well, come on then," he says then starts forward again, across the dry grass and leaves.

And I follow, holding my wallet like a goddamn lifeline.

WHERE DAISIES BREATHE

Releases Oct. 2023 and is the final book in the Star Meadows Duet Series.

Preorder now: Where Daisies Breathe

ABOUT THE AUTHOR

Jessica Sorensen is a *New York Times* and *USA Today* bestselling author who lives in the snowy mountains of Wyoming. When she's not writing, she spends her time reading and hanging out with her family.

For more info:

Facebook: Jessica.Sorensen.Author

Facebook group: Sorensen's Stars

Instagram: jessica_sorensenauthor

jessicasorensen.com

Inspiring You

<u>A Pact Between the Forgotten:</u>

The Art of Being Friends

The Rules of Being Friends

The Art of Kissing (coming soon)

<u>Shadow Cove Series:</u>

What Lies in the Darkness

What Hides in the Darkness (coming soon)

<u>The Coincidence Series:</u>

The Coincidence of Callie and Kayden

The Redemption of Callie and Kayden

The Destiny of Violet and Luke

The Truth of Violet and Luke

The Promise of Violet and Luke

The Evermore of Callie and Kayden

Seth & Greyson

<u>The Secret Series:</u>

The Prelude of Ella and Micha

The Secret of Ella and Micha

The Forever of Ella and Micha

The Temptation of Lila and Ethan

The Ever After of Ella and Micha

Lila and Ethan: Forever and Always

Ella and Micha: Infinitely and Always

Breaking Nova Series:

Breaking Nova

Saving Quinton

Delilah: The Making of Red

Nova and Quinton: No Regrets

Tristan: Finding Hope

Wreck Me

Ruin Me

Unbeautiful Series:

Unbeautiful

Untamed

Tangled Realms:

Forever Violet (can be read as a standalone)

Untitled (coming soon)

Mystic Willow Bay Vampires:

Undead Secrets & Magical Bites

The Secret Life of a Vampire (coming soon)

Mystic Willow Bay Vampires

Tempting Raven

Untitled (coming soon)

<u>Mystic Willow Bay Mysteries Series:</u>

The Secret Life of a Witch

Broken Magic

Untitled (coming soon)

<u>Enchanted Chaos Series:</u>

Enchanted Chaos (can be read as a standalone)

Untitled (coming soon)

<u>Capturing Magic:</u>

Chasing Wishes

Untitled (coming soon)

<u>Guardian Academy Series:</u>

Entranced

Entangled

Enchanted

Untitled (coming soon)

<u>Monster Academy for the Magical:</u>

Monster Academy for the Magical

Monster Academy for the Magical: Hidden Magic

Monster Academy for the Magical: The Monster Trial

Untitled (coming soon)

<u>The Shattered Promises Series:</u>

Shattered Promises

Fractured Souls

Unbroken

Broken Visions

Scattered Ashes

<u>The Fallen Star Series:</u>

The Fallen Star

The Underworld

The Vision

The Promise

The Lost Soul

The Evanescence

<u>The Darkness Falls Series:</u>

Darkness Falls

Darkness Breaks

Darkness Fades

<u>The Death Collectors Series (NA and YA):</u>

Ember X and Ember

Cinder X and Cinder

Spark X and Spark

<u>Standalones:</u>

The Forgotten Girl

The Illusion of Annabella

Confessions of Luna & Grey

Rules of a Rebel & a Shy Girl

Breathing Lies